The Lark Mirror

Adrian J. Smith

Creephouse

© Adrian Smith 2013

All rights reserved

No part of this publication may be reproduced, stored in a retrieval system, or transmitted in any form or by any means, without the prior permission in writing of the publisher, nor be otherwise circulated in any form of binding or cover other than that in which it is published and without a similar condition including this condition being imposed on the subsequent purchaser.

First published in Great Britain by
Creephouse

Cover design by Creephouse

Adrian J Smith studied Literature at the University of Reading (UK). He has written novels, poems, radio plays and songs. His work has been published in The Stand Magazine, Backstreet Heroes magazine and some small literary publications. He lives in rural Oxfordshire.

Would you like an alert when the next book is published? Sign up at Adrian@creephouse.co.uk . This list is used to announce new releases, not for any other purpose.

*For Victoria
and
Marcella
for love, support and refuge*

*This thing of darkness
I acknowledge mine*

*William Shakespeare
(The Tempest)*

1

My name is David Chambers. If you know anything at all about what happened to me and those around me in the summer of nineteen seventy-six it will no doubt be through Margaret Mason's little e-book, *The Magic of the Moors; A Regional History of Cunning Folk*. Yes, I am 'The man who was haunted by his own shadow' as the chapter heading has it. Understand this: I would have preferred that whole sorry business with my shadow to have remained undocumented and forgotten. It's no small thing to be cursed and there is shame aplenty in my story. That aside, the posthumous publication of Margaret's book – her grandson was responsible for *that* little kindness – has caused me no end of trouble.

They are still out there, you see. Even in the age of Google – *especially* in the age of Google – of scientific certainty, mass surveillance and virtual entertainment on tap, they are out there. The would-be Crowleys. The latter-day John Dees. Tarot turners, spell-spinners and rune-witas. Students of *The Key of Solomon*. Hedge witches and wyrd-workers. And in the three years since Margaret's book was dunked into that great over-slopping bowl of esoteric soup from which these characters sup, not a small number of them have beaten a path to my door. 'Doors', I should say; though I have never quit the moors – once the moors have you around the heart you simply have no choice about that – I have been forced to relocate within them several times in the past three years. All because of that damned e-book. All because of that damned grandson. It's true that Margaret had the decency to supply a pseudonym for yours truly, but my tormentors are dauntingly efficient prodders and pokers, ferreters and mousers and the false moniker didn't slow them down for a minute. They come to me in wild-eyed, fevered certainty that I have some great secret to impart. That I hold the key to the wonders of the invisible world. I haven't and I don't.

Moreover, as I have said, this is a story that I didn't want told. But since Margaret has inadvertently let my particular cat out of the bag - and I am more forgiving of Margaret (the writer) than I am of her grandson (the publisher); she was, after all, a victim of the same magic which tossed one huge fuck-off spanner into my cosmic works - I may as well un-bag all of the other moggies, the ones Margaret knew about and the ones she didn't. Yes, by all means read *The Magic of the Moors* (available for download now, as they say) – it's a lively enough read, and I can vouch for the veracity of a good part of it, but the whole story, the *real* dope, is contained within *these* pages. I will leave nothing out – that's my promise to you – and I make it in the selfish hope that it might perhaps stem the flow of magus-minded pilgrims from washing up at my door.

Oh, one more thing before we get going - as a point of honour, I want you to remember that (unlike that idiot grandson) I am only allowing myself permission to make and publish this record because all of the other principle actors in this tragedy are now dearly, and not-so-dearly, departed. Billy Makepiece was the last - Billy succumbed to liver cancer two months ago, God rest his twin souls. Only I remain. Myself and my shadow. And Aunt Alsey of course – I doubt she'll ever die. She may have dropped out of mention – that's the way of today's forward-thinking world – and if any of my visitors have ever found her then they haven't reported back on the matter. But dying would be far too human an affair for someone who I don't believe was ever truly human to begin with.

The Lark Mirror

Trust me when I say – especially if you are *still* tempted to come bothering an old man, *this* old man – that when I set about making that lark mirror I had no idea that it would be my ticket into the heart of the mischief. I certainly didn't expect such a gimcrack, cobbled-together thing as that to attract magic like a magpie to a bauble. And why would I? I knew nothing of magic or curses or cunning folk and cared even less. I just wanted to make a lark mirror – that was all – and the only thing I anticipated attracting to my lark mirror was larks. Well, so much for *that*.

It started, as these things often do, innocuously enough. One sultry, breathless Friday evening in July of nineteen seventy-six, while recovering from a gruelling day's work, I happened upon a brief article in *The Crickford Herald* which snagged my attention - it may have been the 'Times Gone By' feature, though I'm not certain whether *The Herald* ran it back then. The article related how larks were once considered a culinary delicacy (and also kept as caged pets) and how lark mirrors, in conjunction with sprung nets, were used to capture them.

As I progressed through the article – and I would read it again and then again – it became strikingly obvious to me that lark mirrors were marvellous things and equally obvious that I should bodge one together somehow and see for myself what larks did about a lark mirror when they saw one. The sprung net could be dispensed with, since I had no intention of actually *catching* any larks. All I needed was something that would rotate and sparkle in the sunlight and so beguile the larks into swooping down, en mass, from their lofty hoverings. Pure spectacle, I thought, with mounting excitement. My change-of-life move to The Western Moors had set me slap-bang in the middle of lark country and I had high hopes.

Looking back now, I wonder that I got so exercised over such an idiosyncratic, essentially useless project. But I was young then and in any case we probably all went a little crazy in that sweltering, endless summer.

The very next afternoon, as I traipsed sweatily along Crickford high street en route to the butcher's, I spied a music box in the window of a bric-a-brac shop. I made the connection in a flash – the music box was just the thing from which to fashion my lark mirror.

There was no price tag on the music-box - which sat quietly (though for me, full of potential) between a wicker fishing creel and a gramophone with a dented horn - but since the shop lacked the pretension of the up-market antique dealers further along the high street I reckoned it wouldn't be too expensive. Even so, I wasn't exactly overburdened with cash so I stepped closer to the window and studied the music box while I calculated how much I could spare from my wallet while still leaving enough for the butcher, bearing in mind that there were other requirements viz the great lark mirror project.

Though late in the afternoon, the temperature was only now climbing down from a ninety degree high – the thirteenth day in a row of such disabling heat. The accumulative effect of such a record run of 'scorchers' (as the papers had finally grown tired of calling them) had mired the town in the doldrums. Not a car passed. Three doors up, a greying black Labrador was stretched out in front of the butcher's, lassitude having got the better of its appetite. Save that dog, I kept the street alone. The heat rising from the baking pavement was all mine. And so was that music box, if I wanted it. Which I did. And so, without the slightest inkling that I was pricking the flanks of calamity in doing so, I entered the shop.

The proprietor was mopping his face with a handkerchief. It was not a good day to be wearing tweed and he suffered inside a jacket which I suppose he considered some kind of quasi-uniform. After we'd exchanged some obligatory banter about the weather

The Lark Mirror

(thirty-two days without rain) and the ineptitude of the Water Board (bowsers were in short supply and the standpipes seemed placed for maximum inconvenience) I told him what I wanted and he fetched the music box from the window, set it on the counter and turned its key. We watched as the ceramic ballerina atop the box pirouetted to a faltering rendition of *Fur Elise*. It was a ridiculous artefact all in all but I had to admit it had a kind of mawkish charm.

I parted with two pounds fifty for the music box and another pound for a bathroom mirror. It was a little more than I could afford but prudence was no match for the urgency of my idea.

It was past five on that Saturday afternoon when I returned from Crickford with a pound of sausages, some sliced corned beef, the mirror and the music box. Sweat had glued my checked work shirt to my back and my underwear had similarly become an instrument of low-grade torture. Even so, I took a moment to admire my rented cottage. To feel its isolation. It was not as old as some – the walls were of brick rather than beam and white-washed render – and the roof was tiled rather than thatched. But I was fond of it and the isolation which I'd found a little tricky to deal with when I'd first moved here now felt like a privileged embrace.

Once I'd entered the cottage I set down my purchases on the draining board, took off my shirt and rearranged my underwear. The kitchen was relatively cool and that came as a blessed relief after driving home in my white and red-oxide coloured Ford Escort van, which was like an oven even with the windows open. The stink of turpentine which emanated from the rear of the van had made the air feel not just heavy but also noxious.

I really needed a bath but a drought order was in force which limited such a luxury and I, like most people, adhered to the spirit of the edict even though there was no way of such a breach being detected. Besides, the water pressure was now so low that it would take twice as long as normal to fill the tub.

I let the sweat steam off my torso for a minute or two and then I carried the music box into the dining room and set it on the long table where I did most of my quiet activities. I ate there. I read there. I studied maps and sorted fishing tackle there. And now – or tomorrow at any rate – I would construct my lark mirror there.

My appetite had fallen victim to the kind of torpor which often gripped me toward evening of those hot, nineteen seventy-six days. It was like an entity descending. Even so, I managed to flash-cook four sausages and chew on them desultorily until they'd vanished from my plate. All the while I wound and rewound the spring on the music box, watching the ceramic ballerina dance her stiff-armed dance. I continued to study the music box long into the evening, rewinding the spring when it began to flag, smoking cigarettes and drinking tea while I puzzled out how best to adapt the music box to my needs.

At some point I remembered that *A Fistful of Dollars* was on TV, and that I'd quite like to watch it. But the TV was having one of its bad days and Clint Eastwood was only just discernable behind a blizzard of bad reception and so I gave up and went outside to smoke a final cigarette in the relative cool of the evening. I went to bed that night with *Fur Elise* tinkling endlessly in my brain, not knowing how soon everything would change.

Charm or not, when I got to work on that music box the following afternoon I showed it no mercy. I ripped out its voice box and smothered the ballerina with a ball made from chicken wire and papier mache. Then I shattered the bathroom mirror with a claw hammer and used Araldite to fix a rough glass mosaic all over the ball's northern hemisphere. I finished it off by inserting a few left-over shards into the papier mache at various angles.

The Lark Mirror

It was at best a thing of savage beauty, that lark mirror. But if it lacked a certain grace then so what? It would reflect the sun at any angle and that was all that was required of it.

The only thing now standing between me and the mass beguilement of larks was the fact that the glue needed to dry. To speed the process I set the lark mirror on the garden wall to catch the early evening sun. And catch the sun it did. Sparkles like a bastard, I said.

The dusty lane which ran past the cottage was largely untroubled by traffic and on most days I wouldn't see a single soul go by. That being so, I had every expectation, as I went back inside to clear up the mess I'd made, that the lark mirror would remain on the garden wall, un-tampered with and un-pilfered, until I returned to fetch it. And, not for the first time in my life, I was wrong. Because when I went out at sunset to do just that, the lark mirror had vanished.

For a second or two I just gaped like an idiot. Then I sped through the garden gate and into the lane. I peered left into the shadowy tunnel of the beech trees which flanked the lane in that direction and then I squinted right, toward the sunset. Bats aplenty flitted beneath the beech trees. A few rabbits flashed their tails on the grass verges. My van was there too – canted to one side on a weak spring. But of lark mirror thieves there was not a sign. And then there was. The sun's afterglow was smeared across the western sky like an artist's wash. And silhouetted against it, small, far away, fleeing over the crest of a rise, a human form.

I'd been having trouble starting the van lately and I was too eager to apprehend the thief to waste time with the usual cranking and swearing, swearing and cranking routine required to coax the engine into life. Instead, I bolted for the garden shed and dragged out my bicycle, barking my shin in the process.

I launched myself along the lane, pumping the pedals for all I was worth. I crunched quickly into third on the Sturmy Archer gears – and third was as good as it got. The basket clattered about up front and the mudguard rattled behind and a cotter pin creaked on every turn of the crank as I weaved between potholes and dodged moths and swarms of gnats.

The thief had breasted the rise now and had disappeared down the far side. I knew that I must be gaining and I anticipated catching the light-fingered bastard in the next dip, where I would have the full advantage of speed. But speed is not necessarily the same thing as combative energy and after a panting struggle up the rise the last thing I was fit for was battle.

I had to do something, however, because there in the dip – as expected - skulked the thief, shuffling darkly through the gloaming, cowled with some kind of cloak or shawl and burdened with a slung bindle-stiff. I came to a halt and watched the figure take a few more steps. Deciding now that stealth would be my best tactic and greatly encouraged by the fact that the thief was little more than half my size, I pushed off from the verge and free-wheeled down the hill.

As I drew closer, it became more and more apparent that the stooped and shambling figure was an old woman and any lingering doubt was soon dispelled when she stopped abruptly, shifted her feet apart and pissed between her shoes. I braked to a halt as an act of absurd deference. She was probably harmless enough, I thought – just some mad woman or solitary gypsy of the kind that you still saw wandering country lanes in those days – and I had no wish to embarrass her. Nevertheless, there remained the matter of the lark mirror. I waited a few moments to let the old woman put some distance between herself and her

The Lark Mirror

discharge and then I set off again, the bike rattling lightly in the dusk as I feathered the brakes to control my speed.

"Excuse me," I said, when I was comfortably within earshot, "but I think you might have something of mine."

The old woman stopped dead.

I matched her.

In the long moment before she turned to face me, I grew very cold.

"Wha' d'you say?" she creaked out.

She had a face straight out of a story book. A patch covered her left eye, her mouth sucked itself in around a lack of teeth and her nose drooped almost to her top lip. She even boasted a spray of thick, white whiskers on her chin.

Just me, the old crone and the dusk.

I repeated what I'd said.

"No I eren't," she said.

"But I can see it," I said. "You're holding it."

The crown of the mirror-ball showed through the gap in her shawl. It's a wonder she hadn't cut herself on its jagged carapace.

"What? *This* thing ye mean?"

"That's it," I said. "It's mine. It's a lark mirror."

"Aye," she said, "that it be. I *likes* a nice tasty lark. But it aren't yourn. It be mine."

"I'm afraid you're wrong," I said. "It *is* mine. I only made it today. The glue wasn't dry so I left it on the garden wall -"

"I *knows* where ye left it," she said. "Same place as I found it."

"Which means you took it."

"Aye," she said, "which makes it mine."

"I'd like it back, please," I said.

"Can't have it," she said, half turning in a child-like, protective gesture.

"Alright," I said, becoming exasperated, "I'll *buy* it back."

"Don't want yer money," she said. "Nice tasty larks is what I wants."

"But you haven't even got a trap to go with it," I said. I had her there. The lark mirror would only *attract* larks. Without a sprung net it couldn't *catch* anything.

"Don't need no trap," she said and with that she turned and shuffled on.

I was totally thwarted. I wanted that lark mirror but I could hardly fight an old woman for it. Yet neither was I prepared to simply let her carry it off after the effort I'd expended in making the damn thing.

I free-wheeled after her and this time I lay my hand on her shoulder. She smelled rank and I immediately regretted touching her. "Please," I said, "I really want -"

She whirled around and I flinched. "Ye take from me, do ye?" she said, her one good eye burning balefully. "Well, take the blessed thing then …" and with that she raised the lark mirror from the folds of her shawl and dashed it into the lane. It bounced once in the dust and some glass spun off it and then it just lay there, filled with twilight.

I dropped the bicycle into the verge and retrieved my handiwork. It wasn't in good shape – the ball was on skew-whiff and when I shook it I could hear that something inside had broken loose. I was suddenly angry with the old crone.

"There," I said, "now you've broken it."

"Ye take from me," she growled, "it'll cost ye dear."

"Oh, shut up you old fool," I said.

She jabbed at me with a gnarled finger. "*Ye*," she said, "I'll make ye a-feared o' yer own shadder."

I laughed, scornfully and derisively. "What's that?" I said, "a curse?"

"Ye'll see," she said. She spat in the dust by way of conclusion and then turned and humped her bindlestiff onward into the blooming darkness.

2

The next day – Monday - I had to finish a painting job for Mr and Mrs Mason, who were established customers of mine. During the course of the twenty-minute drive over there, the van's exhaust – which had been blowing for several days – grew progressively louder and as I drove between the two stone lions loftily guarding the Masons' gate it finally gave. I rumbled up the drive like Rommel's army and halted in front of the French windows.

Mr Mason was making a long cast down his lawn with a dry fly line. He let the line fall gracefully onto the parched grass, feeding out a little slack even though there was no current to take it. The West Country was suffering badly in the heat wave. Wild fires had broken out across the moors and the trout streams had dried to a trickle. Hence Mr Mason, somewhat sterilely but with obvious enjoyment, casting the driest of dry fly lines along his lawn. He paused and gave me a wave which fell just short of a salute. I waved back, climbed out of the van and looked beneath its belly. Bad news. The exhaust had broken clean in two, just above the box. The better news was that nothing was dragging which meant that I'd be able, fingers crossed, to get the van to Silas Crabtree's workshop on my way home.

It was only eight-thirty when I popped the lid off a gloss can and began to stir the contents into a uniform "Forest Green" but the day was already hot and promising misery. I had a bargeboard to finish and the sun's full glare would beat on that bargeboard for most of the shift and I already knew how I'd be feeling by four o'clock – which was dirty, sweaty and exhausted. The west country was in the grip of the hottest summer in living memory.

As I hoisted up the ladder from where I'd left it on Friday – which was when I'd slapped on the undercoat - the sun was already taking the measure of my neck.

I'd been at it for a while and was progressing nicely along the left-hand slope of the bargeboard when I began to feel a little odd, as if something contiguous with me, but not quite *of* me, was not as it should be. At first I blamed the paint brush, telling myself that a kink was forming in the bristles and that I would have to comb it through with turpentine and a wire brush. But the paint flowed smoothly enough and the brush cut in as it should where the timber met the underside of the roof tiles and I had to admit to myself that it wasn't the brush after all.

I thought about the old crone and her ridiculous curse and wondered if the incident hadn't bothered me more than I'd realised. Which was possible. She'd failed to insinuate herself into my dreams – in fact, I'd slept well in my cool bedroom – but she'd been the first thing on my mind when I was woken (as usual) by two American Phantom jets screaming low over the moors.

"Coffee, David," Mrs Mason called up, breaking my reverie.

"Right-oh," I said. I wiped off the brush on the side of the paint kettle and started down the ladder. A glance at Mrs Mason was enough to put me on my guard. She was sipping a cup of coffee of her own and looked in the mood for a chat. I was careful when dealing with customers not to betray the fact that I was anything other than a man capable of painting windows and fixing leaky guttering. And I had to be especially careful with Mrs Mason because she was herself a former educationalist – a sixth form English tutor – who now self-published books and delivered lectures on local folk-lore, a passion she'd indulged since taking early retirement. If I should ever let slip the truth of my past then my shame would be total. I'd been careless – too careless at times – and had dropped the pretence often enough so that some of my more friendly acquaintances had taken to calling me "Professor". Nevertheless, maintaining the fiction for clients was the one golden rule and as I descended the ladder I was already searching for something suitably bland and unoriginal to say which could be uttered in as few syllables as possible. I needn't have bothered because Mrs Mason pitched straight in.

"Like the head gear, David," she said.

By now I'd donned the wide-brimmed Australian bushman's hat which my friend Billy Makepiece had brought back from a tour of the Antipodes and for extra shade I'd tucked a tea towel inside it so that it hung over the back of my neck.

"Keeps the sun off," I said, setting down the paint kettle.

"Quite," she said. "Very fetching. Very Mesopotamian."

"Mesopo-what?" I said, not rising to the bait.

"Arabs," she said. "Very Arabic."

"Did you say Arabs?" called Mr Mason, who had ears like a bat. He'd been swishing his fly rod like a metronome all the while I'd been painting but now he let the tip fall still. The line collapsed in a loop around him.

"Yes, Dear," Mrs Mason said. "We were talking about —"

"Buggers have got all the oil," Mr Mason said. "Have to get a second mortgage to run the lawn mower any day soon."

"It's going to get pricey," I agreed.

"Can't trust the buggers you know," Mr Mason said, flicking his line back into an airborne roll. "We ought to get in there and take it off their hands."

"Oh dear," Mrs Mason said, lowering her voice a notch or two, "I've started him off now." Then, seeing that I'd lit a cigarette she said, "Oh, David; when are you going to give those silly things up?"

"I'm trying," I lied. Quitting drinking and various peripheral substances seemed sacrifice enough for one lifetime.

"Don't *try*," Mr Mason bellowed. "Just do it. I did." He drove his line forward and let it settle. "Three or four pipes a day. Just stopped. Never regretted it. Sleep better too."

"I'll bear it in mind," I said.

"Don't bear it in mind," he said. "Just do it." Then he went back to his casting.

I looked a little sheepishly at Mrs Mason. She gave me a conspiratorial smile and I caught a twinkle in her eye. That Margaret Mason had been a beauty in her youth was well known (I'd seen plenty of photographic evidence of this as I'd painted and wall-papered my way through the Masons' house) and I'd heard it conjectured that snaring such a beauty accounted for a good part of Charles Mason's border-line arrogance. Hers was that kind of strong, English, country beauty that brings thorough-bred horses to mind. She was now in her early fifties and was still a very handsome woman and despite our age difference I had once or twice been tempted to make a pass at her and might well have done so if not for the photographs I'd seen of a young Mr Mason slugging it out in an army boxing gym.

"Been a bit grouchy since he hasn't been able to fish," she said in an intimate tone. "Still, he enjoys his casting."

"Very impressive it is too," I said, hesitating to vet 'impressive'. I lifted my coffee from the tray that Mrs Mason had set on the patio table and took a sip. Mrs Mason made good coffee – a rare thing in those days. "I'm more of a lead weight and worm man myself, I'm afraid," I said.

"Crude, but effective, I understand," Mrs Mason said.

"It catches fish," I shrugged. I took off my hat and balanced it on a double rung of the ladder so that I could wipe my brow on the towel.

The Lark Mirror

"Of course," Mrs Mason said, glancing towards her husband, "Charles would have you lead-hurlers shot. Something of a purist when it comes to fishing I'm afraid." She returned her gaze to me and a slightly puzzled look crossed her face.

"Have you trimmed your hair, David?" she said.

"No," I said, trying not to sound too defensive. "I washed it last night. Maybe that's it." I was thirty-two years old and my balding state was a thing I was still trying to come to terms with; it would be another year or two before I stopped caring by which time long hair would be out of fashion anyway.

"Well," she said, "there's *something* different about you today."

"Is there?" I said.

"Yes. Can't quite put my finger on it. Feeling alright, are you?"

"Fine," I said, which wasn't quite true.

"Sure?"

"Yes," I said. The sun had started to have some sport with my bald spots so I put my hat back on, minus the tea towel. Then, with no premeditation whatsoever, I blurted out, "Except that I was cursed by some old gypsy woman last night."

"Really?" Mrs Mason said, clearly interested.

"Yes," I said. "She looked like something out of a fairy-tale. Eye-patch and chin whiskers and all. She stole something of mine. When I –"

"Stole something?" she said. "Gosh, how interesting. Do go on."

"Well, she stole something I'd left on my garden wall and when I went after her to get it back she ... well, she cursed me." I laughed at the absurdity of it.

"And ... did you recover your property?" Mrs Mason said. She'd lost interest in her coffee and she set the cup on the tray.

"Yes," I said. "I didn't think she was going to part with it though."

"You weren't rude to her I hope?"

"Not particularly," I said. "Considering she was a thief."

"Oh dear," Mrs Mason said, understanding that my reply implied its opposite. She looked at the bargeboard. "You *will* be finished today, David, won't you?"

3

As it turned out I did finish and in less time than anticipated. Though the sun – as predicted – had been a lesson in brutal and underserved punishment, it did at least increase the flow of the gloss paint which helped speed up the job nicely.

Mr Mason paid me in cash – which is the way I liked it, especially with the nearest bank being sixteen miles from my cottage. As I was strapping the ladder on the van's roof rack, Mrs Mason came out to thank me for a "wonderful job". She made small talk about the drought while I shucked off my bib and brace overalls and she remained in the drive to watch me go. I didn't much care for the look of concern on her face.

I was tired, dirty, paint-sticky, baked and sweaty and I wanted nothing more than to have a good long soak in the bath – the one I'd been saving for days. Nevertheless, as the growl of its exhaust served to remind me, the van was in urgent need of first aid. I consoled myself with the fact that this needn't be too much of a problem; Silas Crabtree's workshop was less than a five mile detour on my route home and it was still only four-thirty – plenty of time to catch Silas before his official closing time of six o'clock. Not that Silas would necessarily leave the workshop at this hour, nor that he'd give me short shrift if I turned up later than six- Silas was amongst that small band who called me "Professor". But *after* six, Silas would start drinking his home-made cider and Silas was a generous man. As things stood I hadn't had a drink in three years, one month and twenty-six days but I felt more than a little vulnerable on that hot, uneasy afternoon and the temptation of a glass of cider might yet make a gutted corpse of my resolve.

Silas's yard sat nestled amongst a small copse of beech trees, a green oasis wobbling in the heat at the end of a half-mile track cutting through a micro-plain of sun-browned paddocks and withered corn fields. The hills to the north had been scorched black by a wild-fire. A half dozen pigs in a wallow at the side of the track lifted their snouts to watch me pass, their jaws working around mouthfuls of pebbles. Three rooks hopped clear of a dead rabbit laying ripped and eviscerated in the lane. The rear-view mirror reflected nothing but swirling dust. It was like driving through the heart of a spaghetti western. I made an earnest plea to fate that Silas hadn't uncorked his cider jug early.

Silas's workshop was nominally a garage. TYRES & EXHAUSTS FITTED/ WHEELS BALANCED/ BATTERIES CHECKED FREE said the sign on the main road. But Silas was more than a mere fixer of cars. He was both artist and artisan and his medium was metal. He could cut it and bend it, chamfer it and weld it. He could drill it, tap it, mould it, turn it and rivet it. A local man was as likely to seek out Silas to fashion a new ploughshare as he was to get him to fit a new alternator; as likely to find him pumping the bellows of his forge or filing the finishing touches into some newly-rendered gear cog as he was to discover him working supine beneath the greasy under-belly of a Hillman Imp. In addition to this, Silas was blessed with a shrewd mechanical insight and he could handle the most intricate of jobs with a surprising degree of delicacy. And on that particular dust-dry afternoon, Silas had been employing his myriad skills to build a new leg for his friend and jug companion, Jed Norton.

Jed's right leg had been amputated the previous year after he'd been infected with yellow spoor, which is a necrotizing dust sloughed off by a certain kind of fungus found around a handful of bogs during the month of May.

Since then, Silas had made several new legs for Jed, each an improvement on the last. Jed had a pair of trousers, shorn at one thigh, which he wore on trial days, so that when he limped out of the workshop's oily gloom the new model was on full display.

I'd parked in the shade and was just closing the van door when Silas followed Jed out, blinking in the daylight.

"There, Professor," Silas said, gesturing to Jed's new leg, "what do you think o' that?"

I strode over and walked a full circle around Jed to view this marvel from every side and angle. I whistled in appreciation. "That's a thing of rare beauty," I said.

"Hear that, Jed," Silas said. "The Professor says it's a thing of rare beauty."

"Will it be strong enough with all those holes in it?" I said. The leg was made of some kind of metal and Silas had cut slots and drilled holes in it here and there to shed weight, thus giving it an odd, skeletal appearance.

"Will it be strong enough?" Silas laughed. "Tell 'im Jed."

"That there's aircraft titanium," Jed said proudly. He rapped his knuckles against his shiny new thigh.

"Got it off the yanks," Silas said with a wink. "You could land on the moon with metal like that. When they cremate old Jed they'll be able to use what's left for a wing strut. Not every man can say that." He pulled a handkerchief from his boiler suit and turned it a time or two in search of a clean spot. If he found one it was discernable only to his eye but he blew his nose anyway. "Show him what you can do, Jed," he said, bunching the handkerchief in his fist and stowing it away.

Jed thrust his hand inside his trouser pocket where a wire disappeared from view. He'd laced a boot onto his new appendage and after he'd fumbled around in the pocket for a few moments a mechanical whirring stirred inside the titanium knee, the suck of hydraulics coursed through the thigh and then the boot began to tap impatiently in the dust.

"See?" Jed said. "Once I get the timing right I'll be able to walk without a limp."

"*Walk*, he says," Silas snorted derisively. "Time we've tuned it right, old Jed'll be the cross-moors marathon champion. Alright Jed, off you go. And for christ's sake take her easy to start with."

Jed made some adjustment inside his pocket and the leg took a step. Jed smiled and matched the step with his good leg. He fiddled some more. The boot tapped three times and then Jed was launched into a purposeful stride, looking very much like a man whose horse had bolted. Across the yard he went – *whir-tap, whir-tap, whir-tap* – out of the shade and into the sun's full glare, the titanium glinting like a mirror.

"Throttle back, Jed," Silas said, a little anxiously.

But whatever adjustment Jed made next was precisely the wrong one and the leg broke into a flat-out gallop down the lane with Jed's good leg swinging out wide in an effort to keep up.

"Well I'm fucked," Silas said, "I didn't think it'd be as quick as that. Come on Professor, we'd best catch him afore he gets to the road."

Jed had built up such speed by now that I had to break into a full sprint to gain on him. Silas plodded on behind with his badger-like gait. I caught up with Jed and jogged along at his elbow.

"Can't you turn it off?" I panted.

Jed took his eyes from the lane for just long enough to give me a fearful glance. He held up his right hand to show me something small and black pinched between his fingers. "The fucking knob's come off," he said.

"Oh shit," I said. "Silas," I yelled back, "the fucking knob's come off!"

"Trip him up," Silas bellowed. "Don't let him get to the road."

Jed gave me another quick glance. "Don't you dare," he puffed, "I'll break my fucking neck I will."

On we ran. *Whir*-slap!, *whir*-slap!, went the leg. Silas had fallen far behind now, his cries becoming distant and almost plaintive. We were still picking up speed and if my own racing heart was any measure then there seemed good reason to fear for Jed's heart, given that he was twenty years my senior. Then I had an idea. There was an electric fence between the wallow and the lane but it was only a low, single strand and I didn't think it would present much of an obstacle. "The pig wallow," I gasped. "Head for the pig wallow."

"Not ... fucking ... likely," Jed panted.

"It's your only chance," I pleaded. "If you get out on the road you won't stop 'til you hit the coast."

"No ... dive... in no ... fucking .... pig waller ..." Jed rasped with what seemed the last of his breath.

Then, no sooner than he'd managed to get those words out than all talk of coasts and pig wallows became redundant. We reached the dead rabbit that the rooks had abandoned and the titanium foot, as if by design, slipped the toe of Jed's boot neatly into the empty cavity of the rabbit's stomach. The leg ripped sideways and Jed went sprawling and rolling through a pall of dust of his own raising. The pigs burst into vociferous complaint and sucked themselves from the wallow. I trotted down to a halt and bent over and drew in great draughts of the hot and empty air. Once I'd recovered some of my breath I straightened to wipe my brow. I'd taken off my hat during the chase and now I used it to fan myself. I turned to Jed, who'd managed by now to sit up. Silas closed the distance between us.

"Are you alright, Jed?" I said.

"'Course he's alright," Silas said. He trudged wearily over to look at the leg. Having come adrift from Jed, it was now kicking in the dust, scrubbing the dead rabbit obscenely back and forth. "Christ, Jed," Silas went on, "I thought I told you to take her easy. You took off like Red Rum with a poker up his ass."

I ambled over, raking my hair across my bald spots and pulling my hat back on.

Jed was dusting down his shirt. "Are you two bastards going to help me up or -" the words died on his lips. He was looking intently at something which seemed to be off to my left. His eyes were wide and his jaw had dropped and for a moment I thought he was having that heart attack after all. Then he pointed.

"Silas," he said. "Silas, look at his shadder!"

Silas looked. "Well, I'll be fucked," he said.

I looked at my shadow. My shadow looked back at me. "Oh, Christ," I said. I reached up for the brim of my hat. I tugged at it to make sure that it was real. My shadow didn't move. It had no hat to tug at.

4

It did, however, have a fine, thick, head of hair and if not for its elongated form would have looked very much like the silhouette of myself as a younger man.

I lowered my hands from my hat brim and still my shadow didn't move. And then it did. It took a wide step away from my boots, paused as if to measure the distance between us, then took another step. It seemed so pleased with its progress that it executed a quick, silent tap dance. Then its long stride carried it over to the titanium leg which was now twitching like a dying fish. My shadow pointed at the leg and doubled over, its upper body rocking back and forth across the dust in silent mirth.

Nobody said a word. We just stared at it in absolute amazement. When I looked at the ground beside me where my shadow *should* have been, I felt as naked and embarrassed as Adam.

"Well," Silas said eventually, with rural understatement, "this *is* a right queer turn."

I was anxious to get out of the sun. I looked up the lane toward the road. The lane was empty and so, as far as I could tell, was the road. But it was not impossible that someone would arrive at any moment and I thought this a delicate enough matter not to want to take any chances. If it were to become widely known that I had lost control of my own shadow then my ostracism would be long and terrible.

Silas tore the dead rabbit clear of the titanium leg and fiddled around until the leg stopped twitching. Then he tucked the leg under his arm and we dragged Jed back to the workshop as if he were a human travois. When I glanced at the shadow of our actions, I, of course, was excluded from the tableaux. Just the shadow of Jed and Silas and the jutting shadow of the leg. It made me question my own existence and an anxious wind stirred in my soul.

As for my shadow – at first it stood slant-wise across the lane and watched us leave but as the distance grew between us it seemed to doubt its independence until, finally, it moped along behind like a truculent schoolboy, trying and failing to kick the shadows out of stones. It hesitated on the edge of the shade cast by the trees around the workshop but as we dragged Jed into the workshops gloomy interior it seemed to have no choice but to follow and I was relieved when it dissolved into the general shade.

Silas had a coffee table at the back of the workshop which he used for playing cards and games of draughts and a matching pair of battered armchairs stood one either side of the table. We deposited Jed into one of the chairs and then mopped the sweat from our brows – I with my shirtsleeve, Silas with his veteran handkerchief.

"We need to make a few adjustments to that thing," Silas said, meaning the leg, which he'd propped against the other chair.

"Oh bugger that," Jed said. "What about the other business?"

"Other business?" Silas said. "By Christ, Jed – you're right. Cider. *That's* what we need."

"I'm not on about *cider*," Jed said. "Though now that you mention it I could use a drop. No, I'm on about the Professor's shadder. You ever seen the like, Silas? Well, have you?"

"You know full well that I eren't," Silas said.

They both turned their gaze on me. I felt like a criminal confronted by his accusers.

"Well, Professor," Silas said, "what the dickens have *you* been up to?"

"Nothing," I said, defensively. "I had a run-in with some crazy old crone last night, that's all. She stole something of mine and - "

"*Stole* something?" Silas interjected. He and Jed exchanged a meaningful glance.

"Yes," I said. "She stole something from my garden wall. Actually, it was a lark mirror."

"A *lark mirror*?" Jed said. "Well, I don't why you'd waste your time on one o' them contraptions. Not much meat on a lark."

"I didn't want to eat them," I said. "I just wanted to know if it would work. By way of an experiment."

"Oh, they *works* alright," Jed said, scratching his stump. "When we was kids ol' Janner Beauchamp had a lark mirror an' we - "

"Never mind all o' that palaver about lark mirrors," Silas said. "What *I* wants to know, Professor, is if you fetched this lark mirror back from this crazy old crone once she'd taken it. *That's* the important thing here."

In my shame and embarrassment, my sense of my own foolishness, I stared at the packed-dirt floor, as if to find solace in the oil drips and dusty sawdust – which was the floor's general complexion.

"Oh dear," Silas said. "Oh deary, deary me." Then, still shaking his head, he waddled off to rummage up a jug of cider.

Silas and Jed passed the jug back and forth while I gave them a synoptic version of the previous evening's events. They listened and nodded sagely and took swig and swallow about.

"Aunt Alsey," Silas pronounced, when I'd finished the telling. "*That's* who it was alright. Must be making the rounds again."

Jed largely concurred, though he qualified this by saying that there was an outside chance that it could be Mother Priest.

"No, no, no," Silas said. "Mother Priest don't know stuff like that. What? Separate a man from his shadder? Not likely. No – Mother Priest would just put snakes in your bed when you weren't looking. Besides, you're forgetting the eye-patch. An' what was that she said again, Professor?: *I'll make ye afeared o' yer own shadder?* Very much like her turn of phrase. *Very* much like. That's Aunt Alsey alright an' no mistake. Well, Professor, I'd say you was in a bit of a fix."

Which was not something I needed telling. What I *did* need telling was who Aunt Alsey was and what I could do about my situation and on *that* subject I was all ears.

Quibbling over points of fact (or conjecture) here and there, they told me that Aunt Alsey was of uncertain origin but was known to be four hundred years old (four hundred and fifty was the figure advanced by Jed) and that every seven years she returned to the area to make mischief for the unwary and the ignorant. She lived by stealing but she didn't usually steal much – some vegetables from the garden, an item of clothing from a washing line, a chicken from the hen coop – and so long as she was left to get on with it was mostly harmless. But upon those unwise enough to thwart Aunt Alsey in the commission of the theft or to try recover what she'd stolen (a pointed glance in my direction) she would surely inflict a curse which would last for a full seven years after which time she would visit them again and, supposing they survived the seven years, give them a chance to rectify the situation. And the only way to rectify the situation was to return to her the thing that you should have let her keep in the first place.

"Seven years?" I said, with a kind of grim wonder.

"Seven year," Silas said, emphatically.

The cider jug passed at an ever-accelerating rate between them and I could tell that Silas and Jed were having a good time – a novelty like this being easily sufficient to take the sting out of the titanium leg's disastrous debut.

At some point, with the evening advancing, Silas had snapped on a pendulant lead lamp and so lent fresh life to my shadow which began to prance around a full twelve feet from my person, making drinking motions with an imaginary jug in an obvious effort to induce me to go for the cider. It made me sick to watch it cavorting like that. I realised now that the process of separation, the blooming of my shadow's autonomy, had already begun back at the Masons' house and I realised too that Mrs Mason – with her interest in local folk lore – had been visited with a strong inkling that it was Aunt Alsey who was at the heart of the brief mention I'd made of my encounter with the old crone. I felt like the butt of a very big joke.

"Seven years," I said again. My shadow seemed to sense my consternation and began to prance around again, gliding over the oil and sawdust and packed dirt with renewed glee.

I wondered how many of my clients would continue to support my business once they'd witnessed the degenerate behaviour of my shadow. The tally was not large.

Then, like a raft on an ocean of madness, a thought bobbed into view. "Has anyone ever tried to beat the seven years?" I said.

Silas arrested the jug halfway to his lips. "Meaning?" he said.

"Meaning," I said, "what if I were able to find this Aunt Alsey and give her back the lark mirror?"

Silas took a drink and thought about it and then turned to Jed. "You ever hear o' that being done, Jed?" he said.

Jed riffled through the archives of his memory. "No," he said, "can't say as I have. No reason to suppose that it *couldn't* be done though." He reached out and relieved Silas of the jug and took a few gulps before issuing a caveat. "Course," he said, "you got to find her first and that *won't* be easy. Fact, it might be next door to impossible. They say that she sleeps in the bottoms of ponds and that she can turn herself into smoke if she's a mind - "

Silas was having none of that. "That's a load o' nonsense," he said. "Surprised you don't know any better'n that Jedediah. Why, Aunt Alsey's just a regular human being like you or I. Just knows magic tricks is all."

"Aye," Jed said "an' one of 'ems turning herself into smoke."

"Not to mention living for four centuries," I said.

"Four and a *half*," Jed asserted. "Listen, Professor," he went on, "I doubt you're the first person whoever hatched a plan like yourn. But I've never heard of any success in the area. And to tell you the truth, I doubt and double-doubt that you'll be the first to pull it off. However, that don't mean it eren't worth a try. Mark my words though, it won't be an easy job sniffing out Aunt Alsey so, if I were you, I wouldn't waste much time."

5

Jed was right. To have any chance at all of picking up Aunt Alsey's trail I would have to leave early the next morning. Of course, I would need my van for such a quest so I did what I had gone to the workshop to do and prevailed upon Silas to repair the exhaust pipe – a job he was happy enough to undertake once he'd got Jed back onto his feet. They both agreed not to risk the titanium leg again until Silas had time and sobriety enough to take a proper look at it and so they buckled on Silas's previous effort which was made of tin with a sprung ankle joint to afford Jed a bit of lift when he climbed his stairs.

While they did this I went out to fetch the van into the workshop. As I un-strapped my ladder from the roof rack I kept an eye out for my shadow but apparently it couldn't be bothered to follow me all the way to the van, though I thought I sensed it watching from the tree-shade.

Once Silas had finished attending to Jed he wheeled over his arc-welder, drove the van onto his ramps and then slid himself beneath it and set to work. The bright, blue, flickering arc-light threw my shadow in grotesque attitudes around the workshop. In one instant he'd be crenellated upright across a shelved wall, in the next he'd be performing a capering jig across the ceiling. It was horrible to watch and it was all I could do not to snatch the cider jug from Jed's grasp.

When the work was complete I reversed the van into the yard and then got out again to pay Silas. My shadow stood in the yard as if transfixed by the blood-red sun. It had grown taller in the evening light. It didn't move except to sweep a hand through its luxuriant shadow hair. I left it to it and re-entered the workshop and handed Silas two one-pound notes. I asked Silas and Jed not to let it get around that I had come adrift from my shadow and then I left. They didn't have much to say on my departure and I had the uncomfortable feeling that they would be glad of my absence in order to have a good chuckle over my predicament. I didn't hold it against them, though it was no laughing matter to me.

My shadow refused to get in the van until I'd opened the door for it. It seemed a superfluous gesture to me, since it was just a shadow, but I decided to indulge it and my shadow behaved itself well enough once it was inside the van. In fact, my shadow seemed to enjoy the ride - even if it had become a little less substantial and well-defined in the light of the moribund sun.

I was halfway home before I realised that I'd left my ladder at Silas's. Not that it mattered; my next job wasn't due to start until Thursday and, in any case, work now seemed to have slipped into the realms of the impossible.

Cursed I may have been but by the time I returned to my cottage I was also ravenous. I usually cooked a decent evening meal for myself (I was a decent cook) but I was in no mood to prepare anything elaborate so, after a quick scrub-up at the kitchen sink, I made a corned beef sandwich – perked up with horse radish - which I ate at the dining room table. My shadow took little interest in what I was doing and just stretched itself across the floor in the light of the wall lamps - which suited me just fine; the less active it was then the less I would have to contend with my nerves. As far as I was concerned, my shadow could be as languorous as it liked.

I'd left the cause of all this trouble on the dining room table and as I ate I studied it. If I was going to find Aunt Alsey and give her back the lark mirror then it seemed a good idea to have it in working order lest she reject it. The few shards of glass that had broken off the globe I deemed

The Lark Mirror

of little importance - since they'd been the ones that I'd added somewhat superfluously at the end of the job - and once I'd straightened up the globe it looked okay. The mechanism, however, would definitely require attention.

Swallowing the last of my sandwich, I fetched a screwdriver and unscrewed the panel on the back of the music box. All that had happened was that the main-spring had kicked free of its peg. It was a simple matter to wind some tension into the spring and notch the loop in its end back onto the peg and I was finished in a matter of minutes.

My shadow had taken an interest by now and had propped itself up on an elbow with its head resting on its hand.

"What are *you* looking at?" I said, sourly. It had made me feel queasy and unnatural to boot fixing that music box without my shadow falling across the table and mimicking my every move.

Later that evening, after seeking out a map of the area, after drinking several cups of tea and smoking several cigarettes; after listening to the radio news and making a packed lunch for the next day's quest, I sloped off into the living room to watch *The Sky at Night*.

Somewhat reluctantly, my shadow tagged along and sat itself in the armchair beside mine. It didn't seem to appreciate *The Sky at Night* and it fidgeted and tapped its foot in a bored manner throughout. When I smoked, *it* smoked – shadow smoke drifting up the wall behind its chair. Even in the dim, flickering light of the TV my shadow seemed to be gaining solidity and definition. It was certainly growing in autonomy and by the time Patrick Moore was issuing a round-up of the coming week's celestial events, my shadow was smoking its own cigarettes at will from a pack it kept in its shirt pocket.

I'd hoped to formulate some kind of plan while watching TV but my shadow had proved too distracting and so, not wishing to have to look at it anymore, I decided to go to bed. I didn't want my shadow in the bedroom and so I thought to deprive it of light – and so the means to manifest itself - until morning. I turned off the TV and my shadow vanished. I headed for the door in darkness. Once there I would grope my way to bed without turning on a single light. There was a gibbous moon that night but I'd fitted heavy curtains over my bedroom window because I would often take a nap in the afternoons. All in all, I thought I could manage things so that I wouldn't have to see my shadow again until morning.

But just as I was about to pull the living room door closed I heard something which made me pause. It was my shadow. It was still there. And I could hear it breathing.

I undressed, climbed into bed and pulled a single sheet over myself. I'd made a point (since the heat wave had started) of keeping the curtains drawn all day and so it was tolerably cool in the bedroom. I lay with my hands tucked beneath my head, staring at the darkened plane of the ceiling. I half expected my shadow to take advantage of the slivers of moonlight at the edges of the curtains but, as far as I could tell, I was alone.

It had been a long, strange day but despite all of that I was sleepy. Nevertheless, if I was going to find Aunt Alsey then it was important to have some kind of plan. Thus far, I'd come up with nothing more sophisticated than driving the moor-land lanes and asking anyone I'd come across if they'd seen the old crone. It wasn't much of a plan and in any case it was one baulked around with difficulty. Quite apart from my nervousness about what the asking of such questions would do for a man's reputation, there was the insurmountable problem of my shadow. There was no reason to suppose that the following day would not be as sun-drenched and glaring as all the days preceding it, which meant that my shadow would be highly visible and it would not take the most observant of interlocutors to spot that there was something aberrant about it. Then again, I wondered if my shadow would even want to come along. It seemed bored by anything I did so maybe it would be content to mooch about the house for the day. In which case I would still be presented with a difficulty for then I would have no shadow at all. As I lay there failing to improve upon my plan, I was already haunted by the fear-stricken faces I would no doubt have to gaze upon before the day was through.

What was needed, I decided, was an accomplice – someone who could make all necessary enquiries while I remained in the relative cover of the van. An accomplice, of course, would have to be in full possession of the facts and there was only one person on the moors I'd trust as much as that and that was Billy Makepiece.

I'd first met Billy at the market in Minch Norton where he'd been haggling over a duck. I'd gone to the market to buy some chestnuts to roast on my open fire. It was to be my first Christmas at the cottage. I'd yet to make any friends and what with no near-neighbours and nothing but snow-blown moor-land around me I'd resigned myself to spending Christmas alone. Because of this, rather than in spite of it, I was determined to make the holiday as cheerily festive as possible.

Billy carried the duck in a wooden cage. I'd grown out of the habit of striking up conversations with strangers but the way Billy squinted at the duck, as if he couldn't for the life of him figure out why he'd bought it or what to do with it prompted me to comment.

"That's a nice duck," I said.

"Isn't it?" he said. "Do you like duck? I'd be happy to let you have it. I'm a terrible cook and I don't want to let it go to waste. All you'd have to do is come and get it when I'm done with it."

"Done what with it?" I said, overcoming the urge to back away.

Billy explained that he was a painter and that he wanted some duck feathers for a mixed-media project. While he spoke, the duck muttered and raked its bill along the bars of the cage, as if it knew what Billy was saying and had decided to plead its case. Ducks are like that.

"Well," I said, "I'm sure it'll make a nice painting." I meant it too. The painter had yet to be born who could render in paint those iridescent greens on the duck's head and neck and I thought it a measure of Billy's humility and genius that he recognised this while finding a way around the problem by incorporating actual duck feathers into the picture.

"It really is a very pretty duck," I said. "Shame to kill it really."

"Nevertheless," Billy said, "I need those feathers. And we can't have the poor bastard running around naked, can we?"

"No," I said, "I suppose not."

I admired a man willing to kill for his art. Moreover, I was quite partial to duck. Before our acquaintance was five minutes old we'd decided that, since we both lived alone (and Billy didn't want to make a 'dreary trip' to visit his 'dreary' relatives) then we should share the duck for Christmas dinner. Billy would pluck it and dress it (he wasn't squeamish; he was just lousy in the kitchen) and then I would arrive at his place – which was a short drive away – in time to cook it.

I roasted the hell out of that duck. I roasted it until its skin was golden brown and crackled like wildfire. When I finally delivered it from the oven's smoking maw we fell upon that duck and tore it apart like Roman senators. We tossed around its bones and wiped its grease from our chins. I even proposed a toast in its honour – Billy raising his glass of wine, me my dandelion and burdock. It wasn't every duck that died for art.

"Bollocks to art!" Billy said. "That was the best damn duck I've ever eaten." He eyed me with growing appreciation. "Now," he said, "what are you like with fish?"

It turned out that Billy was a fellow angler and that – though he confessed a certain weakness for a well-tied fly – he would be perfectly content to throw a heavy lead into a pounding surf. And so the pattern of our friendship was at first delineated by bass fishing trips and (if the trips were successful) home-cooked fish suppers, over which we discussed our shared interests (mostly music and films) and began to develop a mutual appreciation of our respective endeavours. In time I would come to act as supportive critic (not that he needed one) for Billy's painting and I would sometimes help him hang his work if he had an itch to show it in some local gallery. Billy, for his part, had helped me to build an irrigation system for my vegetable patch and would indulge me in my occasional forays into the esoteric and the quixotic (I'd been looking forward to showing him the lark mirror).

There was no doubt in my mind that Billy would rise to the challenge of finding Aunt Alsey – in fact, a job like that would be right up his street. But even so and for all that, part of me thought that it was bad enough that Jed and Silas were aware of my unholy situation (not to mention Mrs Mason's well-informed inkling) and I was reluctant to spread the word any further, even if it *was* only as far as my best friend's hearing.

So, having decided nothing except that *maybe* I'd ask Billy Makepiece to beg off work and accompany me on my quest, I slipped over into sleep. My last remembered thought was that if Billy came along he would at least keep my spirits up.

It was not to be that a better plan coalesced within my sleeping mind ready to present itself to me fully-formed in the morning, because at around one fifteen someone started kicking furiously at my mattress.

"Wake up, Baldy," the mattress-kicker said. "I need a drink and I need one bad."

I snapped on the bedside lamp and had to fend off its glare with one hand until my eyes became accustomed to it. When they had done so, I didn't much like what they saw.

"Yeah, it's me," my shadow said. "Filled out some, wouldn't you say?"

Yes, I thought, I would certainly say that.

My shadow was no longer a shadow but a regular, breathing, talking and walking three-dimensional man, standing there in scuffed jeans and a grubby white shirt. He'd stolen my hat and had it jammed down to his ears. It looked quite good on him, if a little sinister. Now he looked not so much as I had as a younger man but more as if he could be my younger brother. Whereas I'd always considered myself to be unremarkable yet pleasant to the eye, my shadow was more handsome while lacking the pleasantness. Like me, he had blue eyes but there was something coldly mischievous about them and there was a definite and cruel leer about the mouth. On top of this, he had several scars, the most prominent being a white, crescent-moon of raised tissue running around his cheek from his left eye to the corner of his mouth. No doubt the scars were from all the fights I'd chickened out of over the years.

"Well, Baldy," he said, "are you going to lay there like an expectant whore or are you going to fetch me a drink?"

"I don't drink," I said.

"You can suit yourself what you do," my shadow said, "but I'm as thirsty as hell. Thirstier."

"But there's nothing here," I said.

"*Nothing?*" he said. "How can that be?"

"I told you," I said, "I don't drink. I never buy the stuff."

"But you used to. You used to buy it by the gallon."

"Not anymore," I said. "Those days are gone."

The Lark Mirror

"Well," he said, "we'll just have to see about that, won't we? Come on, Baldy – where have you hidden it? A sly bastard like you would have a bottle stashed for an emergency. Guess what?; I'm the emergency. Get up and get dressed. You've got five minutes to remember where you hid your stash. After that, I'll tear this place apart and find it myself. I'm going down for a smoke. Don't waste time."

With that, he headed for the door, his heavy work boots clumping against the floor boards. As he did so, I noticed something which made me groan audibly – a groan of dismay and envy. My shadow was now solid enough to throw a shadow of his own. He was more normal than I was.

He was sitting at the dining room table when I went downstairs, a cigarette clamped in his lips, his hands busy with the lark mirror.

"What the fuck is this thing anyhow?" he said.

"It's a lark mirror," I said.

"What's it do?" he said, turning it over.

"It attracts larks," I said, with a shrug.

"*Larks?*" he said, staring at me with a kind of malevolent sympathy. "What the fuck's happened to you, Baldy? Larks be fucked." Then, something occurred to him. "Worth anything, is it?" he said.

I told him no and he lost all interest in the lark mirror. I was glad to be off the subject and I was cautiously relieved that, apparently, he'd been unable while in his shadow form to comprehend the conversation I'd had with Silas and Jed. When he set it back on the table I had to resist the urge to remove it from his reach.

"So, Baldy," he said, "clock's ticking. What have you got?"

"I told you," I said, "there's nothing here."

"Nothing?" he said, raising his eyebrows in a quizzical way.

"Nothing," I repeated. "Bone dry."
"Then you won't mind if I look around," he said.

He was a fast worker for one so recently created and by the time I'd resigned myself to the fact that I would have to intervene he'd dumped half the contents of the kitchen cupboards onto the floor. When I finally got in there, my shadow was standing in a blizzard of flour, sweeping empty the cupboard above the sink. A jar of jam fell and smashed against the cold tap. The floor was a collage of broken eggs, spilled milk, scattered pasta, dented tins, shattered glass, a desert of rice and half a date and walnut cake.

"I'm starting to think you've hidden it in the shed, Baldy," my shadow said.

"There's nothing there either," I said. "I told you; you're wasting your time."

"Well," he said, "I've got nothing better to do. You go on back to bed if you want to. I can manage just fine on my own." With that he opened the next cupboard and gratuitously shook empty a box of cornflakes into the sink.

"Stop!" I said. "Just wait."

"Time and thirst wait for no man, Baldy," he said. "You should know that. And I am one *very* thirsty bastard."

"Just don't make any more mess," I said, "and I'll get you a drink."

"Get one where?" he said, his interest piqued.

"A friend of mine."

"You've got a friend, Baldy?" he said. "You *do* surprise me."

"Yes, I've got a friend," I said, somewhat defensively. "And what's more, he likes a drink. If you stop what you're doing I'll phone him and see what he's got."

"Scotch," my shadow said. "I want scotch. And I want some wine. Beer if he's got it but I can manage without. Cigarettes, I need. A cigar or two would be good. Oh, and tell him to throw in any drugs he's got. Never know when I might need a pick-me-up."

"Is that all?" I said, managing to muster some sarcasm.

"It's a start, Baldy," he said. "It's a start."

6

I had no qualms about ringing Billy Makepiece at that hour. Billy was more owl than lark and I thought there was a good chance that he'd still be up, brooding over the painting which had claimed so much of his attention lately, or else trying to tease out a witty and memorable slogan for one of his ads. Billy was a copywriter in his day job – a successful one – for a big London agency. He would commute to work two or three times a week for meetings; the remainder of his work commitments would be scratched out with pencil and pad in his cramped office at the rear of his cottage. He worked irregular hours because he liked to reserve as much daylight as possible for his painting.

My phone was in the hallway at the bottom of the stairs and I went to it and dialled Billy's number. I let it ring for a long time but Billy didn't answer. It had grown very quiet in the kitchen and I suspected that my shadow might be listening.

"Billy," I said into the ringing line, "it's David. Listen, I haven't got time to explain but I need something to drink. Can I come over and grab a bottle or two? (pause) Yeah, fifteen minutes." Then I hung up.

I wasn't unduly bothered that Billy hadn't answered his phone. It was his habit to ignore a ringing phone if he were deep in thought or even, as I'd witnessed him do, if he were simply reluctant to break off a conversation. "Oh, that'll just be Colfax about the Wheaty Grain account; let him stew," he'd say, or, "That'll just be Mother – her leg's playing her up again; she'll ring back." Though at that hour he was more likely to be copywriting than painting, I imagined him that night, brush poised over palette, waiting for the phone's intrusive ring to quit so that he could regain his creative composure sufficient to make an important daub in just the right place. The painting he was working on then was large and serious and smouldered in his mind like no painting he'd ever before painted and my imagined solemnity of the moment seemed right.

I hadn't seen anything of the painting since the day he'd started it – which is to say I'd seen nothing more than a canvas of roughly the dimensions of a wide, full-length mirror blocked out in warm grounds with enough charcoal line to suggest that its subject was a woman, standing alone and facing the viewer in a room which was probably a hotel room. In the back-ground was a bed on which sat an open suitcase with various items of clothing spilling from and strewn around it.

Billy wouldn't talk about the painting – not directly – but he did let slip that the subject of the painting was the most beautiful woman he'd ever seen. I'd found it amusing to witness a man in the throes of creating a masterpiece while trying not to let on.

As I say, it didn't bother me that Billy hadn't answered his phone – it by no means meant that he wasn't home. And in any case, it wasn't impossible that Billy was sleeping and that was a thing which was easily solved. So, when I returned to the kitchen to speak with my shadow, I had every confidence that I could secure him some booze.

"Well?" he said, trying not to sound anxious.

"All set," I said, taking the van keys from their hook. "I'll be half an hour," I said.

"Whoa – hold your horses, Baldy," my shadow said, "I'm coming along for the ride."

"I don't know if that's a good idea," I said. "Too much explaining to do."

"How do I know you're not running out on me?" my shadow said.

"Because I live here, you idiot," I snapped, finally running out of patience. "What's more, you've got work to do."

"*Work?*" my shadow said. "Have you stripped a fucking gear? I don't *work*, Baldy. That's your job."

"No," I said, "fetching your booze is my job." I opened my cleaning cupboard and took out a broom. "I reckon you'd have this place cleaned up by the time I get back if you were to start now."

He took the broom grudgingly. "Alright," he said, "but if you're not back in half an hour I'm going to make match-wood and brick dust out of this shit-hole."

I was glad to get out from under the shadow of my shadow. It was a cool night for that summer. The moon was approaching full and there was a suggestion of mist along the banks of the lane. The van fired on the eighth or ninth turn of the key – which wasn't bad.

I drove in the same direction in which I'd chased Aunt Alsey the previous evening, with the moon riding to my left, failing to cast my shadow across the van's interior. Even though I'd not brought the lark mirror along I kept an eye out for the old crone, just in case. When I drove past the spot of our encounter I was seized by a shiver.

In the dips in the road the mist gathered in white drifts. I snatched glances across the open moorland as I drove, looking for that shuffling form, but I saw only a fox and a couple of deer. And sheep of course. Plenty of sheep.

I drove on for four miles until I reached Billy's hamlet. Unlike me, Billy had a few neighbours. They were not intrusively close, for Billy loved his solitude – the nearest house to Billy's was on the far side of a green with a well and a hand-pump – but close enough that I risked waking them. With this in mind, I coasted down the slight gradient to Billy's cottage with my foot on the clutch and the engine idling. I even turned off the lights for good measure.

The Lark Mirror

Billy's garden was an overgrown affair and I was grateful for the moonlight as I scraped and brushed my way between shrubs and bushes which encroached ever more tightly upon the winding path which led to Billy's door.

I was glad to see that a downstairs light was burning and my only remaining practical problem, as I tapped lightly on the door, was that Billy might be reluctant to furnish me with booze. Billy respected and supported my determination to remain teetotal and though I knew he'd prefer it to be otherwise (so that he had someone to drink with after fishing trips) he had never once complained or tried to induce me to drink. In short, I was about to present Billy with a moral dilemma.

I was hoping to get in and out of Billy's ill-lit cottage without him noticing anything amiss – I had yet to decide as to whether to include him in my plan (such as it was) to find Aunt Alsey and, either way, I had no intention of telling Billy about my shadow at that point, if only to save time. And so I was just concocting some guff about an unexpected visit from a distant relation when the door failed to open. I knocked again, louder this time.

The door remained closed. I flipped open the letter box and called inside. This time, I was rewarded by a quiet sound from within – which I took to be the thumb latch of an interior door being depressed. I let the letter box fall closed and waited while the key turned in the lock. Finally, the door opened a few inches and someone peered out through the gap. I didn't think that it was Billy. Then the door opened all the way and I *knew* that it wasn't Billy.

Because, standing in the soft light spilled from Billy's living room, was a woman. But not *just* a woman. She was, without doubt, the most beautiful creature I'd ever seen and for a full five seconds my heart seemed to stop. Her hair was dark and her mouth was dark. Her eyes were darker. Her skin, however, was as pale as cream and I couldn't help but imagine her naked in the moonlight. For a long moment I forgot all about my shadow and his need for booze, about Aunt Alsey and her seven-year curse. I just stood in stunned silence and drank this woman in.

Then she smiled, as if she knew me.

"Is late," she said. "Please to come in."

I closed the door behind me and followed her into Billy's living room, more perplexed and confounded than ever. You didn't hear many Russian accents on the moors in nineteen-seventy-six.

A half-empty wine bottle and a glass with a mouthful of red wine remaining in it stood on the small round table that also held Billy's globe. It was the place – because it was just a pace or two from the liqueur cabinet – that Billy usually poured and mixed his drinks and I took it as sign that the goddess was familiar enough with Billy's habits to take some of them as her own. It irked me that this wonderful woman had escaped Billy's mention but then it was fair to say that we didn't live in one another's pockets and in any case they may have been at the very start of the thing – I hadn't seen Billy in a week and a half after all.

Before she spoke, the goddess poured more wine and as she did so I couldn't take my eyes off her. She was wearing a long, black evening dress with a distinctly old-fashioned look which left one creamy shoulder deliciously exposed. Around her neck was a long string of pearls which fell just so between her cleavage. On her feet, I now noticed, were a pair of elegantly-made boots which should have looked incongruous with the dress but which somehow didn't.

"I would offer drink," she said, at last, "but I think that you are David. And David, I think, does not drink. This is so?"

I almost threw everything over right then, just to have a drink with her. I was still finding it hard to breathe and I was grateful for the room's width of distance between us.

The Lark Mirror

"How do you know who I am?" I finally managed to say.

"Who else to come at this hour?" she said. "Billy speaks of you. I hear engine, I hear knocking. I think, this must be Billy's good but crazy friend, David. I am Anushka, by the way."

"Anushka," I said, tasting the word on my tongue, sweet and dark. "It's a beautiful name."

"No," she said, "is ordinary name. Is just strange to your ear, that is all."

"Your accent," I said, "I can't help noticing …."

"I am from Russia," she said. "My father was diplomat. I travel more freely than most." She sipped at her wine and there was something so shockingly sensuous about it that I didn't want the moment to end.

"Have we met before?" I said. My question surprised even me. Given the things that Anushka was making me feel then no doubt I would remember a previous encounter (and probably recall it every day since), which I didn't. Yet there was something familiar about her reflective pose and the way she fondled the wine glass; something very de ja vu.

"No," she said, without any pretence of recall, "I would remember." She took another sip of wine. "You wonder why am I here …"

Actually, I'd taken a moment's time-out to wonder if my shadow had recommenced the wrecking of my home but this concern receded from the power of that mesmerising voice.

"I am here because Billy wished to paint me," Anushka explained. "In fact, Billy *has* painted me, but he has been slow about it."

"*You're* the woman in the painting," I said, sounding like some star-struck fan. The most beautiful woman I've ever seen. Those words of Billy's came back to me now. I'd never imagined for one moment that the woman in Billy's mysterious painting was one derived from flesh and blood. I'd always assumed that he'd been mooning over the object of his own imaginings, or else some composite melded together from the various models Billy was lucky enough to work with. It dawned on me that Billy had been gazing at Anushka for hours on end. No wonder I hadn't seen much of him lately. No wonder he'd seemed so distracted when I *had* seen him.

"I've only met you in charcoal before," I said.

She smiled at the joke and the smile was devastating.

"The picture, it is almost done now. We wait only for the paint to dry. So," she said, changing the subject, "you are in trouble, yes? Or why else the hour?"

"Yes," I said, "I need to speak to Billy." It was the first time since Anushka let me into the cottage that I'd even got close to addressing the reason for my visit and I realised fully and perhaps for the first time how powerful was the spell that she had cast over me.

"Billy is not here. Billy is called away on emergency. Work," she said, batting away the word "work" with a dismissive gesture.

"An emergency copywriting job?" I said, finding it easier to focus now that we were talking about practical, quotidian matters. "What happened," I said, "biscuit sales collapsing?"

"No, is not biscuits," Anushka said. "Somebody has made a trouser press which is better and cheaper than The Seam Butler. They launch this week. The I.C.B.M. electrical people cannot make a better, cheaper Trouser Butler in such short space of time so they must make better marketing campaign. Yes? And so Billy took taxi to station to go to London to help out. Is no matter; perhaps I can help you. This trouble you are in …?"

"Oh, it's not really trouble," I said breezily, "I just need something to drink, that's all."

It was a curious thing to witness but a fleeting look of alarm – of panic even – swept over Anushka's features then and I wondered about the size and scope of Billy's yarns when he'd explained to Anushka that I didn't drink and why.

"But you no drink," she said. A fur stole that I'd half-noticed was draped over the back of a chair close to Anushka and, as much to cover her embarrassment as anything else, she took it up and let it fall over her shoulders.

"No, no, I know," I said, attempting to reassure her. "It's complicated and it's late and I haven't got time to explain. All I can tell you is that it's not for me. Oh, and that I need quite a lot of it."

Anushka considered this while she drew the stole close to her throat and then relented. "In any case," she said, "is not mine to refuse. What do you need?"

"Whisky," I said. "Definitely whisky."

7

When I left Billy's cottage that night I carried a cardboard grocery box that chinked merrily in the moonlight. I was still in a state of shock and emotional confusion and my mind was burning with questions. We'd talked a little as we'd filled the box but I hadn't managed to get to the bottom of Billy's relationship with Anushka. Was it strictly professional or something more? I hadn't wanted to pry – or, more accurately, hadn't wanted to hit a wrong conversational note with this woman I was so much in awe of – for the fact was that Anushka owned my heart from the moment she'd opened the door. Such moments occur - if ever – only once in a lifetime and it was just my luck to have to rush off and deal with my thirst-tormented shadow when it happened to me.

Anushka, for her own part, had grown a little more reticent and introspective, as if she were still learning the rules of a game she hadn't quite yet decided to play. Then, with the box almost packed, she revealed the reason for her change of mood. "Billy will not return for a few days," she said. "Perhaps you would like …. Perhaps you will have dinner with me."

I couldn't believe my luck.

"Perhaps tomorrow," she said. "Is good for you?"

Tomorrow was an unknown quantity of course and I was trapped in an agony of indecision. All my life I'd wanted to be in a position to tell a truly beautiful woman that I was too busy to make a date with her and here I was in a position to do just that and *mean* it. But it just wasn't in me.

"I'm quite busy," I said, "but if we make it fairly late I ought to be okay."

"Is good," she said, satisfied. "You will come here, yes? Eight o' clock." she said.

"I will come here, yes," I parroted. "Eight o' clock."

It was then that something happened – just a small, queer moment – which I have thought about often ever since. Possessed of an itch behind her ear, Anushka unselfconsciously scratched at it with her index finger. A puzzled look showed briefly on her face and she glanced at her finger and then rubbed at it with her thumb. Though the light was low, I could see very clearly what had vexed her. Spread across the first two joints of her finger, discernable by the difference in shade against her creamy skin, was a thin smear of flesh-coloured paint. She shrugged. "It gets everywhere," she said.

I dumped the box in the passenger seat of the van and, seeing that Anushka had followed me as far as the garden gate, I thought to walk back to her to say a final goodnight. I had not been too concerned about my lack of a shadow while inside Billy's cottage. The light in there was diffuse and varied and in any case there had been other claims on my attention. But now that I'd moved away from the safety of my van's shadow and was standing in a quiet lane in bright moonlight I felt as naked as I ever had. Realising too late what I'd done, I stared at the moon-silvered ground where my shadow should have been and I knew, with horrible certainty that Anushka was doing the same thing. That I had exposed myself.

"Yes," she said, "I think that you *are* in trouble."

"I've lost something, that's all," I said, hoping like hell that one of the things I hadn't lost was a dinner date with a woman who made Helen of Troy look like a dentist's x-ray of a diseased tooth.

Anushka looked at me for a long time. "We speak of this tomorrow," she said. "Good night, David. Enjoy your party."

"Goodnight," I said, my crest not as fallen as it might have been. I climbed into the van and risked the wrath of the hamlet when I began to crank the engine slowly towards ignition.

8

My shadow was waiting for me at the door. "About fucking time too," he said, snatching the box from me. He headed straight for the dining room and dumped the box on the table. "I'd almost given up on you, Baldy," he said. He began to rummage through the box, murmuring his approval. "You did good, Baldy," he said, when he'd finished.

From where I stood I had a depressingly unobstructed view of the kitchen floor. "I thought you were going to clean up this mess," I said.

My shadow shrugged. "Got bored," he said.

"Well, someone's got to do it," I said, knowing full well who that someone would be.

"Jesus, Baldy," he said, "you sound like your mother. Relax. Have a drink for fuck's sake."

"I told you," I said. "I don't drink."

"So you did, Baldy. So you did. My guess is you don't have any fun at all." He glanced at the lark mirror. "Not unless you count larks, which I don't. Can't even eat the scrawny bastards can you? No, you took off down the wrong road somewhere back there, Baldy, and you need putting right. All you've got to do is reach into this box and we can have a fine old time."

I looked at the box and I looked at my shadow and I had the dreadful feeling that he was right.

"I'd better clear up that mess you made," was all I said.

"Suit yourself," he said. "Now, where's the corkscrew?"

I got to work on the kitchen while my shadow got to work on the booze – a task for which he seemed blessed with super-human alacrity. By the time I'd binned the glutinous mountain of debris that my shadow had simply swept into the middle of the floor and then abandoned; by the time I'd wiped up the jam and the egg yolks and the half can of spilled treacle, great clouds of cigar smoke were billowing out of the dining room and my shadow was engaged in some kind of conversation with himself.

I put away the broom and dustpan and rinsed out the filthy cleaning cloths and then, bracing myself, returned to the dining room.

"Know what we should do, Baldy?" my shadow said, pouring more wine into the half-pint mug he'd taken from my glass cabinet. "We should go away somewhere for a few days. Spread our wings a bit. Always fancied Mexico myself," he said. "Wild peyote and tequila. Suit you, Baldy, would it?"

It was going to be a long night. Of course, like any drunk, he was going to have to be humoured. So, with grim resignation, I made myself a cup of tea and settled in opposite him, with the lark mirror, the ashtray, the box of booze and four wine bottles between us – three of them empty.

"So Baldy," my shadow said, "what do you do for women around here?"

"To tell you the truth," I said, thinking of Anushka and how desperately I hoped that things in that department were about to change, "I don't bother much."

He looked at me as if he suspected something and then he winked and leered. "You," he said, wagging a finger at me, "you, Baldy, are a sly old dog."

I smiled back in an aw-shucks, simpering, self-deprecating manner which shames me to this day. But, as I say, I was just trying to humour my booze-hound tormentor until he was drunk and lost enough for me to leave him and get to bed. I had a long day ahead of me, after all, and dawn was heaving inexorably into view. I was going to need at least a couple of hours sleep if I was going to function in any way efficiently.

The Lark Mirror

So I sat there, smiling like an idiot. I lit a cigarette and took a sip of tea.

"Hands are shaking, Baldy," my shadow said.

"Nerves," I said.

"Nerves, or nervous," my shadow said.

"Nervous, I suppose," I said.

"Of what?"

"Of you."

"Of me? Well, don't you worry on that score, Baldy. I'm not going to hurt you. We're pals, aren't we?"

"Maybe you're not going to hurt me –"

"There's no maybe about it –"

" – But you could make a lot of trouble for me."

"I *could* do that, Baldy," my shadow agreed. He jabbed his thumb at the box. "But so long as you keep the sweet stuff coming then you'll get no trouble out of me. Course," he went on, "I'll have other requests from time to time but they'll be easy enough bridges to cross."

He drank off a near-full mug of wine and then emptied the bottle into the mug and took a more modest sip. He smacked his lips and regarded me thoughtfully.

"Thing I don't get, Baldy," he said, apropos of nothing, "is why did you set fire to the school?"

I thought very carefully before I answered him. My estimation of the trouble he could cause had just increased a thousand-fold. On top of that, I sensed that he was lying; that he knew full well why I set fire to the school even if the reasons now seemed a little cracked.

"I didn't," I said, finally. "You did."

"No, Baldy, see ... you *think* I don't remember things and I *do* remember things. And I remember that it was *you* with the can of petrol and *you* with the box of matches…"

"Right," I said, bitterly, "and you were just tagging along."

"That's right, Baldy, I just tagged along like a good shadow."

"Except that you've never been that kind of shadow. Have you?"

"Now, don't be getting all deep and philosophical on me, Baldy," he said, relighting his cigar. "You know that stuff bores me. I'm surprised you're not banging on about Carl Jung already. He's one of your boys, ain't he?"

"I taught maths. You should know that," I said.

"Yeah, but you're the kind of boring fuck-wit who likes his extra-curricula bullshit. Have you any idea how many conversations you nixed with your theories on this, that, and the flip-side of the fucking universe?"

He was right about that, I knew. "Sorry," I said, and meant it.

"Oh, forget about it," he said in a conciliatory way. "It's all just water gone under. I'm in the mood to reminisce is all …"

And so we reminisced. He couldn't quite bring himself to let the night in question go and so we talked about *her*, about how she wasn't exactly your average geography teacher and about how her short skirts drove me wild and about her minxy ways (his phrase) and about how I drank back then and how it had seemed an act of righteous retribution to burn down the geography room – which is where she worked - when in fact I'd just been muddled and confused and deeply vexed with an underlying depression and almost too drunk to stand to boot.

Then, having (thankfully) put that topic to bed, we rehearsed some slightly less uncomfortable episodes. We did the blow-job in the back of the taxi (which my shadow claimed was a classic) and we did the stolen car and the cannabis raid and a few lesser adventures until we'd whittled down our material to a handful of anecdotal fillers, by which time I'd begun to wonder a) how I'd managed to hold down a teaching job for as long as I had and b) if my shadow was now drunk enough to be left safely to his own devices.

The Lark Mirror

I studied him carefully and judged that he was. He was a good way into Billy's bottle of very fine scotch by now and his eyes kept closing and he'd let his cigar go out.

"I'm going to bed," I told him. "You can sleep on the couch."

"Bed, Baldy?" he said, trying to rally. "But we've just got going."

It was a valiant effort but even my shadow had his limits - he'd drunk four bottles of wine plus the scotch in a short space of time. It was possible – likely even – that he'd hit a second wind at some point but if that happened I thought that he would most likely sit where he was and mumble to himself or else sing some song he only knew half the lyrics to. It's what I used to do, after all.

Either way, I was determined to exploit the hiatus in order to get some sleep and so I stood to fetch my shadow a blanket from the airing cupboard. When I returned with it I pointed to the couch to make sure he understood. Then I left him to it.

But before I could make good my escape, with one foot already over the threshold, my shadow stopped me.

"Baldy?" he said.

I turned back to him. He looked as if he were enjoying a momentary flash of sobriety and I knew I wasn't going to like what he had to say. I was right about that.

"That was a cruel and terrible thing you did," he said, "cutting me out of your life like that. But now I'm back. And I like it here, Baldy. I like it a lot. Which is why I'm going to stay. Only *this* time, I'm going to stay for good."

9

Two American Phantom jets split the air above the moors. My head hurt and the birds were singing. It was time to begin my quest and I was as tired as hell. I forced myself out of bed and got dressed.

When I went downstairs my shadow was snoring loudly from the couch. I checked that the lark mirror was still intact and then gave the detritus on the table a more general perusal. In addition to the tally as it stood when I retired for the night my shadow had also drained four cans of beer – which had exhausted the contents of the booze box save for a bottle of Babycham. I remembered back to my own drinking days and guessed that he'd had the beer for breakfast. With any luck, I thought, the bastard would have to sleep all day. Of course, such convenience would carry a double edge; if my shadow remained at home while I went about my quest I would no doubt be persecuted by the worry that he would rally enough to go around spreading wild and true rumours about me. I pondered that, factoring in the distance between my cottage and anywhere else, and told myself that he would not relish such a long walk on a hot day in his condition (and it was a condition I well-remembered). Besides, it was clear that things would be worse in so many ways if he were to come along. With that in mind, I crept around so as not to wake him.

My thoughts, as I closed the kitchen door to contain the noise of the boiling kettle, turned to Anushka. If success in my quest were denied me, if only a trial of frustration, failure and humiliation awaited me, then there would be Anushka, on the far shore of it all. Nothing could spoil the fact that whatever happened today, *tonight* I would be having dinner with such a fabulous woman. What's more, a woman who had seen my lack of shadow the night before and had not fled in horror.

And so it was that I was feeling oddly buoyant as I made my coffee and took it out to the doorstep to drink with a cigarette. The day was already warm even though it had yet to be light for an hour.

I drank my coffee and smoked my cigarette and mulled over the task ahead. Needless to say, what with one thing and another, my plan had advanced not one jot. Neither did anything fresh come to mind as I sat there. I decided to ignore Jed's speculation that Aunt Alsey slept in the bottoms of ponds and could turn herself into smoke. It's not that I disbelieved him entirely – though he'd stretched credulity – it's just that such a person would be hard to find (as Jed himself had pointed out) and I needed hope. After all, my shadow might be all that stood between me and the realisation of last night's brief, delicious dream in which I was riding to hounds across the Russian steppes with the wonderful Anushka at my side. Anushka had ridden beautifully in the dream.

I decided that I would treat Aunt Alsey as if she were simply a flesh and blood creature (which she was) and so bound to travel by road just like any other human being. My plan then, would remain as initially conceived. I would simply drive west (since that was the direction she'd shuffled off in) and keep an eye open for her while doing so, making a few discreet inquiries along the way if circumstances allowed. At her rate of travel I didn't think she'd have covered more than twenty miles even if she'd done nothing but walk – no stopping for meals, no rest, no sleep, no stealing.

Of course, she could have diverged down any number of country lanes but if I kept the western boundary of the search within twenty miles then I thought I could grid off an area that was searchable in a day.

When I crept back into the dining room my shadow was still snoring. He'd turned over in his sleep and a string of drool connected his mouth to the cushion he'd been using as a pillow. I noticed my hat crushed beneath his elbow but, as tempted as I was to reclaim it, I didn't want to risk waking him by teasing it clear.

I wrapped the lark mirror in a towel to protect it and then put it inside my haversack. I shoved my map and a notebook and pens in there also and then took my haversack into the kitchen to add a flask of tea and the sandwiches I'd made to its load.

I slung the haversack over one shoulder, took a last look at my shadow and then carried myself back outside and into the sunny morning air. I considered locking the door. I seldom bothered to do this and decided not to break the habit. What good would it do to lock my shadow inside the cottage anyway? If he did recover sufficiently to want to escape then I had little doubt that he had it in him to do so, locked door or no.

The van started on the third turn of the key, which I took for a good sign. As I drove slowly along the lane, gold finches flitted among the sparse hedgerows and, knowing nothing about gold finches nor their place in the folkloric imagination, I decided to take this as a good sign also.

I kept to a low speed so that I could safely scan the moors as well as the lanes and roads. Above the moors, the larks were already ascending into the pristine blue of a sky which, in that moment, was not even defaced by the contrails of American jets. It was a beautiful day for a witch hunt.

My initial optimism, however, was misplaced – and badly so. I was spat at by cats and attacked by dogs. Wherever and whenever I was unwise enough to step from my van to make an enquiry I was greeted with signs of the cross and slammed doors. In Halfpenny I was set upon by a gang of boys from which I escaped with a busted back

The Lark Mirror

light but no serious injury. I was mobbed by rooks and chased by horses. I was run off a farm at gunpoint and, just outside Benchback, I was almost trampled to death by a camel attached to a travelling circus.

By which time I'd had enough and I returned to the cottage like a broken crusader minus his horse and lance and little to show for his journey to the Holy Land besides tales of torture and deprivation (and a full flask of tea).

From now on, I vowed, I'll travel only by night.

But that wasn't to be, because the first thing I noticed was that my shadow was no longer sleeping on the couch and, what's more, a search of the cottage revealed that he wasn't anywhere else under its roof either. Damn it! His recuperative powers and reserves of energy were obviously far greater than I'd given him credit for.

I flopped into the armchair by the kitchen stove and, needing a moment to gather my thoughts, poured myself a cup of tea from my flask. As I hadn't run into my shadow on my return journey it seemed reasonable to assume that he'd turned left on the lane, immediately upon leaving the garden. It also seemed reasonable to assume that he wouldn't have gotten very far on foot – and I doubted anyone would offer him a lift in his state.

Whether or not he had a destination in mind was a harder thing to fathom. I didn't know how much he knew – or otherwise – about my life since I'd "cut him out of it", so I couldn't really guess as to the extent of his geographical knowledge of the area. As far as I knew he had no money in his jeans and so-

I stopped right there.

I rose from the armchair and crossed the kitchen and reached up to the top of the cupboard above the sink. I groped around until I found the small milk jug I kept hidden up there, my heart already sinking from the knowledge that the jug had been moved. I took it down and looked inside. Whereas it should have contained the several notes which made up my grocery money, it now contained only a dead woodlouse.

The bastard!

I kicked the cupboard under the sink and did a couple of circuits of the kitchen to calm myself. When I happened to glance out of the window I noticed that the shed door was hanging open. I went outside and picked my way through the lavender along the path to the shed. I peered inside. The hatchet was still embedded in the chopping block where I'd left it at close of winter; my fishing rods still hung on their pegs; the mice were still shitting on the workbench and a string of onions still hung from a nail in the roof beam. Everything was as it should be except that my bicycle was gone.

It was hard to imagine my shadow, hung-over as he was and hungry too no doubt (I assumed he needed food as well as alcohol), tearing across the moors on a bicycle on such a hot day. Nevertheless, that was the only narrative in town and the only one I had to work with.

But where would he have headed for? My shadow didn't strike me as the type who'd be happy just riding around and enjoying the countryside and besides, the stolen money smelled of a plan.

Then it came to me. Corny Cross. He'd gone to Corny Cross.

A man with my shadow's proclivities would need no prior knowledge of Corny Cross. He'd sense it and smell it and, in his deep heart's core, would hear it calling him across the moors.

Corny Cross stood on a rise overlooking the distant sea. It was ten miles from anywhere and to say that local people didn't think that distance enough was an understatement. The deeds committed there were so vile, the commerce so strange, its reputation so damnable that there was always some petition or other doing the rounds to demand that a by-pass be built around the place to prevent tourists visiting it by accident. It was, apparently,

The Lark Mirror

verboten to even mention Corny Cross in the tourist information centre in Crickford.

My shadow would feel very much at home in such a squalid hole. The more I thought about it the more I thought that it would be a miracle if he'd gone anywhere else. Yes, he would feel right at home in Corny Cross and it was going to be a tough job to get him out of there.

As urgent as the need was to get after my shadow straight away I wanted a moment or two to collect myself and think things through. I sat in the kitchen and munched on a cheese sandwich and wondered if I should take a rope or some weapons with me. When and if I found my shadow it would be unlikely that he'd come quietly. And then what?

I'd never been much of a fighter and I doubted that I could beat him if it came down to it. Could I bribe him somehow? But then what could I offer him that he wouldn't, in any case, be able to find in Corny Cross?

As I worked my way through various scenarios, each more lurid and unsettling than the one before, I was acutely conscious that I would have to negotiate the streets and inns of Corny Cross minus a shadow. Given that morning's setbacks, it was not a prospect which filled me with joy.

On the other hand, I thought, rising from my chair, if there was anywhere on the moors where my lack of shadow would be met with little more than profanity-ridden acceptance then it would be Corny Cross. After all, the towns own mayor was a known transvestite and its vicar was said to moonlight with a local coven.

Not forgetting my larger purpose, and even though Corny Cross lie well outside my search area, as I hit the road for the second time that day I once again carried the haversack containing the lark mirror. Just in case.

Adrian J Smith

10

They say that you can smell beer and catch clap a full five miles from Corny Cross if you stand downwind of the place but all I could smell as I paused on the rise to view the town and the sea beyond was the dead dog that someone had hung from a fence. Rooks were perched along the fence posts but they had little interest in the dog and I wondered if they thought it was rabid.

I drove on but before I'd got very far I saw something glinting in the shallow ditch and I slowed as I approached to see what it was. What it was was the buckled rim of the front wheel of my bicycle. I got out of the van and dragged the bicycle from the ditch. There was a rock back along the verge on the van's side of the road and it seemed obvious that my shadow – probably spurred on by his thirst into a last minute burst of effort and perhaps with the sun in his eyes – had hit the rock, dusted himself down and then, the cavalier bastard, simply slung my bicycle into the ditch and recommenced his journey on foot.

I opened the back doors of the van and hefted the bicycle inside. It was a strange thing to see that bicycle shadow moving around like that, without my own shadow to explain its movements.

I entered through the arch of the town gate and drove the narrow, winding, high-walled road into the market place. I parked near the church and surveyed the scene. Even though the market was on, it was a slow day in Corny Cross.

I watched two whores cross the square arm in arm and I watched some old women lolly-gagging around the place and I studied their shadows and noticed that they were not long shadows, it still being early afternoon. I stepped tentatively from the van. A large grey dog lifted its chin from the cobbles and marked my lack of shadow but didn't seem to care. A man wheeling drunkenly out of an inn doorway also took note but just muttered to himself and staggered off toward his next port of call. One boy nudged another and pointed but the other boy was too sun-sapped to care. They were used to strange sights in Corny Cross and it was apparent that my condition need not disturb the surface of the day. Not that I could be tardy or complacent – when the shadows lengthened then my aberration would become more and more obvious and it wouldn't pay to linger long enough for aberration to become abomination and so I set to work.

Of all the inns in Corny Cross the Blue Boar had by far the worst reputation, which made it a good place to start. It stood on the far side of the square and I threaded my way toward it through the market in order to take advantage of the shadow-cover offered by the stalls.

The market was the usual Corny Cross affair. Pigs' ears glazed with honey. Cider by the gallon, chickens live and dead; salt fish, jam and chutney. The lord mayor himself (wearing a sensible skirt and a pink blouse) was selling cartridges for an elephant gun. And that was all. So far as I could tell, there was nothing out of the ordinary.

Except this.

The mayor had found a buyer for the elephant gun cartridges. *That* struck me as odd, since there weren't any elephants on the moors and, even if there were, I was pretty certain they'd be protected. But what had really piqued my curiosity was that the buyer looked vaguely familiar. He wore a kind of safari jacket complemented by a wide-brimmed hat and his deep tan told anyone who cared to listen that this was a man not unacquainted with the outdoors. He exuded calm and confidence as he pointed at two boxes of cartridges and held up three fingers.

Sweating in his too-thick blouse, the mayor shook his head and held up four fingers. The buyer smiled and shrugged gamely, shelled out four notes and then put a box of cartridges into each waist pocket of his safari jacket. You could see the weight of them by the way the jacket tugged down at the shoulders.

Try as I might, I couldn't quite place the man and so I let it go and continued on my way to the sign of the Blue Boar.

The Blue Boar was as dim and smoky a tavern as any you'd find in a gothic tale and – in the sense that not a single person in the room threw a shadow – very egalitarian. I hadn't set foot in a pub since I'd quit drinking and the smell of beer and smoke and the general hubbub of voices hit me with a wave of nostalgia almost too powerful to bear. However, if the smell of beer and smoke remained a constant the hubbub of voices diminished and then died altogether before I'd taken more than a few steps into the room. People began to nudge one another and to point in my direction and I knew beyond doubt that my shadow had made some kind of impression here.

The conversation picked up again but it never achieved its previous level. I looked nervously around for my shadow but could neither see nor hear him anywhere. When I glanced at the bar I saw that the landlord was staring at me. He didn't look happy. I felt the dread of the parent when the police come knocking.

I sidled to the bar as casually as I could manage.

"You'll be looking for your brother, I expect," the landlord said.

"Yes," I said, grateful to be handed a ready-crafted lie. "I'm afraid he's been off on one of his tears."

"Out back," the landlord said, jerking his thumb over his shoulder.

"Out back?" I said, surprised. I hadn't expected my shadow to content himself with a beer garden when there was a room full of poachers and sailors and scrimshankers and whores and gamblers and thieves and end-of-voyage fisherman for him to play in.

"Here," the landlord said, "you'll be needing this." He fetched up a key from beneath the bar and offered it to me. When I went to take it he snatched it back. "That'll be ten quid, if you please," he said.

"A tenner?" I said. "What for?"

The landlord regarded me as if I were an idiot and I must say I felt like one. "For your brother," he said.

"What is this?" I said. "A ransom?"

"A ransom," the landlord said, for the benefit of the room. "He wants to know if it's a ransom." The room appreciated the humour of that but I was damned if I could see anything to laugh about.

"I'm sorry," I said, "but I haven't got a clue what's going on here."

"It's quite simple," the landlord said. "Your brother is out back. If you want him returned to you then you'll need this key. And the loan of this key will cost you ten pounds as issued by the Royal Mint."

"Right," I said, still flustered. Luckily, I had the Masons' money in my wallet. It was quite a large sum for those days and I was careful not to expose it to view as I peeled off a ten pound note, which I made to hand to the landlord.

"It's not for me," he said. "See the lady behind you."

I'd noticed when I came in that one whore in particular had skewered me with an especially vicious glare and it was in her direction that the landlord now pointed. She sat at the closest table to the bar – along with two companions – and so I didn't have to stretch far to hand her the note. She snatched it from me and tucked it inside her bra.

"That your brother out there?" she said. "He looks like you."

The Lark Mirror

"Apparently so," I said, to both clauses.

"Well, you tell you brother he shouldn't take things if he can't pay for 'em. Ooo," she said, "he *is* a filthy beast."

"You always was too proud, Serry," one of her companions chipped in.

"Well, he was," said the first whore. "Just plain filthy. I eren't never even heard of half the things we just done."

"Sounds like an education to me dear," said the other. "What about you?" she asked me. "Educated man like your brother, are you? You can teach me a thing or two if yer like."

"Er, no thank you," I said.

"Only a tenner," she said. "Same as your brother. 'Cept you won't hear me complain about the novelty. *Some* of us appreciate a thing like that."

"No, really," I said. "It's alright, I've got a dinner date."

"Suit yerself," she sniffed. "Can always come back another time; I'll be here."

"I'm sure you will," I said, turning back to the landlord. I relieved him of the key and he lifted the bar hatch to let me through. He ushered me to a door at the rear of the inn. He swung open the door for the sunlight to pour in and then he left me to it, too busy to even notice my lack of a shadow.

The sunlight was so fierce as I emerged from the gloom that at first I couldn't see anything. Then, when I *could* see, it took me a few moments to make sense of what I was looking at.

My shadow had been placed in a set of stocks. Him and that set of stocks were the only features of the landscape – which was basically an enclosed yard with bare earth that looked to have been recently pecked over by chickens. My shadow's trousers and underpants were pooled around his ankles and, since I was standing behind him, I could see that the cheeks of his ass had been striped with a garden cane. This, he would later explain, was the standard punishment for failure to pay a Corny Cross whore following satisfactory delivery of service.

I walked around to look my shadow in the eye. His head and hands hung limply from their respective holes in the stocks. He appeared to be asleep and so I assumed that he must be a lot more comfortable than he looked. Then again, he also looked very drunk.

Not knowing what else to do, I gave him a gentle slap to wake him. It wasn't a deep sleep and he roused himself readily enough. He raised his head and blinked a few times until I came into focus. "Baldy," he said, "am I glad to see you. Look what those fuckers have done to me."

"It's about what you deserve," I said. "I ought to whip you myself for stealing my grocery money and wrecking my bike."

"Bike, Baldy?" he said. "I don't know what you mean. I haven't had your bike."

"Stop lying," I said. "I found its body."

"Oh," he said. "Well, alright, I borrowed it. That's all. It's not my fault if they want to scatter rocks all over the damn road, is it? What kind of place is this anyhow?" he wanted to know. "Throwing innocent strangers in the stocks. Beats me why you moved here in the first place, Baldy."

"Nobody asked you along," I said. "Nobody forced you to come to Corny Cross either. You're lucky you didn't get your throat cut. And if you want to know the truth I came to the moors to get away from *you*."

"No, Baldy – you came here because you set fire to the school."

"Which amounts to the same thing," I said. "In any case we've been over that ground and if you want me to get you out of there then I wouldn't mention it again."

"Why, Baldy," he said, "does that mean you've got the key?"

I showed it to him.

The Lark Mirror

"Well, don't just stand there," he said, "get the fucking lock open."

"Maybe I don't want to," I said. "Maybe I'd prefer to leave you here. In fact, now that I think about it, that seems like quite a good idea."

"Don't be a cunt about it, Baldy," he said. "I'm your pal."

"A pal who nicks my grocery money and wrecks my bicycle."

My shadow spat. "Alright, Baldy," he said, "let's stop fucking around here. We're not pals in any way, shape or form. But I *am* your shadow and that binds us. If you don't get me out of here then when I *do* get out – which I will – I'll make such trouble for you that this time you'll have to move to fucking Siberia."

"I've got two weeks' wages in my pocket," I told him. "I could give that landlord enough money to keep you here for a week. Do you think anyone's going to help you in a place like this? No. In fact, the way your ass is hanging out, they're more likely to come and *do* things to you."

"Be wasted on me, Baldy," my shadow said. "I'd think that was more your line, you fucking pansy."

Despite his bullying, his grossness and his empty defiance, I could tell that I'd hit home.

"If I really stretched the budget -" I said, " – and I'd consider you worth it – then I could even pay the landlord *not* to feed you."

"I don't eat much," he said.

"But you *do* eat," I said. "And a week's a long time."

"Alright, Baldy," he said, "you've got me. So what are we haggling over here?"

"I want promises."

"Name them."

"Firstly, *if* I decide to let you out, you'll get straight in the van without any trouble. Secondly, when we get home, you'll get yourself cleaned up and then stay out of my way. Watch TV, read a book. I don't care. Just no more fuss and noise. Thirdly, I'm going out tonight and I want your promise that while *I'm* out, *you'll* stay in. No more wandering off. Not tonight. Not ever. And there'll be no more all-night drinking nor stolen money nor wrecked bicycles."

"Is that all?" my shadow said. "Baldy, you've got a deal."

I didn't exactly trust him to come through on his promises but I'd made him realise that I wouldn't put up with his antics without a fight and that was as much as I'd really hoped for. I was even feeling a little conciliatory at that point – he was my shadow after all and it gave me no pleasure to see him in such a wretched state.

When I freed him from the stocks he pulled up his underwear and trousers and rubbed at the chaffing on his wrists. I picked up my hat from where it lie in the dirt. As tempted as I was to reclaim it I decided that it would be easier just to let my shadow keep it for now and so I handed it to him. He put it on and then strode over to the nearest wall and urinated up it. I could tell that he was feeling more himself already because when he'd finished urinating he said: "Now, Baldy, about that money …."

11

Nevertheless, he was as good as his word and took 'no' for an answer and I was able to get him to the van with a minimum of fuss. Once inside the van though, he began to babble on about his day and the verbal torrent was only stemmed when, halfway back to the town gate, he was forced to wind down his window and vomit on a small child.

No sooner were we on the main road when we came across a Land-rover with steam pouring from beneath its open bonnet. I slowed and stopped beside it. Staring into the engine compartment was the man who had bought the elephant gun cartridges from the mayor. It seemed entirely fitting that he should have a Land-rover to go with his safari jacket and elephant gun cartridges.

"Now, don't you say a word," I told my shadow. "Just shut up and let me do the talking. Alright?"

"Fine by me, Baldy," he said. "You do your good Samaritan routine and I'll have a little snooze. You can wake me up when we get home."

The passenger window was wound down but I didn't want to speak across my shadow so I got out of the van and called to the man over the roof.

"What is it?" I said. "Radiator?"

"I'm afraid the old girl's cooked," the man said.

"I can run you back into town if you want to call the AA," I said, remembering that there was a phone box in the market square. I quickly pondered the likelihood of an un-vandalised phone box standing right in the centre of Corny Cross and added: "Or I can take you on to the next phone box if you like." The next phone box stood at a lonely cross-roads about eight miles further on.

"No good I'm afraid," the man said. "Not a member."

"You could call Silas Crabtree," I suggested. "I'm sure he'd come out."

"Still no good," the man said. "Thing is, I'm in rather a hurry. Some urgent and important business at home. I don't suppose I could prevail upon you chaps .... ?"

"Where do you live?" I asked.

"Just outside Crow Norton."

I deliberated for a moment. On the one hand I had to get my shadow home and cleaned up and settled and then I had to get my own self cleaned up and calm and with any luck rested in time for my dinner date with Anushka. I'd barely slept the night before and I didn't want to be yawning my way through such a promising occasion and had hoped to snatch an hour or two's sleep. On the other hand, here was a man stranded on the moors beneath a baking sun almost within spitting distance of the most disreputable town for miles around. A man, moreover, I was curious about. I was still trying to figure out from where I knew his face and I was intrigued by the elephant gun cartridges and it was within the scope of my plan – wasn't it? – to look for clues and signs no matter how vague or tenuous. Crow Norton was twelve miles or so out of my way. I calculated that the extra miles would cost me about forty-five minutes, which didn't seem so bad.

"It would mean an awful lot to me," the man said. "I really have got the most appalling spot of bother to clear up."

"Okay," I said. "I'll make some room."

While the man slammed down the bonnet and secured the Land-rover I roused my shadow and shifted him into the back of the van. He lay down beside my wrecked bicycle and used some of my dust sheets for mattress and pillow.

The Lark Mirror

The man climbed into the passenger seat and I pulled away.

"This is awfully decent of you chaps," the man said. "And you, Sir," he went on, turning to my shadow, "are a gentleman. I wouldn't have objected to riding in the back, all things considered."

"Should've mentioned that before Baldy threw me out the shotgun seat," my shadow said, tersely.

"Shut up," I said. "You're lucky I didn't leave you where I found you. Pay no attention to him," I told my new passenger. "He drinks too much."

"Well, never mind," the man said, "we all like a little snifter from time to time. But how rude of me – I haven't even introduced myself. I'm Major Cecil Pikestaff," he said, holding out his hand for me to shake. Which I did, if a little awkwardly.

"David Chambers," I told him.

"And your friend?" the Major said.

"Brother," I said. "He's my brother. Er … Sid."

"Pleased to make you acquaintance, Sid," the Major said but my shadow, whether dozing or not, ignored him.

I spoke the Major's name silently in my mind a couple of times. It definitely had a familiar ring to it. Then it came to me and I knew where it was I'd seen him before. "You're the monkey-dog hunter," I said.

"Ah," he smiled, "I'm afraid you've got me there. Amazing what a little exposure on television will do for one's public profile isn't it? Of course, it distorts the picture. My pursuit of the monkey-dog is only really a sideline. Big cats; that's what I'm known for by my colleagues and rivals. And then there's the bread and butter work of vermin control – rabbits, rats, foxes. And corvids of course. Mustn't forget corvids."

But I wasn't interested in corvids. "This monkey-dog business … " I said and then failed to follow through.

"You want to know if he's real," the Major said.

"Is he?" I'd been following the monkey-dog story since my arrival on the moors when, during my very first perusal of the *Moorland Quarterly Gazette*, I'd happened upon an article which adumbrated how farmers were complaining about menaced flocks and missing lambs and savaged ewes and strange footprints in the earth. All of that and an otherworldly howling beneath the moon. I'd been keeping an open mind on the subject for this reason and this reason only: the monkey-dog was a new phenomenon. It hadn't been revived from legend by superstitious moorsmen. There was no mention of it in either the written annals or in living folk memory until only several years ago. (It had been about eighteen months since I'd first seen the Major on the local TV channel, speaking authoritatively on the subject of the monkey-dog, even though he confessed to not, at time of speaking, having got so much as a decent look at the creature.) That the monkey-dog shared some physical attributes with a dog, others with a monkey, was the common thread which linked purported sightings of it – hence the name – but there was little agreement as to how this chimerical beast was actually arranged. Did it possess the body of a dog and the head of a monkey (for instance) or vice versa?

"Oh, he's real alright," the Major said.

"Have you seen him?" I said, excitedly.

"You want to know what he looks like?" the Major said, somewhat evasively, I felt. "Let me put it this way, old chap," he said, "I'm very close to him. The world won't have to wait too much longer before it can gaze in wonder upon the monkey-dog." Which effectively closed down all further discussion on the matter.

We drove on for a while until, finally, the Major broke the silence. "Couldn't help noticing, old boy," he said, "that you seem to be lacking a shadow."

I nearly drove into the ditch.

"Unusual state of affairs, eh?" the Major said. "You know, old boy, if I were forced into making a guess, I'd say that you'd been bitten by a certain person who goes by the name of Aunt Alsey."

Again, the ditch beckoned.

"You know about her?" I said.

"Oh, it's much more than mere knowledge, old boy. In fact, I'm afraid that you and I are in the same leaky old tub, as it were. I think that perhaps we should have a little chat, don't you?"

"Has this got anything to do with elephant guns?" I said.

"You'll see," he said. "You'll see."

12

For pretty much the remainder of the journey I recounted my brush with Aunt Alsey and the events of the last couple of days, rattling on in a very unguarded manner and retaining barely enough prudence to omit mention of how I set fire to the geography block at my old school.

The Major expressed some interest in the lark mirror, saying that he'd once seen a 'similar contraption' used to snare eagles in Kazakhstan (though what he was doing in Kazakhstan he didn't say) and I would have shown him the lark mirror if not for the fact that my haversack was behind my seat and I didn't think I could retrieve it without waking my shadow, who was now snoring loudly.

"Of course," I said, probably redundantly, "his name's not really Sid."

"Turn right here, old chap, if you don't mind," the Major said, when we were roughly a mile shy of Crow Norton. By now the open moorland had given way to a more wooded country and when I turned as directed I found myself driving down a winding lane through a deep wood. The shade was a blessed relief.

As we crossed a humped-back bridge over a trout stream I glanced up the stream, where there stood an old mill. Water spurted through its mill race but the mill wheel had come adrift from its axis and was canted to one side and some of its paddles were broken off.

"Shame about that, isn't it?" the Major said, perceiving the direction of my gaze. "It was fine until a few days ago."

"Really?" I said. "What happened?"

"Something smashed it up, old boy. I'll tell you about it when we get to the house."

The Lark Mirror

I drove on down the lane to where the woods ceded ground to a clearing and in that clearing was a house so incongruous that it seemed to tell lies about its own history. It was built in the style of the French Chateau, with slate turrets and a spire. There was a stable block off to the left of the house and plenty of lawn around the place and the whole thing was circumscribed by a moat. There wasn't a single duck paddling in the moat – it's funny how you notice the small things.

We rattled across the moat bridge and the Major instructed me to park facing on to the end of the stable block, on a bare, oil-stained patch of earth which was roughly the base dimensions of a Land-rover.

"What about him?" the Major said, as we clambered out of the van.

I looked at my shadow, who was still snoring and drooling into my dust sheet. He stank of beer, cigarettes and vomit – which is pretty much how I'd smelled in the mad days leading up to my infamous arson attack. "Let him sleep it off," I said.

The Major led me past the stable block and around to the back of the house, fishing a key from his trouser pocket as he did so. There were more woods on the far side of the moat and the shadow of the woods was just then encroaching onto the back lawn, something which the Major remarked upon.

"Haven't got long," he said, cryptically.

I noticed, as he let us into the house, that a stake had been driven into the lawn a few paces from the moat, and that a rope trailed from the stake as if it had been used to tether some animal.

I followed the Major through the kitchen and then along a hallway - where trophy heads (a bear, a leopard and various kinds of antelope) stared glassy-eyed into endless space and where a suit of armour, stripped of one glove and gauntlet, stood propped in asymmetric splendour – and then into a kind of long drawing room with French windows that opened onto the lawn and which the Major did indeed open.

He held up a finger. "Listen to that," he said. "Not a single bird."

I listened. He was right. With no birds and no wind to rustle the leaves and no other sound close by save a solitary bee making the rounds of the honeysuckle that grew around the French windows, it was quiet enough to hear the water in the mill race back along the lane and I sensed some connection between the lack of bird song and the smashed water wheel.

"Won't be long now," the Major said. "Take a seat, old boy." He gestured to the large table which dominated the room.

The table was a testament to the Major's occupation and pre-occupations. If I were the kind of person who wondered about other people's marital status and other domestic arrangements (which I wasn't, particularly – though, of course, I would make an exception in Anushka's case) then that table would have told me all I needed to know. No woman, especially a woman of the Major's stamp, would tolerate such clutter in her domain. Bills, maps, fishing tackle, magazines – *Trout and Salmon, National Geographic, The Rat Catcher* – vied with handguns and knives and boxes of shells for my attention. They failed miserably, because it was the thing with its barrels resting on a stack of old newspapers which claimed the majority share of my interest. The barrels were about three fingers thick and half as long again as the barrels on the average shotgun. A hammer as big as a clothes peg protruded either side of the breech. It must be – could *only* be – an elephant gun.

I took a seat. Before me was a yellowing newspaper cutting with the headline 'Monkey-dog Madness' which seemed to be a round-up of sightings and speculation of the kind which ran about two or three times a year in the local press. Scrawled across the article in heavy, black felt-tip pen were the words: UTTER BALDERDASH!!!

"Can I get you a drink, old boy?" the Major said. "I usually go for a gin round about now."

"No thanks," I said. "I don't drink."

"Lemonade?" the Major said and, since I was thirsty, I accepted. The Major opened a cocktail cabinet and poured the drinks. Then he returned to the kitchen to put some ice and lemon into them.

In his absence I allowed myself to grow nervous about the time – blowing a dinner date with Anushka was the kind of thing that could haunt a man all his life. If I was going to learn more about Aunt Alsey, however, I was just going to have to be patient and let the thing develop at its own pace.

The Major returned, handed me my lemonade and then took a seat at the head of the table. He took a good long look through the French windows followed by a thoughtful gulp of his gin and tonic.

"Where to start, old boy," he said, as if to himself. "Alright," he decided, "let's start here."

He slipped his hand beneath a copy of *Guns and Ammo* and produced a dog lead and a collar. He let the collar dangle from the lead so that he could be sure I knew what it was and then he tossed it onto the table. "I used to have a Labrador to go with that," he said. "Sweet-natured chap. Good for pheasants but not for much else. A wonderful companion though, especially since the old memsahib left me. Only a few days ago I was grooming him out there on the lawn. Now he's gone."

"What happened?" I said.

The Major pulled a grim smile. "Something ate him, old chap," he said.

"Was it-" I started, to say.

"No," he said, almost laughing. "It wasn't the monkey-dog. I'm afraid it was much worse than that."

It was hard to believe that there was something more ferocious and terrifying than the monkey-dog loose on the moors and I said as much.

The Major took off his hat and ran a hand through his thinning, sweat-damp hair. Without his hat, he looked older than I'd taken him to be.

"Signal crayfish," he said. "Ever hear of them?"

I hadn't. It would be several more decades before they'd colonised every river in the country. My only knowledge of crayfish was of something not much bigger than my thumb. I doubted that a thing like that could eat a Labrador.

"Big, brash, American bastards," he said. "About so big." He indicated something roughly ten inches in length, which was a monster compared to the crayfish I'd just had in mind but still not big enough to tackle a Labrador. "Lord knows where they came from," he went on. "Maybe from the yanks along the way there," by which he meant the air-base. "I know they like to eat the damn things. Maybe they've been farming them and let some escape. Or maybe," he added, a little mischievously, "they've been using them for some kind of experiment in one of those laboratories they have out there."

"Like the monkey-dog," I said. One theory had it that the monkey-dog was a product of the mysterious laboratories which were reputed to be part of the air-base – a thing of darkness created for deadly purposes and impervious to Russian bullets.

"Quite taken with this monkey-dog business, aren't you, old chap?" the Major said, with a smile. "But let's just stick to the crayfish for now, eh?"

"Alright," I said.

"They got into the trout stream some time back," the Major said. "Buggers breed at an alarming rate. One day they seemed not to be there at all, the next day the stream bed is crawling with the damn things, undermining banks and eating all the trout spawn. Easy enough to trap but a full-time job – an *impossible* job – to eradicate once they get a foothold. Or, indeed, a claw-hold. Even so, up until recently, they hadn't made it into the moat."

"And now they're there too?" I said.

"Oh yes," the Major said. "Even as we speak we're surrounded by the ugly little brutes. Except that they're not so little anymore." He eyed the shadows on the lawn.

"You mean they've grown?" I said.

"Just a tad," he said, sardonically. "But don't worry, old boy," he added, brightening, "I've got just the remedy." He took a box of the elephant gun cartridges from his pocket, opened the box, and then started dropping the loose cartridges back into his pocket, as if for ready access.

"But surely," I said, watching him, "they're not big enough to shoot with *those*. With *that* thing." I nodded toward the elephant gun.

"That instrument is all that stands between them," he said, gesturing toward the moat, "and the destruction of all my hard work." He drank some more gin. "Several evenings ago – it was just about getting dark – I was returning from the woods with Blackie. He liked to go in there to flush out a bird or two, whether or not I had a gun. As I came around the last bend in the lane I saw an old woman leaning over the bridge, dangling a line into the water."

"Aunt Alsey," I said.

"It would appear so," he said. "And just as you described her – shawl, eye-patch, chin-whiskers and all. I wasn't in the best of moods, I freely admit. I'd hit a glitch – a delay anyway – in one of my projects – my chief project actually – which was causing me some unexpected aggravation. So, when I saw this old woman with the line my first thought was that she was fishing for trout; poaching. And being in a bad mood, and, idiot that I am, I tore her off a strip and told her to clear off back the way she came. 'Can't' she said. 'Wants me supper'."

"To hell with your supper' I said. 'You're not going to batten down on any of *my* damn trout.'"

"Don't want no trout,' she said. She pulled the line clear of the water and hoisted it up to show me the small sack on the end of the line. The sack was moving and I realised immediately that what she'd caught could only be crayfish – she must have had some old meat or something in the sack to attract them. You wouldn't think that a man with a military career behind him would lose his cool in such an innocuous situation as that, nor that a man in my line of work would lack patience. And you would think – wouldn't you? – that in addition I'd be grateful to that old woman – to anyone come to that – for removing some of those damn pests from the stream. But my bad mood and her intransigence and, to be honest, the purely repulsive appearance of the old hag ... well, let's just say that it was a combination which proved detrimental to a harmonious outcome. Plus, there was the fact that she was trespassing and that she was very close to the house. And, I'm afraid, I have secrets to protect."

He took another drink.

"No offence intended, dear boy," he said, "but you're only sitting where you're sitting because, as I say, we seem to be in the same leaky tub and there's a chance we may be able to help one another. Pool our information, that kind of thing. Anyway, back to the night in question. So, the old woman, this Aunt Alsey, she'd pulled the sack clear of the stream to show me and, as I say, I could tell right away that it was only crayfish she'd caught. 'Nice tasty crayfish is what I wants,' she said. And, of course, I should have let her keep them. But instead, my temper was such that I snatched the sack from her and tipped the crayfish into the lane. There were five or six of the beggars and the sight of them raised my ire even more. I started to stamp on them with my boot and I kept on stamping until there was nothing much left of them. Even Blackie looked embarrassed."

"The old woman spat at me then. 'Ye keep 'em then,' she said. 'An' may they increase.'"

"'Ha,' I scoffed, 'a gypsy curse to have me over-run with crayfish. Not only superstitious twaddle,' I said, 'but superfluous twaddle too.'"

"'Ye'll see,' she said. 'May they increase and separate ye from yer prize.'"

"'Go on,' I said. 'Get the hell off my property.' The last I saw of that old woman she was towing the wet sack back up the lane."

He sipped his drink again. "Funny word that, 'increase'," he said. "Apart from any archaic meanings it can mean *either* to increase in amount, *or* –"

"To increase in size," I put in.

"Quite," the Major said.

13

"Well," the Major continued, "the first I knew something was amiss was when I saw the mill wheel all smashed up like that. I wasn't here when it happened so I didn't hear a thing and when I saw it the next day I couldn't for the life of me think what might have caused so much damage. Now, of course, I *do* know. One of them, maybe several of them, had got jammed in there. And they were by then so big and powerful that they smashed their way out of the damn thing. Seems silly now," he went on, "but at the time, having more pressing matters to attend to, I just put it out of mind. And I suppose the next thing that happened was the ducks began to disappear from the moat. They'd migrated that far by now, the enterprising little bastards. There's a trickle-ditch from the stream to the moat, which is what keeps it topped up. Either they'd already migrated using that means, or else they'd just marched from the stream to the moat using the lane. They can survive for long enough out of water to do a thing like that, even when they're of regular size – and it's an open guess as to their condition when and if they did that and it's a thing the mind recoils from, imagining the possibilities."

He glanced outside again and looked a little wistful. "Had some nice big tench in that moat," he said. "I expect they're gone too. Takes a long time to grow a tench, old boy."

"That *is* a shame," I said. I was fond of tench and hadn't seen anywhere near enough of them since I'd moved to the moors.

"The next thing," the Major continued, "was Blackie. It was early evening and Blackie was just bumbling about on the lawn. He'd just cocked his leg up some stinging nettles when it happened. I was trimming the edge of the lawn – don't usually garden but it was expedient to give Jim the week off. I heard Blackie yelp – not bark, mind you; poor beggar didn't have the chance to bark. Just a surprised yelp. And when I looked up, I saw it. Saw its claw. It had Blackie around the ribs and it just lifted him off his feet and took him into the moat. Just like that. Dear old Blackie didn't stand a chance."

He took another drink while he thought about Blackie. "You know," he said, "when I've sorted out what needs to be sorted out here, I'm going to catch that old woman and put her in a cage."

In that moment I realised what a very bad enemy the Major would make. Which was, of course, not a thing I was going to say out loud.

"Jesus," I said, "how big *are* these things?"

"You'll see soon enough," he said.

His choice of words made me worry about the time again. "How soon?" I said. "Only, I need to get back home. I've got –"

"Relax, old boy," the Major cut me off. "You haven't long to wait. A mere matter of minutes now. They're much bolder than they were. They still won't emerge in direct sunlight but once there's enough shadow on the lawn ... well, you'll see."

"And then you'll shoot them with the elephant gun?"

"It's the only way," he said. "Tethered a goat down there yesterday to draw them out so's I could get a decent shot. Thought I'd thin them out with my Enfield. Lost the goat and didn't kill a single one of the brutes. Scared them off and wounded a few is all. Even broke an upstairs window with a ricochet, what with their shells being so hard. And the very devil of it is old boy, they're getting bigger by the day. It's now or never at Chateau de Pikestaff, I'm afraid."

"This all very well," I said, with uncustomary assertiveness, "but how does any of this help me with my shadow? I mean yes, you *say* you're going to put Aunt Alsey in a cage, but we've got to find her first."

"Don't worry about that, old boy. You're forgetting, *finding* things, *catching* things – well, that's my meat and potatoes, isn't it? Now, I've a feeling it's going to take on shades of the Alamo around here in a few short minutes – hopefully, with a different outcome. There are plenty of guns. You help me now; help me fend them off, and I'll catch our Aunt Alsey and have your shadow returned to its rightful place and station."

"But I don't know how to use a gun," I protested.

"Yes you do. You just point it and pull the trigger. Couldn't be simpler, old boy."

"That doesn't mean I'll be able to hit anything," I said.

"You will," the Major said. "Once you see them, you'll see."

Which was not a comforting thing to hear. "But what's the point?" I moaned on. "You said yourself that only the elephant gun will do the job."

"Yes," the Major said, "*I'll* kill as many as I can. All *you* have to do is hold them off flank and rear. The reload rate on the elephant gun is slow. Don't want them gaining ground while I reload. I just have to keep them from the prize for one more night. That's all. They know what they want and without your help, they may just get it."

"Alright," I said, "but what is this prize?"

Smiling to himself, the Major stood up with alacrity, unearthed a large revolver and a box of shells from amidst the detritus on the table and handed both items to me.

"You can have a practise shot if you like," he said, "but you probably won't need it. Now, I'll just secure the perimeter and then I'll show you my prize. I'm fairly certain that you'll like it."

The Lark Mirror

Securing the perimeter, it transpired, was simply a matter of the Major glancing out of the windows on the other three sides of the house. When he returned, he had nothing to report. Meanwhile, I'd figured out how to swing out the cylinder on the revolver and I'd even managed to load three of its chambers by the time the Major returned.

"You see?" he said, marking my progress. "Like a duck to water." I expected him to pick up the elephant gun and lead us out through the French windows. Instead, he checked again on the lawn shadows and led me back toward the kitchen, telling me to leave the pistol on the table for the time being. As he passed the suit of armour in the hallway he paused and rapped his knuckles three times against its breast plate. "Chin up, old chap," he told it, breezily. "Won't need to lend a hand for much longer." He laughed at his own joke, which wasn't a joke I really got until we reached the kitchen and the Major opened one of the cupboards and from it produced the suit of armour's missing gauntlet.

"Here," he said, handing me the gauntlet, "see if it fits."

It was so heavy that I almost dropped it – not something that bode well for my up-coming debut with a live, bucking pistol. I recovered and managed to get my fist inside the iron glove. The gauntlet came up to my elbow and I couldn't feel the end of the iron fingers.

"See if you can effect a grip," the Major said.

I flexed the fingers into a half-grip, as if I were grasping an upheld, invisible sword – though I must admit I felt more perplexed than martial.

The Major stepped to the fridge and took out a whole leg of lamb. "How about this?" he said, slipping the shin bone into my waiting grip. I had to flex my muscles to hold up the combined weight of lamb and iron but this time I succeeded in not looking like a total weakling.

"Your shadow," the Major said as he led us outside, "just wondering; any good with a shotgun, is he?"

"I don't think that's a good idea," I said.

Once outside, I lugged my burden over to my van for a quick peek through the window. My shadow was still sleeping soundly with his head all but wrapped in a dustsheet.

I deliberated as to whether or not to wake him. Even in his sorry state I doubted that he'd sleep through the racket generated by an elephant gun (a racket which would be supplemented by my own sonic contribution by means of the revolver – which I now knew was a forty-five because it was stamped on the bullets I'd fed it). On the other hand, there might not even *be* any shooting. The crayfish could fail to show; indeed, they may not even exist. (Though I was indisputably in the grip of one of Aunt Alsey's curses – with the product of that curse even now in view – a giant crayfish was a big thing for a sane imagination to swallow and I must admit - not to my credit - that I wasn't *entirely* convinced.)

I decided in the end that it would be better to leave my shadow to his nap. At least that way I would know where he was and I wouldn't have to worry about him wandering into the house while my back was turned. The potential for mayhem if he found his way into the Major's drawing room, chock full of guns and alcohol as it was, was enormous.

I rejoined the Major at the front of the stable block, where he stood rattling a bunch of keys. He stepped towards the door of the stall closest to the house (the stall, that is, against the end of which my van was parked) and I noticed that it was the only stall with a padlock on it. In fact, it had three. A couple of the other doors hung ajar and I guessed that those stalls now housed the Major's lawn mower and other gardening equipment. It was certainly a long time since any of them had seen a horse.

The Major inserted a key into the first lock to free a kind of inspection plate fashioned into the upper half of the stable door. He opened it and looked through it cautiously. Then he stood aside to let me have a look.

"It's in there," he said.

I peered through the hatch. It was very dark in there. The hatch was only about a foot square and there were no windows. I couldn't see very much of anything and I told the Major so.

"Right-hand corner," he said.

As my eyes adjusted I *was* able to make out a form of indistinct shape and, as I watched, I heard a kind of snuffling sound and the form moved slightly, as if migrating from one phase of sleep to another.

"What is it?" I said. It could have been almost any largish mammal.

"Oh, I think you know," the Major said.

"It's *not*?" I said, half incredulous, half stuck by awe and wonder.

The Major nodded. He was puffed full of pride and I didn't blame him. He had snared the monkey-dog and as far as I was concerned (and I knew it wouldn't be a minority view) his achievement could not have been greater if he'd netted a mermaid or lassoed a winged Pegasus.

"He's a bit groggy, I'm afraid," the Major said. "I've had him under heavy sedation. He should be coming round though. I unchained him and stopped giving him the sedative this morning. If those brutes *should* break in here then I want him to have a chance of escape. I'd sooner have him running free again than chopped into fish bait."

"Or crayfish bait," I said, all doubts on the subject quashed. How could you doubt a man who'd captured the monkey-dog?

"Quite," the Major said. "When this is over, of course, I'll sedate him again and get the chain back on him. This stable won't hold him for long without the chain and sedative. Tomorrow I've got a hand-picked team of zoologists and publicists – with a couple of bods from National Geographic thrown in – coming out here to fetch him. One more night and he'll be someone else's responsibility. He should have been gone by now except that Morley, my most trusted man, is laid-up in Africa with a touch of dengue fever. Which was, you may as well know, the delay with which I was so vexed when I bumped into Aunt Alsey on that ill-starred evening."

But just for once, and only in that single, discrete moment, I'd lost all interest in Aunt Alsey. "How did you catch him?" I said.

"Ah," the Major said, "ordinarily the answer to *that* question would come under the heading of 'trade secret'. However, since we are now to some extent partners in an endeavour I'll make the exception. I discovered that our friend here has quite an unusual behavioural trait which I was able turn to my advantage. You see, I noticed that from amongst a flock of sheep or a herd of deer he would select an individual animal as his quarry. Nothing particularly unique in that. Except that *this* chap, having once made his choice, will pursue the unfortunate animal relentlessly until he's caught it. Nothing will deflect him – not even an easier opportunity if presented. Space and time are no obstacles. I'd observed that if he were forced to abandon a hunt due to some extraneous factor, something spooking him, say – and those damned American jets will do it – then he would simply pick up where he left off the previous night, pursuing exactly the same quarry as before. One night I spotted him close to a flock of sheep. He was too far off to hit with the hypo gun and so I waited until he'd made his selection and then I scared him off with a rifle shot. After that, it was just a matter of catching that particular young sheep and I had

The Lark Mirror

the perfect bait for an ambush the following night. Simple really," he said.

"If you know what you're doing," I said. I stared back through the hatch. "Can't really make much out," I complained. "Is there a light in there?"

"Oh, we don't want to wake him *too* suddenly, old boy," the Major said. "Temperamental kind of soul. Doesn't like too much light. Sunlight especially. Strictly nocturnal this fellow. Wouldn't want him to turn ugly and bust out before I can sedate him again."

I thought about the monkey-dog's reputation for ferocity and found that I couldn't have agreed more.

The Major scanned the perimeter again and marked the shadows on the lawn. "Haven't got long," he said. "Let's rouse him with some lunch and get you better acquainted. Put the meat through the hole, old boy. That leg is from the animal I used for bait. A good sniff of that ought to do the trick. Go on, give it a go. Only don't drop it, otherwise he'll just take it and slope off where you can't see him."

Dolt that I am, I belatedly realised why I was wearing the armoured gauntlet.

I pressed the leg of lamb through the hatch – it just about fit – and then squinted over the cuff of the gauntlet and down the length of my extended arm. "Here boy," I said.

The monkey-dog made the same snuffling sound I'd heard earlier and then raised its head, which is something I more sensed than saw, since I was blocking out most of the light. I heard it sniffing the air. When the smell of the lamb reached its nostrils, the monkey-dog let out a low growl followed by an un-earthly screech and then, without further preamble, launched itself at the door. Claws tore against wood and the doorframe creaked as if it would split. I almost dropped the leg of lamb and might well have done so had not the monkey-dog seized it between its teeth. My arm was jerked this way and that as if I were being electrocuted. I'd pulled my head back from the hatch but managed to recover my nerve enough to peer down the length of the gauntlet again. All I saw was teeth and blood and shredded meat. It was like an industrial process that had turned on its masters, with everything moving so fast that it was impossible to discern whether the teeth most resembled those of a dog, or a monkey.

When the frenzy was over the creature let go of what was left of its feed and began to prowl around in the dark, growling quietly to itself. I pulled my arm clear of the hatch. The lamb's leg was entirely stripped of meat.

"Good God," I said.

"Imagine *that* chap locked onto your trail," the Major said. "You know, in some respects he'd be the perfect assassin. Too crude for black ops, obviously. But imagine him in the field. Makes you wonder about all that speculation surrounding those Yanks and their labs, doesn't it. Eh?"

It certainly did. Of course, I had a hundred and one questions to ask about the monkey-dog but just then, from somewhere in the moat, came a sound very much like the breeching of a whale and our focus of attention shifted.

"There she blows," the Major said. He quickly closed the hatch and locked it. "Time to break out the ordnance, old boy," he said.

14

For a man in his predicament I must say that the Major went about things in a very calm manner. Of course, I lacked his military experience as a bulwark against panic and I pretty much hopped around nervously as I awaited my orders, the first of which was to fill a bowl with ice; the second of which was to set the smallest of a nest of tables on the lawn; and the third of which was to carry out the gin, the tonic, the lemonade, the glasses and the bowl of ice to set on the table. Obviously, the wholesale slaughter of giant crayfish was going to be a thirsty business. As I walked back and forth over the lawn – the tray's shadow floating across the grass without my shadow to support it – I noticed something which I hadn't spotted through the French windows. The lawn was littered with spent shotgun cartridges and empty bullet casings of several different calibres. The Major had obviously had a very tough and busy time of it in defending his 'prize' and I marvelled again at his equanimity.

For my own part, with those breaching whale noises now emanating from all quarters of the moat, I was nothing short of terrified. With the refreshments laid out to the Major's liking we loaded our ordnance (to use the Major's term) and took up our position on the lawn.

The Major fixed himself a gin and tonic. "Damn," he said, "forgot the lemon. Best go get one. Not the same without."

As he spoke, something crashed heavily against some moat-side vegetation. "You're not leaving me?" I said, in utter panic.

"Won't be a moment, old boy," the Major reassured me. "If you see anything, just pop away until I get back.

Oh, you might want to release the safety catch on your weapon." He showed me how to do it and then gave me a bracing slap on the back. "Chin up, old boy. If we bag some of these brutes then it'll be a bonus for those *Geographic* bods I told you about. You'll be famous. Might even be some money in it." And with that, he went off to fetch his lemon, leaving me to rake an increasingly threatening world with a badly-shaking gun sight.

The moat was boiling with activity now and the brush was crashing all around. Shades of the Alamo, the Major had said and I would have done anything to exchange this impending horror for the known quantity of the Mexican army. Then, talking of armies, I saw the first claw waving above the bank like a vanguard banner. A thing of plate and bone, olive green in colour save for an aggressive flash of red, it was easily as big as a dustbin. It snapped like a pair of secateurs in the hands of a rose-pruning gardener who was just getting his eye in. Freshets of water ran from it as it snapped back and forth. I took a wild shot and, predictably, missed. I heard a large branch break and fall in the woods across the moat. The second claw appeared and I fired again. By some miracle I hit the first claw but the bullet just spun away in ricochet with a high whine.

Then the thing's feelers came up, as thick as willow branches, followed by its eyes, followed by the rest of it. For a moment, I was just too transfixed to do anything. The beast dragged itself onto the lawn and stood, rising and falling as it tensed its eight, awful, spider-like legs. Then, with a loud hissing sound, it expelled great draughts of muddy water from vents along its body.

With its claws snapping menacingly, it made its lumbering way towards me. Its pace and gait seemed unsteady and laboured, as if it carried too much weight for its legs to adequately support. I fired the pistol again and managed to hit it somewhere, though I couldn't tell where. It raised up the foremost part of its body and waved its

The Lark Mirror

claws high, its feelers lashing the air like bullwhips. Then it let out a terrible shriek of outrage.

Despite everything, I heard the answering screech of the monkey-dog and I hoped that the Major had not miscalculated regarding the level of sedation.

I emptied the revolver to no good effect and I must admit that all notions of a partnership to find Aunt Alsey dissolved in my mind. I've got *my* problems, my coward heart said, and the Major has *his*. And the Major was welcome to them. Which is to say that I had just turned tail and would have bolted if it hadn't been for the Major's return. He was ambling sedately down the lawn with a knife in one hand and a lemon on a small china plate in the other.

"Don't worry, old chap," he said. "This one's mine." He set the knife and the plate on the table and hefted up the elephant gun from where he'd left it laying on the lawn. "Couldn't slice up that lemon, could you?" he said. "There's a good chap." And with that, he shouldered the elephant gun, thumbed back one of its great hammers, and shot the creature in the face.

It's head exploded like a pumpkin hit with the blunt side of an axe and its legs buckled and the whole thing crashed onto the lawn. Its claws came down last – *thump, thump* – like the first two beats of a drum tattoo which failed to develop.

"Good shot," I said. I cut a slice of lemon and managed to nick my thumb my hands were shaking so badly. I put the slice of lemon into the Major's glass and handed it to him, succeeding, against all the odds, not to spill it. My ears rang from the report of the elephant gun but I could hear the Major clearly enough when he spoke.

"Cheers, old boy," he said. He took a drink. "That was an old one, by the way," he explained. "Too heavy. The younger ones are a bit nimbler on their feet. Might be a good idea if you handle those. Pistol alright for you, is it?"

Before I could answer, one of the younger creatures he'd just mentioned crabbed its body from behind a box hedge to our right. I snatched up the revolver and let the beast have six clicks of six empty chambers.

Luckily, the Major despatched it with a single shot that blew it backwards with a dying squeal into the box hedge.

"Might be a good idea to reload," The Major said, good-naturedly.

I spilled half a box of shells in doing so, but I was able to shake six of them into the waiting chambers. While I was thus preoccupied, the Major fired twice more. I was dismayed when I looked up to see that there were about half a dozen crayfish of various sizes heading our way. Two of them were as big and lumbering as the first but the rest were all nimble side-step and parry and thrust. I emptied the pistol again in their general direction and brought one of these smaller ones to a dead, twitching halt. The Major fired again, killing one and mortally wounding another.

"Not bad sport, eh?" he said. All in all, and despite his more overriding concerns, the Major seemed perfectly happy to be spending his afternoon this way. Perhaps all this rapid-fire action and the smell of cordite had transported him back to a happier, simpler time.

I reloaded with a bit more proficiency this time and then fired all six rounds into a crayfish which had snuck up behind us and which was far too close for comfort. I emptied and reloaded that pistol over and over until the barrel grew hot. The Major continued to despatch our assailants with great efficiency and skill – pausing for refreshments now and again – until their hideous, still-clacking bodies began to pile up on the lawn.

Even so, they just kept on coming and I started to consider our position doubtful. The Major's remarks grew less flippant and jolly as his rate of fire increased until he was barking out orders as to where to concentrate our aim. Forget 'doubtful'. It was now clear to me that our situation was fast approaching one which might reasonably be called desperate and so I suggested a tactical retreat to the house (albeit in more demotic terms than expressed here).

"What? And cede ground?" the Major barked. "Pull yourself together, man. And keep firing."

I did as I was told while the Major got back to work with renewed ferocity. "Try to steal my prize, would you, you hell-spawned bastards?" he bellowed. One of the big crayfish reared up in front of him and he shot it through the chest so that it crashed down with a long, pneumatic wheeze. "How do you like *that*, you ugly brute?" he asked it. If he was growing increasingly short of good humour he was growing long on fighting spirit and, despite the way he'd barked at me, I was full of genuine admiration for him. That this man, this *warrior*, was now my partner in the quest to find Aunt Alsey afforded me, despite my terror, a fleeting moment of buoyancy.

Then, like some quotidian sound cutting through a nightmare – a nightmare of snapping claws and horribly articulating alien forms – a familiar churning noise reached my ears.

During the skirmish I'd forgotten all about my shadow. But now, wide awake and cranking over the engine of my van, there he was to remind me. The bastard! He was going to flee and leave me! Not only that, but if he got loose with my van I'd never get him back.

The imperative of that thought alone drove all other considerations from my mind and so, without seeking the Major's permission, I turned and legged it across the lawn toward the sound of my dryly cranking engine. How could I have been so stupid as to leave the keys in the ignition?

"Come back here!" the Major commanded but I ignored him because just then the engine caught and, hard on the heels of that news, came a painful grating noise from the gear box.

One of the smaller crayfish had interposed itself between me and the house. I emptied all three of my remaining bullets into its flank, leaving it too broken and crippled to be of further threat. Having no more bullets about my person, I tossed the pistol aside as I ran on.

But before I'd made it to the corner of the stable block the Major called out again. "You damn coward!" he bellowed. "Come back here." He fired a warning shot which blew the back door of his house from its hinges and this time I *did* stop.

When I turned around I saw to my great horror that my exiting the field had caused the Major to take his eye off the ball and for too long. And this time, it was my turn to shout. "Look out!"

But the warning came too late. Before he had a chance to heed it, a giant claw had seized him around the waist. A look of surprise came over his face and the elephant gun was discharged sky-wards. Then, as swiftly as a well-honed scythe laying low a thistle, the two halves of the Major's body were separated one from the other as thoroughly as the Major now was from his prize.

Within a heartbeat, the rest of them were on him. If our engagement had started out as the Alamo, it had ended with a more than passing resemblance to the Battle of the Little Big Horn.

15

I lingered no more to gaze on that awful scene because by now my shadow had been stirring around in the gear box for long enough to find a gear and the van's wheels were spinning furiously.

I scuttled around the corner of the stable block. My shadow was gibbering in terror. He had the van in reverse gear with the accelerator jammed to the floor. For all that, the van didn't budge an inch. And it didn't budge an inch because one of the smaller crayfish – which must have scuttled up the lane - had jammed itself under the back bumper. I froze in panic for a second. The crayfish reached its claws around and started pounding on the van's side panels.

Snatching a glance over his shoulder my shadow caught sight of me. He hadn't had a chance to put his hat back on and his hair was pressed flat on one side of his head and was flecked with lint from the dustsheet.

"Get in, Baldy, for fuck's sake," he said. "There's a giant fucking bug in the road!"

I leapt onto the bonnet and down the other side and yanked open the door and swung myself into the passenger seat.

"Put it in first!" I said.

The gear box crunched horribly.

"*First!*" I reiterated, louder this time. He was so cack-handed that I immediately regretted not turfing him out of the driving seat when I had the chance. But, with the shadow of another crayfish now looming into view at the corner of the stable I knew that the moment for that had passed.

"Press the fucking clutch in," I said. I slapped his hand clear of the gear stick and put it into first for him. "Go on," I said. "Easy."

We rolled forward and the van became un-jammed. The crayfish let out a pained screech.

"Clutch," I said, and then banged the gear stick back into reverse. "Now, fucking floor it!" I said, meaning the accelerator.

My shadow was more than happy to oblige and we smashed the crayfish back a few feet. Then we became jammed again and the wheels stopped biting and once again spun uselessly in the dirt.

"Clutch," I said, and put the van back into first. We rolled forward again and then stopped. That is, we were stopped. You could hear the bastard scrabbling around under there. Then came a sickening renting of metal and my just-recently-repaired exhaust began to blow again. The engine was revving almost to detonation point and the wheels span and then suddenly, something gave. We shot forward as if launched from a catapult and my shadow couldn't find the brakes in time.

As swiftly as it happened, it felt as slow-motion as a Sam Pekinpah indulgence, the event rolling itself out with horrible inevitability. On we catapulted until the van's front end punched a hole through the end wall of the monkey-dog's cell. Then the engine stalled. The boards directly in front of the windscreen remained intact so we couldn't see anything. We could, however, hear plenty.

The screeching, yammering and snarling – as unsettling as it was – was about what I'd expect from an un-sedated and very excitable monkey-dog. The thing that really threw the alarm switch was the ugly sound of the radiator grill being ripped clear of the front of the van. If the monkey-dog got its teeth inside the engine compartment, we were toast.

The Lark Mirror

My shadow, to his credit, needed little fresh instruction. He cranked the engine furiously until it caught and then jammed down the clutch. "Find the gear, Baldy," he said.

I shoved it into reverse and he popped the clutch. The grill was wrenched from the front of the van as we shot free of the stable.

The crayfish, meanwhile, had managed to pick itself up but we'd placed enough distance between us and it and now had enough momentum to roll right over it. It clung to the underside of the van for a few feet until we wrenched off one of its claws and then it fell away, sprawling through a dusty tumble in the lane.

As we tore off in reverse towards the moat bridge I snatched a glance at the hole we'd punched through the stable wall. My radiator grill was spat out of that hole like the product of a much-needed Heimlich Manoeuvre.

"Keep going," I said. "Get us out of here."

I turned my head to look out of the back window, fearing that the incompetent bastard would crash into a tree. But however inept he'd been with the gear box, my shadow was proving to be more effective at steering at speed in reverse.

On we veered, the exhaust growling from its fresh injury and something else clanking around under there as if it didn't want to be excluded from the party. We backed over the hump-back bridge which spanned the stream and only then did I look forward again. The elevated position allowed a good view of the stable and the lane leading down to it. And bounding, loping, lumocking along the lane, hot on our trail, was the monkey dog. I couldn't tell – to answer the conundrum – whether or not it was more dog than monkey nor which part most resembled which. I *could* tell a) that it ran on all fours, b) that it was far from slow and c) that it looked very angry – angry enough to temporarily overcome its aversion to sunlight.

"Jesus," I said, "can't you go any faster?" The answer was not meant rhetorically but it may as well have been since the engine valves were bouncing in the cylinder head.

Finally, we burst out of the end of the Major's lane and tyre-screeched onto what passed for the main road. I thought we were going to blast straight across it and into the ditch opposite but my shadow yanked the wheel hard to the left and braked to a halt.

"Get out," I told him.

"Don't worry, Baldy," he said. "I'm getting the hang of it now." But he put the lie to that when he started crunching around in the gear box again.

"Get out!" I said. "Unless you want to be stripped to the bone."

My shadow didn't relish that anymore than I did and without further quarrel we both jumped out of the van to swap seats. From below us, echoing through the woods, came the monkey-dog's irate snarl.

"Christ, Baldy," my shadow said, "I knew we should have left that silly old fool in the road." By which he meant the Major.

I slammed the van into gear and we tore away from Crow Norton, the exhaust blowing and the engine rattling and the undercarriage clanking so that all in all we sounded like a Sopwith Camel that had taken a bullet in its vitals. Several bullets. Big ones.

I drove for a full mile, my eyes fixed on the rear-view mirror, before my heartbeat returned to anything close to normal and it was another two miles before I let out a long sigh of relief and slowed to a less dangerous pace.

"Baldy," my shadow said, lighting two cigarettes and passing one to me, "I've got to admit that hanging around with you is no-where near as dull as I thought it'd be."

"Never mind that," I said, snatching the smoke, suddenly angry with him, "you were going to leave me - weren't you? - you bastard!"

The Lark Mirror

"No, Baldy," he said, "you've got it all wrong. I was just warming-up the engine."

"Liar," I said. I sucked at the smoke. "I thought *I* was supposed to be the coward in this outfit."

"And so you are Baldy. And so you are," he said.

"Fuck you," I said. "I should've left you in Corny Cross with your ass hanging out, you evil bastard,"

"Well, that might have been better than being left in this crate. Jesus, Baldy, I was like a fucking sardine in a can. That fucking bug would've gobbled me down double-quick if I hadn't woke-up when I did."

I conceded to myself that he had a point. "It was a crayfish," I said, calmly, "not a bug."

"Are you sure about that, Baldy?" he said. "Where I come from they're little squitty things about yea big."

"I know," I said, "but these ones were American."

Something started dragging underneath the van and I pulled into a passing place in the full glare of the sun to take a look. The claw we'd ripped off the crayfish was pinched to the axle casing and had swung down to drag in the road. I had to prise the damn thing off with a nail bar.

I tossed the nail bar into the back of the van and then gave the van a cursory inspection. My heart sank. One headlight and both tail lights were now smashed. The radiator grill was missing of course so that the radiator was exposed like that of a Keystone Cop car. The side panels were dented and it would be a miracle if the exhaust held together long enough for me to get us home, let alone cover the extra miles to Billy Makepiece's place where Anushka would be awaiting my arrival. I felt a real pang at the thought of letting her down. Would she forgive me? My entire longed-for future hung in the balance.

"Fuck it!" I yelled at the sky.

"Fucking, fuck it," I screamed at the surrounding moors.

My shadow was out of the van by now. He'd jammed his hat back on and had taken off his shirt in order to cool down. I noticed that his muscles had better definition than mine. I wasn't the least bit surprised.

"Calm down, Baldy," he said. "Just needs a touch-up is all."

"Oh shut up, you idiot," I said. "Just shut up."

16

Once I'd calmed down, I deliberated for a moment or two as to the best course of action. We were at a point in the journey where Silas Crabtree's workshop stood closer to hand than did the cottage and no doubt Silas, seeing a chance to update the gossip-mill, would welcome me with open arms. But now, of course, my shadow was more than mere shadow and I didn't want to risk exposing him to any talk of finding Aunt Alsey, since a successful outcome on this score would guarantee his demise and so he was bound to act up if he got wind of it. (I'd taken enough of a risk speaking on the subject with the Major, while my shadow was sleeping.) And on top of this was the practical consideration that it seemed unlikely even Silas could repair such extensive damage in time for me to make my dinner date. He had a courtesy car – you could call it that – but I had no way of knowing if it was available or not until I got there. And if it *wasn't* available, then I'd be stuck.

Working on the assumption that the van had but one last gasp left to it, I decided that the only sensible thing to do would be to use that last gasp to return home and then (assuming my luck held) phone Silas and get him to fetch the van from the cottage with his breakdown truck. I'd then have the option of either riding with him to fetch the courtesy car if it were available, or walking to Billy's if it wasn't.

To my relief (and mild surprise) the van *did* make it home and my shadow's first complaint on getting there was that he was hungry. He'd dumped himself in his usual seat at the dining room table, where he sprawled scratching at his bare chest as if he had lice, his shirt rolled up and deposited in the neighbouring chair. I made him a plain corned beef sandwich to shut him up. This prompted his second complaint, which was that the bread was stale (he was right about that, in fact).

"Tough," I told him. "It's like it or lump it time. Since *somebody* spent all my grocery money."

I left him crunching his way through his sandwich and went to phone Silas. It took but a few words for my plan to fall apart. Yes, Silas would be happy to do the work and the courtesy car was available but no, he wouldn't be able to come and fetch the van since he had some kind of emergency to deal with at the workshop. I would just have to hope like hell that the exhaust would hold for a few more miles and get the van to Silas's myself.

"I'm going to get the van fixed," I told my shadow. "While I'm gone, I want you to have a bath and bollocks to the water. You stink like a polecat."

"Never mind a bath, Baldy," he said. "A drink's what I need. That sandwich has lodged in my throat."

"Haven't you had enough for one day?" I said, knowing the answer to that; knowing the answer my old self would have given.

"Tell you what," I said, realising it was the only way that I was going to get him to behave, "you have a bath and I'll fetch you some cider from Silas's."

"*Cider?*" he said. "I said I wanted a drink, Baldy. I wouldn't use cider to clean my fucking teeth with."

"This stuff's different," I said. "This is Silas's good stuff. You won't be disappointed."

By the time I got to Silas's I'd lost the back section of the exhaust entirely and what was left was loud enough to drive the pigs from the wallow. I parked in the shade and got out of the van, relieved that at least this part of my mission was now safely accomplished.

The Lark Mirror

Silas was in his yard, standing at the foot of the ladder which I'd left behind on my previous visit. The ladder extended into the branches of one of the beech trees. As I strolled over, my gaze climbed the rungs of the ladder until they reached Jed, who was stretched out on a thick limb of the tree like a resting leopard – so much so in fact that he was fast asleep. He was held in place by several bindings of rope – one around his upper torso, another around his waist and yet another around the thigh of his good leg. The titanium leg seemed not to be well-buckled and it hung down from the branch at right-angles, the toe of its boot twitching restlessly.

"Hello, Professor," Silas said. "Any luck with Aunt Alsey?"

I was standing in the shade and I might have lied if not for the fact that Silas's courtesy car was parked in full sunlight and so getting to it would trap me in the lie. That being the case, I thought it more prudent to take control of the narrative from the outset.

"No," I said. "No luck yet. Got some promising leads though."

"Shadder still acting up, is he?" Silas said.

"He *was*," I said. "Luckily he's tired himself out. He's at home having a rest."

"My, my," Silas said, "he *has* come adrift."

"That he has," I said, omitting to mention that my shadow was now endowed with all the attributes of a flesh and blood man and had a taste for the flesh-pots of Corny Cross. It was a good time to change the subject, and luckily I didn't have to look far for a fresh one.

"Is this the emergency you mentioned," I said, meaning Jed.

"It is," Silas said. "I was hoping I'd be able to get him down myself but I reckon I'll have to get the fire brigade out after all. Can't wake him up, see," he added.

"I must say he looks very content up there," I said.

"You'd look the same way too," Silas said, "if I dosed you up with horse tranquilizer like I did Jed."

"Why did you do that?" I said. Though I was in a hurry to get home it wasn't every day that you saw a one-legged man in a drugged stupor lashed to a tree limb twenty feet above the ground.

"I didn't think I'd get 'im down without it," Silas said. "Trouble is," he went on, "I misjudged the dose. See, what happened was … I sorted out that problem we had with the leg –"

"You put the knob back on?" I said.

"*Right*. I put the knob back on. But while I was about it I gave it a few tweaks to help Jed with the stairs. Lot of stairs in Jed's house."

"But you misjudged that too," I guessed.

Silas nodded, a little shame-facedly. "Went up there like a fucking Polaris missile," he said. "He managed to grab that branch and pull himself up. Trouble is, Jed's got a deadly fear o' heights. I fetched the ladder for him, as you can see, but Jed … well, he were so frozen up with fear that he wouldn't move. *Couldn't* move. He just clung on like a cat. So I went to fetch him some cider to calm his nerves enough for him to swing his good leg onto the ladder and while I was about it I remembered I had some horse tranquilizer in the back there, so I put a dose of it in the cider afore I give it to Jed. *That* did the trick. I've never seen Jed more relaxed. Look at 'im. Trouble is, like I say, it were a bit more powerful that I thought. Took hold just like that. It was all I could do to tie 'im in place afore he fell an' broke his neck"

"Is there anything I can do?" I said, confident that there wasn't.

"No, no," Silas said. "It's alright. I'll fetch the boys out soon as you're gone." He ran his quick, professional gaze over my van. "My, my," he said, "she *has* taken a beating. Not having a very good week, are we, Professor?"

The Lark Mirror

"Not really," I said, "but I've got a feeling my luck's about to change."

Silas's courtesy car was a three-wheeled wonder, a model proprietarily labelled a Reliant Robin but known throughout the land as a plastic pig. It had a fibre-glass body – shit-brown in colour – and a 700cc engine, which was about on a par with a large motorcycle of the day. To drive it well required observation of wind speed and direction bordering on the nautical. With a good wind to its blunt stern it was capable of hitting ninety miles per hour. With the prow to the wind, however, the intrepid pilot of this vehicle would be lucky to witness the needle grace the number forty on the speedometer, while a savage cross-wind could easily lift one of the rear wheels from the road.

Happily for me, there was no wind to contend with and, laughable as the vehicle was, it was generally considered that it's name – Reliant – was not a misnomer. Also, though the tales I'd heard of plastic pigs being able to circumnavigate the globe on a single tank of fuel were no doubt fanciful, the light fibreglass body combined with such a small engine made it very economical to run.

The plastic pig was the non-deluxe model which had pretensions of being a van – which meant no seats or side windows in the back – and when I pulled out of Silas's yard, with the engine farting along happily, I had utilized this rear space not only to stash my haversack, but also to store two translucent plastic flagons of cider and a jar of horse tranquilizer.

I'd told Silas that I was suffering from insomnia – which he obviously thought plausible, given my cursed state – and he'd laced one of the cider flagons with about half the dose he'd given Jed (which he was sure would afford me a good night's sleep) and then let me have the remainder of the jar so that I could adjust the dose if necessary.

All of which is to say that when I said my farewell to Silas, my hopes for a trouble-free evening were high.

17

When I got home my shadow was sitting at the table scribbling on a page he'd torn from one of my notebooks. A cigarette was clamped in his mouth and he had one eye squint against the smoke. He'd obviously taken a bath because he smelled better and was now wearing my bathrobe, the cheeky bastard. He barely looked up when I entered the room.

I raised the cider flagons ostentatiously to gain his attention, the dosed one in my left hand, the un-dosed one in my right. My shadow didn't seem to care very much about cider at that moment and my heart skipped several beats.

"What are you writing?" I said. "Your memoirs?"

"No, Baldy," he said. "I'm making a list of things I want to do before I get old."

"Maybe you're not going to get old."

"Everybody gets old, Baldy. That's why you have to make the most of *not* being old. Which is something I understand even if you don't."

I ignored the jibe. "Maybe you're different," I said. "Maybe that doesn't apply to you."

"And why would that be, Baldy?" he said, distractedly, as he jotted down the next item on his list.

"Well," I said, "you've already violated the usual laws. I mean, you were only born yesterday and you're already thirty-two."

"Thirty-one," he said. "And don't be a stupid cunt all your life, Baldy; I've been here all along. I was with you when you set fire to the school. Remember?"

"I thought we weren't going to mention that again," I said.

"Listen to this," he said, ignoring my reproach. "Item one: learn to play the guitar. Open brackets, *slide*, close brackets. Item two –"

"Wait, just wait a minute ..." I said, falling into his logic. "I used to be in a band. It was *you* who made me quit."

"*Bass*, Baldy," he said, with real venom. "Fucking *bass*. Plunky, plunky, fucking plonk all fucking night. And not even proper rock'n'roll at that. I want to play something with some fucking *fire* in it."

"Alright," I said, slightly hurt but somewhat relieved that his list had got off to such an innocuous start. "Item two?" I prompted.

"Wall of death," he said.

"Are you sure you've got the nerve for that?" I said, recalling his disgraceful behaviour that afternoon.

"Oh, I've got the nerve, Baldy," he said. "Besides, I was made for the carnival life."

The word "carnival", when uttered by my shadow, had such fearful connotations that I thumped down the cider flagon in my left hand. "Here," I said, "that looks like thirsty work."

"Never mind that," he said, "I'm thinking. Item three ... listen to this one, Baldy. You'll get a kick out of this. Item three: shack up with a foreign bird for a bit. Open brackets. Broaden my cultural horizons. Close brackets. You like that, Baldy? Broaden my cultural horizons?"

"Very admirable," I said, trying not to let my voice convey anything but sarcasm. "Any particular nationality in mind?"

"I'm glad you asked me that, Baldy, because I've been giving it some hard thought. Chinese girls, I like. Throw in some opium and you've got a fine old time. But then again, Spanish .. Italians ... they've got a bit more spirit. Nothing like good hard loving after a lively fight. Americans? Too gobby. So, I was thinking ..."

The Lark Mirror

"Do you want a drink or not?"

"I was thinking, Baldy – if you'll let me finish – I was thinking maybe a Russian." He looked at me steadily for the first time since I'd entered the room. "What do you think, Baldy? Think that's a good idea?"

"You won't find many Russians living here," I said. "In fact, you won't find any."

"Oh, I don't know, Baldy. I wouldn't rule it out. Sometimes when you want a thing badly enough, it just appears right in front of you."

"I've had enough of this nonsense," I said. I snatched the list from him. "Here," I said, "drink your damn cider. I'm going for a bath."

I left him with the drug-laced cider and took the other flagon into the kitchen and pushed it to the back of the fridge. When I walked back through the dining room, he just watched me pass, a satisfied smile plastered across his face. Climbing the stairs, I could hear him chuckling to himself as he chinked around for a glass. Drink up, I thought. Drink up.

The first thing I noticed when I entered the bathroom were the two sopping towels my shadow had simply dumped on the floor. The second thing I noticed was the open bottle of calamine lotion he'd left on the window sill. I'd bought it at the start of the heat-wave when I'd been negligent enough to get sunburned and it had remained in the bathroom cabinet ever since. What the hell did my shadow want with it? - that was the question. Surely even that debased bastard wouldn't stoop to drinking calamine lotion. Then I remembered the welts on his buttocks from the caning he'd received in Corny Cross and it was my turn to chuckle.

While I ran the bath, I perused my shadow's mid-life crisis list. You couldn't fault his creativity when it came to depravity and by the time I got to the final item (which makes me shudder to this day) I had dredged up a good deal of sympathy for the whore in the Blue Boar. When I'd finished reading it, I tore up the list and flushed it down the toilet.

Soaking in the tepid bath (my shadow had used up most of the hot water) I mulled over item three on the list. Coincidence? I would have liked to think so, but I just couldn't make it stick. He'd had that sly look on his face which said anything but coincidence. Did he know about Anushka? Was there some kind of psychological link between us? And if so, did he know anything about Aunt Alsey and what it meant for him if I found her?

My one consoling thought, as my mind kept flipping between yes and maybe as possible answers to these questions, was that the horse tranquiliser would, if used with care, neutralise his ability to do anything about it.

I dried myself off and towelled what was left of my hair. I put on a clean blue shirt and the kind of flared trousers which makes men of my generation burn entire photo albums in order to rid the world of the evidence of their ever having worn them. Then I put on my one and only smart jacket which had a long service history and had seen action in job interviews, christenings, weddings and a couple of court appearances. Which is to say that the jacket was looking a bit threadbare (which at least went well with my scalp) and, more to the point, was not quite as voguish as it once was - especially since it was something approaching plum in colour. My only hope was that Anushka, being Russian, would have at best a scant knowledge of such local matters as sartorial fashion.

Downstairs, my shadow was happily slurping his cider. He already looked a little squiffy – it really was good cider – but not particularly sleepy. I wasn't unduly concerned; he was bound to have more resistance to the horse tranquilizer than had Jed, given his experienced hedonist's constitution. Moreover, he hadn't got very far down the flagon and so had a good deal of it left to get through. Even so, I'd started to wonder if I ought to find a way to lace the second flagon without arousing his suspicions, just in case, when I caught him stifling a yawn.

"How did you like my list, Baldy?" he said.

"Very interesting," I said. "You've obviously got literary talent. But I've got a list for you: item one; rinse the fucking bath out when you're finished."

"There you go again, Baldy," he said, "sounding like your mother."

"It's common courtesy," I said. I studied him for a second or two. "You look tired," I said.

"Been a long day, Baldy," he said, lighting a cigarette. "Don't worry though, I'll rally. You enjoy yourself now. And if you should happen across any Russian beauties, then for fuck's sake do yourself a favour and dump the monkey jacket. You look fucking ridiculous."

"Thank you," I said. "Hope the calamine lotion did the trick."

"Took the sting out of, Baldy," he said. "Thanks for asking."

He yawned again and I gave him an indulgent smile.

"I'll see you later," I said. "Try not to burn the house down."

18

On the way to Billy Makepiece's I lit a cigarette and saw that my hands were shaking, which told me how nervous I was. I'd never been on a date where I hadn't had a bracing drink before-hand and several drinks during and I recalled with a deep pang just how useful alcohol could be at a time like this. The more I thought about it the more panicky I felt and I was almost overwhelmed by the likelihood that I would be rendered tongue-tied and embarrassed, awed by Anushka's beauty; mocked and tortured by my own ridiculously high expectations of the evening.

"Relax, Baldy," I said, "its just a dinner date for christ's sake." Then, peeved at the fact that I'd just used my shadow's name for myself, I tossed my half-smoked cigarette out of the window of the plastic pig and pressed hard on the button which squeezed the windscreen washer. Silas had neglected to fill the washer bottle (and I'd neglected to check it) and an inverted dribble was all that the washer could manage, which was unfortunate since it was that time of the evening when the lanes were full of flitting insect life. I put on the wipers anyway and they creaked across the windscreen with dry reluctance, smearing the mashed bodies of moths and insects into red and puss-yellow rainbows across the glass.

Having achieved very little, I shook another cigarette free of the pack and put it to my lips. I changed my mind before I lit it and stuffed it back into the pack, not particularly caring whether I broke it or not. It was a funny thing, but the more my shadow smoked, the less I seemed to want to.

The Lark Mirror

As I approached Billy's cottage, I was stricken with the certainty that I would not be well-received. That Anushka had invited me merely out of pity or politeness or boredom or even out of some kind of Russian perversity as revenge for some or other proxy humiliation suffered by her homeland in the on-going cold war. It would be just my luck to become embroiled in global politics at such a difficult time.

But, after I'd parked the plastic pig and messed about with my hair in a vain attempt to deny my biological inheritance, after fretting that I hadn't brought any flowers or chocolates or even a bottle of wine (much less a replacement for all the alcohol I'd commandeered the night before), after knocking on the door and shuffling around like a shy teenager on the doorstep, the welcome I was given banished all such worries and fears.

Anushka's smile on opening the door was wide and genuine and friendly. Her cheeks were flushed and her eyes glittered and when she kissed my cheek I could smell wine on her breath. My old friend alcohol had ridden to the rescue after all.

The kiss left me stunned for a moment — so unexpected was it, so warm, so moist, so ... *luscious* ...

Anushka laughed. She was wearing the same dress as the previous evening and I didn't hold it against her one bit.

"Perhaps now is time to close mouth, David," she said. "Unless you wish to choke on moth."

When I did so, my teeth snapped together audibly.

"So," she said, "please to come in."

The cottage was redolent with the smell of cooking and, until it hit my nostrils, I hadn't realised how hungry I was. Food had been the last thing I'd been thinking about — "dinner" having been reduced in my mind to being merely a vehicle which would deliver Anushka to me for a few precious hours. Now, however, my stomach juices began to gurgle in anticipation. I knew the smell too – it was connotative of mine and Billy's first dinner together. A roasting duck. I was a little surprised. Roast duck seemed un-seasonal, plus it was a lot of trouble. I was not, however, the kind of man to reject a duck dinner on grounds of season and, besides, the fact that Anushka had taken the trouble to cook duck bode well for the evening ahead. Nobody cooks duck as a formality.

"I cook duck," Anushka said, superfluously. "Billy says you like duck."

"Oh, I *love* duck," I said. "Billy's not here is he?" I mentally kicked myself at the transparency of the question.

"No. Is no need for worry," Anushka said. "We are completely alone." And with that, she disappeared into the kitchen to check on the duck.

I almost followed her in there – it was, after all, more my domain than Billy's – but with Billy absent I thought it might seem presumptuous. Besides, it didn't take two to baste a duck.

I lingered in the living room where Billy and I had chatted away many a pleasant hour but, what with Billy's absence and Anushka's presence and my lack of shadow the room and I felt like mutual strangers. The armchair by the fireplace – "my" chair – no longer said "sit in me", the books on the shelves no longer said "dip into me" and the ashtray on the coffee table no longer said "fill me". Left alone like that, my nervousness returned and I paced the threadbare rugs and carpets like a man awaiting his imminent moment in court.

Finally, Anushka returned. She held a glass of wine and a tea towel was draped over her bare shoulder as if she had just been overcome with modesty.

"The duck," she said, "it is almost ready. You are good cook, Billy says. I am not such good cook."

"I'm sure it'll be delicious," I said.

"We will see," she shrugged. She set the wine on the table which held Billy's globe then snatched the tea towel from her shoulder and began to wipe what I assumed was duck grease from her fingers. Once again I was struck by the familiarity of this and I wondered about it for a second or two before it came to me. When Billy was painting, he habitually slung a piece of rag over his shoulder where it was readily available to wipe his brushes or, when he took a break, his fingers – just as Anushka had done. Even then, I had a job dismissing this as coincidence. Were she and Billy close enough for such gestures to be picked up in an osmotic fashion? In which case – and again – how had she escaped Billy's mention? And how was it we had failed to meet until last night? Then, dunder-head that I am, it came to me. I didn't know Billy at all. That is, I didn't know the whole of him. I knew the painter – the *artist* – the drinker, the angler, the raconteur. And while it was true that he did some of his copywriting work at the cottage it was also true that the rest of his professional life was an unknown to me. Billy in a suit. Billy at some kind of meeting in a room full of stuffed shirts. Billy taking a timorous secretary out to lunch somewhere swanky. Billy- and this was the most pertinent piece of conjuring - ... Billy having dinner with Anushka (not swanky this time; an intimate setting) before taking her to bed – at her house? In his hotel room? All of this in London, where I had never been with Billy.

It was a lengthy mediation and when I returned to myself I saw that Anushka was eying me quizzically.

"I was just wondering where you and Billy met," I said.

She sipped her wine. No, actually she took a good belt of it – just as my shadow would; just as Billy would.

"Billy and I," she said, "we meet at exhibition." It was a story she seemed reluctant to tell, or, perhaps, one she needed to brace herself to tell. She took another belt of wine. I'd noticed already that she was drinking from Billy's "goblet", which was a glass big enough to hold almost a half bottle of wine, something which saved Billy the trouble of bestirring himself to refill it any more often than he had to.

"I work at embassy," she went on. "Is my job to procure furnishings. Paintings. I look for English landscape paintings to put visitors at ease. So. I go to exhibition and Billy is there. We strike conversation. We talk about painting – which is hobby of mine also – and then one thing lead to other and Billy ask can he paint me. So. I come here and here Billy paints me. But forget Billy. Is you and me only and I wish for you to have good time."

"I *am* having a good time," I said.

"No," she said. "You are nervous and worried and wishing you had not worn that jacket. The jacket is fine. The nerves will go. As to the worry, this we discuss over dinner. You will see that I am not so scary. Not so *untouchable* as you seem to believe. Besides," she added, "you are here because destiny willed it."

"Am I?" I said.

"Yes," she said, "you and I are supposed to be together this evening. Not some other evening. *This* evening. Together, alone. I come from an old people and we know many things. This is one of the things that we know. We wait for people, David. We may not know it, but it is so. We wait for them perhaps to help, perhaps to fight, perhaps even to kill. And sometimes, perhaps, to love. You and I have waited for one another for a very long time. And now we have found one another. This should please you? Yes?"

"That's very ... profound," I said.

"Yes," she said, with a knowing smile that turned my bone marrow to molten ooze, "it pleases you." Then, somewhat bathetically, she said: "I will go see to the duck."

But she turned at the threshold and said: "It is no small matter for a man to lose his shadow. And this, we must correct. When I want a man, David, I want the all of him."

You can imagine what an erotic whirl was my mind following her exit.

The Lark Mirror

Dinner was a torture. It wasn't that, for the most part, the meal was virtually inedible (Billy's cooking skills or lack thereof was something else that seemed to have rubbed off on Anushka) - with the duck being undercooked and packed with grease where she had neglected to prick the skin, the potatoes rendered into lumps of coal-lite, the cabbage so over-boiled that it actually slipped through the tines of the fork while the carrots had retained enough of their crunch you'd think to hear us that we were two ponies accepting a treat – no, what was unbearable was that Anushka had seated us at the large dining room table, where Billy and I sometimes took our meals and, just as on those occasions, we sat at opposite ends of the table and so were separated by about a furlong of family heir-loom. That distance between us seemed to nullify all of the erotic promise which Anushka had so cruelly ushered into the evening.

Add to this the embarrassment of having to talk about my errant shadow and all the lies I had to utter in the telling. I told her about Aunt Alsey and the lark mirror; I told her about the seven long years the curse would last and I even told her Jed's notions about Aunt Alsey being four and a half centuries old and able to turn herself into smoke and about her sleeping in the bottoms of ponds. I told her about that morning's aborted search and the difficulties I'd encountered.

What I *didn't* tell her was that my shadow was now made of flesh and blood and was possessed of a free and mischievous will of his own. Neither did I mention the monkey-dog, giant crayfish or the glorious last stand of poor Major Pikestaff. I *did* mention that I'd had trouble with my van which was why I was driving the plastic pig – I'm not sure why, except that it was the kind of vehicle which begged explanation.

She listened to my heavily-edited version of the story so far without interruption (save to apologise for her cooking) and then said: "In Russia we have women like your Aunt

Alsey. They give much trouble to the peasant class. Much sour milk. Many chickens which do not lay. And sometimes, much, much worse. There is old story from time of Gulags. Such a woman was turned away from camp in Siberia without – how you say? – alms? She cursed every man there. Within one week – though it was summer; though the rations were not short – cannibalism had swept through the camp and everyone had been eaten by everyone else until one man only survive. The relief officers who found him say that he was cooking his own leg. There are other stories. Some worse."

It was hard to think of something worse – which is saying a lot when you've witnessed a man being chopped into chum by oversize crustaceans – and I didn't try. "Sounds like I got off fairly lightly," I said. "All things considered."

"No," she contradicted, "your case is bad. This situation, we must rectify." It was full dark now and she looked at the wall behind me which was where my shadow should have been thrown by the candlelight but wasn't. "It is … forgive me … but is creepy for a man to have no shadow."

"Creepy?" I said, my hopes all but dashed.

"Perhaps is wrong word. *Weird* is better word. Yes?"

"Weird is *just* the word," I said.

She drank more wine. "So," she said, "I think you will be better man when you retrieve your shadow. And, since I have waited for you for so long, I will help you."

"You will?" I said.

"Of course. It will perhaps be not so hard as you think. This Aunt Alsey, she is bound to curse others. No? So, she will leave a trail. So, we drive around, we ask people, we look for anything … *weird* …. And this will lead us to her."

The plan, I have to say, was a disappointment and, save that it was delivered with a Russian accent, sounded not dissimilar to my own, which was of course a proven failure.

Except, I suddenly realised, it wasn't. There was one crucial difference. This time I would have Anushka at my side to make enquiries on my behalf. And nobody, in their right minds or otherwise – not even a gang of vindictive boys – would willingly drive Anushka from their sight.

"Alright," I said, "we'll give it a go."

"We will give it many goes," she said, "until you have recovered your shadow. The dinner is ruin. I am sorry. We will abandon it, yes? So, we will go and be more comfortable in other room.

19

"This lark mirror," Anushka said, as we entered the living room, "you have it with you? Perhaps in plastic pig?"

"Yes," I said. "I've been carrying the damn thing around with me just in case I bumped into Aunt Alsey."

"You will fetch? I am curious to see this artefact."

I did as I was bid and went outside to fetch it, detouring into the kitchen on the way for a jug of water with which to fill the plastic pig's washer bottle. The moon was up now and a breeze had risen with it and on that breeze, very faintly, I could smell burning. I couldn't see the horizon up-wind because of the hedges and the lie of the land but I scanned the sky for smoke. Nothing. Just a big round moon and an easterly breeze – the kind of breeze that always makes me feel that something somewhere is going wrong for somebody. I sniffed again but the burning smell was gone. I put it out of mind (for a while at least). As I've said, there were a lot of wild fires on the moors that summer and that faint whiff of burning could easily have originated thirty miles distant.

I groped around under the plastic pig's engine hatch for the washer bottle, uncapped it and emptied the jug into it. Then I grabbed the haversack from the rear of the pig and took it inside. I returned the jug to the kitchen and then joined Anushka in the living room where she was sitting in Billy's fireside chair, her legs folded beneath her. She was drinking her wine and watching me with the calm imperiousness of a cat.

I sat in the chair on the other side of the fireplace ("my" chair) and unfastened the haversack and took out the lark mirror, which was still wrapped in its protective towel. I set the bundle on the coffee table. Anushka leaned

The Lark Mirror

toward it expectantly, like a prelate about to receive the first glimpse of the holy grail. When I unwrapped it, the lark mirror failed to live up to the occasion – which should have been expected given that it was just a wooden box with a ball of smashed glass sitting atop it. We both felt the disappointment.

"You need to see it working," I said. I wound it up and set it down on the hearth. We watched the ball rotate and imagined it throwing off sunbeams (rather than the dim illumination of Billy's wall lamps), imagined the larks spotting it from their lofty hoverings and thronging to it, a great convocation of song and chattering …. or, at least, that's what I was imagining.

When I looked up at Anushka I saw that she was watching me.

"You are fascinating man," she said. "Is why Billy thinks so highly of you."

"My talents don't compare to his, I'm afraid," I said, truthfully. An entire series of Billy's paintings flashed through my mind and, inevitably, one of their number was the (at the time of my viewing) unfinished painting which had conjured Anushka into my life. "Well," I said, "now that you've seen my masterpiece I think it only fair that you show me Billy's."

"And which is this masterpiece of Billy's?" she said, playfully.

"That would be his portrait of you," I said.

"I'm afraid is not possible," she said. "The room is locked."

"I know where he keeps the key," I said, suspecting that Anushka knew too.

"No," she said. "Billy said no one is to see. Not until he returns."

"Not even me?" I said.

"He said no-one. You understand."

"Yes," I said, "of course." Though in truth I was a little put out.

"Is no matter," Anushka said. "You will be first to see when time comes. In meantime, you have me. *I* am here."

As if some proof of that were necessary she set down her glass and with a feline fluidity of limb slinked out of her chair and into my lap and before I could even begin to come to terms with this delicious turn of events her mouth was on mine, her strong fingers caressing my face. Time stood still. She pulled away and looked into my stunned face. "I have loved you for a long time," she said. "And I wish for you to make love to me."

Which I was more than happy to do and would have done so if not for the smell of burning which again reached my nostrils – this time through the partly-opened window.

"Can you smell burning?" I said.

She sniffed. "No. Wait. Yes. But is no matter. Is not our concern."

She was right and I almost succeeded in no longer caring about that burning smell. But then other thoughts and dark possibilities stormed the castle of the moment. The very last thing I'd said to my shadow was: try not to burn the house down. What if I'd unwittingly handed him the idea on a plate, with a side order of matches? What if he'd failed to drink the drugged cider and had devoted his energies instead into turning my cottage into a smoking ruin? What if none of that happened but in his drugged state (assuming he'd drunk the cider) he'd fallen asleep and dropped his cigarette onto something flammable, like the folds of a couch? I must have been mad to leave him alone and madder still to think that my curse was as bad as it could get. Aunt Alsey had *killed* Major Pikestaff; it would hardly trouble her conscience further to burn my house down.

"Jesus Christ!" I said. "Let me up."

Anushka drew back in surprise and I leapt out of the chair – or tried to, at least. The truth was I was somewhat hampered by my erection. I hurried outside as best I could, adjusting the relationship between my manhood and my underwear as I went.

The burning smell was strong on the breeze and smoke now drifted across the moon. The sky above the hedgerow – the sky in the direction of home – held an ominous glow.

"The dirty bastard!" I said. "He's done it. He's really done it."

"*Who* has done *what?*" Anushka said, from the cottage doorway.

"I've got to go," I said. "My house is on fire."

"I come with you," she said.

"No," I protested, not wanting her anywhere near my shadow or his handiwork. "Stay here."

"I come," she said. "You no argue. You want lark mirror?"

"No," I yelled. "No time. It's safe where it is. Just lock the door and get in if you're coming."

I had the keys to the plastic pig in my jacket pocket and before Anushka had pulled on her boots and an old wax jacket of Billy's I'd fired up its engine and jounced it around in a circle so that its prow pointed towards home. I turned on the wipers and pumped at the washer bottle until the screen was clear of smeared insects.

Anushka jumped in and slammed the door and I popped the clutch with such brutality that the plastic pig almost pulled a wheelie. We shot along the lane, the engine humming along gamely, the leaf-springs creaking from the potholes. The hedges fell away behind and we were soon on open moor-land so that we could see the fire, a far-off orange intensity that bobbed in and out of sight with the dips in the road.

As I drove, I raged in and out of coherence. I must have been a treat to listen to.

"That bastard," I ranted. "He's done it this time. This time I'll *kill* the bastard and bollocks to the consequences. It was him," I said, "it was *him* who set fire to the fucking school. I should've known better than to leave him alone …"

"Who is this man you must kill?" Anushka said, managing to sound amused, despite the obvious gravity of the situation. "Who is this school burner?"

"My brother," I said, maintaining just enough presence of mind to hold a lie together.

"You have brother?" Anushka said. "Billy make no mention –"

"Long lost," I said. "He's been gone for a long time. And now he's back, the bastard."

When we finally reached the fire there was neither a fire crew nor a malevolent, gleeful, pyromaniac shadow dancing around the fire-stripped corpse of my home. In fact, the fire was a good distance short of the cottage. In my defence, I'd like to say that from my earlier vantage point the fire *was* in the direction of my cottage and that distances on the moors are notoriously hard to judge, especially at night. A further fact – if I'm going to be truthful about it – was that I'd have to say that the fire which was now consuming both banks of an empty road for a distance of about two hundred scorched yards was at – or close enough to – the spot where I'd tossed my lit cigarette from the window of the plastic pig on my outbound journey.

"Oh," I said, feeling foolish.

"So," Anushka said, "a wild fire. That is all. Perhaps now we return home." The hand she placed on my thigh had obvious implications.

It was the acme of temptation to do just that. But since we were now closer to my cottage than to Billy's I thought I may as well go and check that my shadow had taken his medicine and gone to sleep. My evening – my *night* – would be all the more enjoyable for knowing that I could relax on that score. I saw little risk either; I'd already blurted out the lie about my brother and I was fairly sure that my shadow would be in no condition to contradict the lie. And if he *hadn't* drunk his cider and gone under? Well, that would be a thing I needed to know about and a thing I would have to deal with as best I could. The bottom line was that I knew I would be distracted in my love-making if I didn't know for certain one way or the other.

"Alright," I said, "but I want to just check on my brother, see if he needs anything."

"This bastard you want to kill? Now you worry over his welfare?"

"It's complicated," I said. "He's a very sick man, my brother."

The breeze had abated a little but it still drove the fire relentlessly towards us. You could hear it crackling through the dry grass, just above the purr of the engine. There wasn't so much smoke that we couldn't see all along that burning length of road. I thought about how hot it would be at the mid-point of that fiery gauntlet and I thought about the plastic pig being made of flammable fibreglass and decided that a detour would be prudent.

There was no reversing light – or if there was, it didn't work – but the moon and the fire threw plenty of light for me to see by. I reversed for several hundred yards until I came to the left hand turning (left, that is, when facing forwards) for a track which I knew dropped down into some bog-mired bottom-land with sparse copses of gnarly trees before looping back up to join the "main" road about three quarters of a mile the other side of the fire.

I drove down the track into a world of moon-shadow. We'd gone less than a few hundred yards – the glow of the fire above us and to our right – when, just rounding a bend, the dim headlights picked out a shuffling figure in the road. No sooner had we spotted it than the figure stepped off the road and down the slope which led to the bogs. Even so, that glimpse was enough. The shawl cum cloak, the stooped shuffle, the bindlestiff.

"Jesus Christ Almighty!" I yelled. The brakes creaked us to a halt at the figure's point of departure from the road. "It's her. It's Aunt Alsey!"

I glanced across at Anushka in short-lived triumph.

"The lark mirror," she said. "We do not have it for to give to her."

"Oh shit," I said in despair and frustration. "Oh, bloody, fucking, shit."

I jumped out of the plastic pig regardless and ran to the verge. "Aunt Alsey?" I called down into the hollow.

I couldn't see her. Then I could. She stood stock-still, half turned toward me, as if listening. Then she turned and continued on her way down the slope.

"Aunt Alsey, please wait" I pleaded. But, with a few more shuffling steps, she was lost from view.

"David," Anushka called through the open window, "you waste time. We must go for lark mirror."

If the plastic pig had been a team of horses I would have flogged the hide from their rumps and burst their poor hearts. Be in no doubt, you *can* corner hard enough in a Reliant Robin van to lift a rear wheel from the road, just as you *can* raise the front wheel like a motorcycle ace tearing clear of the start line.

When we arrived in a skidding halt amidst a pall of dust back at Billy's cottage I snatched the key from Anushka and fumbled it into the lock and all but kicked Billy's door off its hinges. I stormed into the living room and quickly wrapped the lark mirror in its towel and shoved it into my haversack.

Back inside the van I dumped the haversack into Anushka's lap without a word and slammed the plastic pig into gear. I drove with no less urgency than before until we reached the place where the old crone had shuffled down the bank – the fire having burned to a place just short enough of the turning for me to safely access the lane.

I snatched up the haversack and got out of the plastic pig. "Are you coming?" I said.

"No. Is your affair," Anushka said. "Perhaps is better for you to go alone. Better I am not seen by her."

"Alright," I said, pulling the haversack onto my shoulders.

"Good luck," Anushka said. "Perhaps you return as whole man."

I descended into that place of blue light and shadow, fern beds and knotted tree roots. Further ahead there was mist where the bogs were. I looked in vain for Aunt Alsey. Once or twice I called out, my voice sounding small and far away - even to me – but all I heard in response was the ribbeting of frogs. Then, as I traversed a shoulder in the land form, I saw, down in some little gulley, the glow of a fire. I stumbled toward it. My foot snagged a tree root and I fell into ground so soft and mossy that it felt like an embrace.

When I got back to my feet and looked for the fire again it seemed to have moved. Just a trick of the night, I thought, making my way toward it. But the next time I looked it had moved again to a place deeper into the boglands. I stumbled on, noticing now how the fire burned more blue than yellow. Then the fire winked out and reappeared in yet another place. I chased it down until it moved once again, drawing me ever deeper into the mist. I turned to look back toward the plastic pig, as if for reassurance, but it was hidden from view. I saw another fire behind me and the penny finally dropped and rattled to a halt. Bog sprites. Will o' the wisps. Walking fire. Ignis fatuus. Call it what you will, it was not the camp fire of Aunt Alsey and I'd been on a fool's errand chasing fool's fire.

Feeling utterly defeated and depleted, I sat against a bank on the edge of the bogs and let out a sigh of despair. Aunt Alsey was not to be found here and if she was then she'd be asleep and out of reach in the bottom of one of the bogs or else had turned herself into smoke and mingled with the mist just as Jed had said.

I lit a cigarette, my own light in the darkness. I called Aunt Alsey's name one more time and the words came out enfeebled and devoid of hope.

"What do ye want with Aunt Alsey?" creaked an old voice.

It will stand as one of my more minor confessions that I started like a hare and let out a little cry that you'd have to call feminine.

I sought out the source of the voice, which had come from my left. There was a single, well-crowned hawthorn bush a dozen yards away and, in its shadow, sitting on an exposed root, I could now discern the form of an old woman. In my peripheral vision, another bog sprite flared up.

"Aunt Alsey," I said, "I've brought you the lark mirror."

"Lark mirror?"

"Yes," I said, grinding out the cigarette and slipping off the haversack, "the lark mirror you wanted. I took it off you and I'm sorry." I got to my feet and held up the haversack as I carried it toward her. "Look," I said. "I've got it here. You can have it. Will you take it, please? And then will you give me back my shadow?"

"Don't want no lark mirror," the old woman said.

I paused. Confusion and dread welled up inside me.

"You *do*," I said. "You want it to catch nice tasty larks with."

I began to move towards her again with faltering steps. "You took it from my wall and I chased you and took it away from you and I shouldn't have and I'm sorry but here it is. I just want my shadow back, that's all."

The old woman began to chuckle. "Lark mirror," she said. "What would I want with a lark mirror? Can't stand larks. Scrawny devils."

The Lark Mirror

"But you *do*," I pleaded. "You love larks. You said they were nice and tasty."

"Not me," she said. "Can't give you no shadder neither. All I gots to give you is these." She stood and stepped into the moonlight, her face remaining hidden by her cowl. She hitched up the hem of her cloak and several darkly-glistening things flowed out of it.

Snakes.

They slithered towards me, hissing.

She pulled another snake from the folds of her cloak and tossed it amongst the others.

"I don't *want* snakes," I said, backing away, "I want my shadow."

"Then ye'd best find the person who robbed ye of it, ye young fool," she said. She raised a hand and pulled back her cowl. Her features were as old and craggy as mountains but there were no chin whiskers and no eye patch nor any of the other story-book conventions that formed the features of Aunt Alsey.

"You're not her," I said, barely able to believe it. I tripped on a root in my retreat from the snakes and the old crone chuckled again.

I got to my feet. "Who are you?" I said.

"Ye tell anyone who asks that ye've seen Mother Priest, an' that Mother Priest is real an' not summat made-up. An' ye tell 'em there'll be snakes aplenty fer them as says otherwise. An' as fer yer Aunt Alsey, I'd as soon spit on her as kiss her I reckon. If ye be looking fer Aunt Alsey then ye're in the wrong place. Where ye finds Aunt Alsey ye won't find Mother Priest, an' where ye finds Mother Priest ye won't find Aunt Alsey. An ne're the twain'll meet."

"Then I don't suppose," I said, without much hope, "that you know where I *can* find her?"

"Ye'll find her in a place like this, I shouldn't wonder," she said. "An' if ye *do* find her, tell her I hopes the devil takes her liver."

When I got back to the plastic pig I slumped into the driving seat and stared through the windscreen in disbelief.

"David?" Anushka said.

"It wasn't her," I said. "Can you believe it? There are two semi-mythical old crones wandering this particular patch of earth. Most people live here their entire lives without bumping into either one. Now I've met them both. What's the opposite of serendipity?"

"So, this person- this was Mother Priest?"

"Yes," I said. "It was Mother Priest. Snakes and all. Oh well," I said, "may as well go and check on my brother."

I'd driven for a quarter of a mile or so before a question occurred to me. "How do you know about Mother Priest?" I said.

"Billy," she said. "He tell me."

"Billy's got every subject covered," I said.

"Billy is big talker," Anushka said. "But I tell you before – forget Billy. Billy is not here. There is only us two. And later, when I get you home, that is all you will care about. You will see."

With this reminder of things to come nestled warmly in my heart and groin, I managed to background my recent disappointment as I urged on the plastic pig a little faster.

20

My shadow was *not* sleeping soundly when I arrived back at the cottage. In fact, he wasn't sleeping at all. He was drinking gin and smoking a cigar and making lists and all in all he seemed to have made a pleasant evening of his solitude. He'd divested himself of my bathrobe and was now wearing a clean white shirt (mine), a pair of moderately-faded jeans (also mine) and the pair of almost-new cowboy boots that I'd been breaking-in piece-meal - the whole ensemble topped off with my bushman's hat.

"Don't lurk in the doorway like that, Baldy," he said. "Come on in if you're coming." He looked up from his fresh list – or at least from the fresh page of an ongoing list (there looked to be about a dozen of them) – and regarded me drunkenly with one eye closed. "Got some stuff here I'd like a little feedback on. Sit yourself down, Baldy. Even a dull, kill-joy bastard like you ought to appreciate this. Listen," he said, "you know how you always wanted to go to Morocco? –"

"Did I?" I said, declining his offer of a seat and looking forlornly at the flagon of cider which seemed to have barely been touched in the time I'd been gone.

"Yes, Baldy, you did. You've just forgotten the fact. Well, lucky for you, I'm here to remind you of all the fun things you've chickened out of these past few years."

"Didn't you want your cider?" I said.

"Don't bother me with extraneous details, Baldy," he said, squinting back at his list. "Of course I want the cider. Just saving it for later is all. By the way, there was a fire along the road earlier. You could see it through the bathroom window. Wouldn't know anything about it, would you, Baldy?" He swivelled his eye in my direction and gave me a good going over. "Look at the state of you," he said, "you've certainly been up to *something*."

"Never mind that," I said, not wishing to dwell upon how ridiculous I looked in my bog-ruined monkey jacket, "where did you get that gin?"

"At the getting place, Baldy, is all you need to know. Now listen," he said, "about Morocco -"

He stopped abruptly and his jaw dropped. He was looking past me, both eyes sprung open now. I turned. Anushka had decided to follow me in. I hadn't invited her to do so but neither had I forbidden it. I'd just expected her to wait in the plastic pig while I checked on "my brother".

"Whoa-ho!" my shadow cried. "Look what Baldy managed to catch."

"This is Anushka," I said. "Anushka, this is my brother, Sid."

"Now, Baldy," my shadow said, "you know that's not my name."

"Really?" I said, wearily, "then what *is* your name?"

He stared at me for a moment or two with a mischievous look in his eye. "Sidney," he said. "You *know* I prefer Sidney. Got more dignity to it. More *gravel*, if you know what I mean."

"You mean 'gravitas'," I said.

"No Baldy," he said, emphatically, "I mean 'gravel'."

"Pleased for to meet you, Sidney," Anushka said, ignoring our pseudo-fraternal dispute.

"Likewise, my dear," my shadow said. He tipped me a lascivious wink. "Well, come in," he said to Anushka. "Don't wait for Baldy to grow any manners. Baldy doesn't know the first thing about how to treat a lady." He picked up the gin bottle. "Reach the lady down a glass, Baldy, for Christ's sake," he said.

"She won't be stopping for a drink," I said.

"Says *you*," he said. "Would you like a drop of gin, my dear? Don't let Baldy sway you."

"I *told* you," I said, "she won't be staying for a drink."

"Actually," Anushka declared, "I think I *would* like some gin. Just small glass."

"There, you see, Baldy? Now, hand me down a glass."

Even though he was closer to the glass cupboard than I was I did as I was ordered just to shut him up, though I made sure I knocked off his hat with my elbow as I reached above him, just out of spite. He gave me a mean look as he put the hat back on but he didn't say anything.

I slammed the glass onto the table and my shadow poured in some gin and slid it in Anushka's direction.

"Perhaps is better with water," she said.

"You heard the lady, Baldy," my shadow said. "Go fetch some water."

I threw Anushka a glance as I headed for the kitchen, intending it as a signal for her to follow me in there so that I could warn her about the cider. But she failed to catch my meaning and I was annoyed with her for that as I sought out the milk jug that used to hold my grocery money. I ran the tap for a good long while until the water ran cold. Anushka and my shadow were already getting along nicely, judging by her laughter. It was the first time I'd heard her laugh and by the time I left the kitchen my internal weather was ruffled by a bitter squall of jealousy which blew an exceptionally wild gust when I saw that Anushka was now seated at the table and leaning expectantly toward my shadow as if hanging on his every word.

I set the jug on the table and Anushka poured water into her gin. "Your brother is amusing man," she said.

"Isn't he?" I said. "You should see him in action when he hits his stride."

"Now, Baldy," my shadow said, "don't you be telling tales on me."

Anushka picked up her glass, said something in Russian and then downed her gin in a single gulp.

"*That's* what I like to see," enthused my shadow.

Anushka wiped her mouth on the sleeve of Billy's waxed jacket. "Is how we drink at home," she said.

"And where *is* home, my dear," my shadow enquired, solicitously.

"I am from Russia," Anushka said.

"*That's* what I thought," my shadow said. "Soon as I saw you. I bet you're of noble birth too, aren't you, my dear? A princess of some kind?"

"They haven't had princesses in Russia for some time now," I said, somewhat superciliously. "Haven't you heard? A little thing they had over there called a revolution."

"There you go again, Baldy," my shadow said, "bleaching out all the mood." He poured Anushka some more gin and added a splash of water. "Here," he said. "Don't worry about Baldy. Baldy hasn't got a romantic bone in his body."

"Oh," Anushka said, "I think is not so."

"Trust me," my shadow said, "not a single one. He's only ever once done a romantic thing that I ever heard of. ..."

I shot him a glance, which he ignored.

"... One moment of burning passion in thirty-two years," he went on.

"You are hard on him," Anushka said, a little too coquettishly for my liking.

"No," my shadow said, "Baldy's hard on himself. But don't you worry, my dear; I'll show you a fun time."

It continued like this for five minutes or so – five minutes during which Anushka slammed down three more belts of gin. It was a relief when she declared that she needed the toilet. I directed her to it and she took off her boots and jacket and left the room - a little unsteadily it has to be said.

My shadow's eye followed her, taking in her lovely exposed shoulder before lingering on her backside.

As soon as she'd left, I turned on him.

"Stop chatting her up, you bastard," I said.

"Relax, Baldy," he said. "Just trying to provide a bit of healthy competition. It makes me sick to see you so coy and tardy around the woman. Besides," he added, tipping me another of his obnoxious winks, "I thought maybe you'd brought her home as some kind of present. There I was only today telling you how I'd like to shack up with a Russian bird for a change and you, you sly old dog, you bring one home. And what a fucking beauty too!"

"Well," I said, "you've got *that* all wrong."

"Have I?" he said and the way he said it made me go cold inside. I thought it best to go back on the offensive so as to back-foot the bastard.

"I asked you where you got that gin," I said. "You stole it, didn't you?"

"No, Baldy, a passing eagle dropped it into my waiting palm. Course I fucking stole it."

"From the Major's?" I said, remembering his bundled shirt when we'd arrived home following that unfortunate visit.

"Well, Baldy, you didn't think I was going to sleep through *that* racket, did you? Sounded like the fucking siege of Stalingrad. So, while you were popping away I just happened to wander into the house …"

"And there it was."

"Yep, that's right, Baldy; there it was. A very well-stocked place, the Major's. Wish I'd had more time there. You want to see what else I got?" He hitched up his shirt and from the waistband of his jeans pulled out a small pistol. I recognised it as the one which had been sitting atop a pile of folders in the Major's rumpus room.

"Give that to me, you reckless bastard," I said.

"Oh, I don't think I'll be doing *that* any time soon, Baldy," he said. He spun the pistol by its trigger guard like a B-movie western hero and then tucked it back into his jeans. "No," he said, "I think it's best if it stays just where it is – with me. Makes a difference, a thing like that. I've got a feeling things are going to change around here, Baldy. I reckon I'm due a bit more respect than you've shown hitherto and that's the *first* thing that's going to change."

"Bet its not even loaded," I said, uncertainly.

"Oh, it's loaded alright," he said. "It's true that I didn't have time to hunt up any spare ammo, but six bullets is plenty enough to get the job done."

"And what job would that be?" I said.

He just smiled pityingly, as if to tell me not to be so dim.

"You can't shoot me," I said. "It'll be the end of you if you do."

"Maybe it will and maybe it won't. That's a thing neither one of us knows for sure, Baldy, one way or the other. Either way, you haven't got the guts to call me on it. Anyhow, let's not let it spoil the evening. You just do as I say and everything will be tickety fucking boo. By the way," he said, "I've been learning some new tricks."

The gin bottle contained about an inch of gin. He picked it up and poured the gin down his throat and then set the empty bottle back down, smacking his lips appreciatively. "No, Baldy," he said, "*that* wasn't the trick. *This* is the trick. Now watch this."

He reached for the bottle again but instead of grabbing it he made his shadow's hand grasp the neck of the bottle's shadow. He lifted the bottle's shadow clear of the bottle and had his shadow hand waggle it a couple of times before setting it down, where it sat a foot from the bottle. Then his shadow hand slid the bottle's shadow back to its rightful place.

I felt sick. My shadow's shadow could now perform tricks. "Well, aren't you the fucking metaphysical marvel," I said, bitterly.

"What do you think, Baldy?" he said. "Think I could make it into the carny with an act like that?"

I can't tell you how relieved I was when he uncorked the cider and filled his glass with it - so relieved, in fact, that I sat down in order to study its effects in comfort.

He took a drink and again he smacked his lips but this time in disapproval. "Got a queer taste, this stuff," he said. "It's why I left off it earlier."

"It's scrumpy," I said. "It's supposed to taste like that."

"I *know* how scrumpy is supposed to taste, Baldy," he said. He tipped the flagon this way and that, stirring up the sediment and frowning at it the whole time. "At least there don't seem to be any rat's eyes in it," he said. "I fucking hate finding a rat's eye in my drink. Don't you, Baldy?"

Despite his obvious reservations he began to tuck into the cider with increasing alacrity. "Where's the Russian, Baldy?" he said. "Do Russians always take so damned long to go to the toilet?"

"I don't know," I said. "I've never met a Russian before."

When Anushka finally emerged from the toilet (and even my shadow was too much the gentleman to ask her what had taken so long) we were discussing guitars and other musical matters. He'd rewritten the original list that I'd flushed down the toilet and he'd become fixated on that item.

For my own part, I'd become increasingly fixated on the contents of the cider flagon and his progress in diminishing it. The first thing I intended to do, once he'd been bitten hard enough by the horse tranquilizer, was to relieve him of the pistol. I was willing to make any number of conversational concessions to keep him at his ease and keep him drinking.

He wanted a Fender Strat (to start with), he said, because he considered himself more a chord-monger than a noodler and he thought that said instrument, combined with a Marshal amp, would be best for the kind of choppy chord changes he had in mind. He wanted to leave things hanging, he said; to violate time (which didn't surprise me, since violation was pretty much his stock in trade).

"You know what makes me sick, Baldy?" he said. "Mozart, that's what. Fucking Mozart. Know what it sounds like, Baldy, do you? Like a fucking mathematician playing the piano. Only he's more interested in the maths than the music. Which, bearing all that in mind, Baldy, is how *you* used to play."

Which was the moment that Anushka arrived back in the room. It was clear that in the interim, the wine and (especially) the gin she'd drunk had made itself ever more strongly-felt. She surveyed the table with a prospective eye. "So," she said, "there is no more gin."

"Don't worry, my dear," my shadow said, with exaggerated civility, "the cider's quite palatable."

"Oh, I don't think you'd like the cider," I interjected, trying to keep the panic from my voice. "It's pretty rough stuff."

"I am used to rough stuff. So, please to pour me a little cider, Sidney," she said.

"Why, of course, my dear," my shadow said.

The only positive element I could find in the moment was that my shadow was now slurring his words. He seemed a little dismayed at how thick his tongue had grown and he frowned at the flagon doubtfully as he poured Anushka some cider.

"Now, Anushka," he slurred, " – can I call you Anushka?"

"Of course," she said, "is my name."

"And what a beautiful name it is too, my dear," my shadow said. "Now, Anushka, my sweet princess, I want you to tell me the story of your life, from your birth onward."

"This is big story to tell," Anushka said, taking an experimental sip of her cider.

"Well, I *like* a big story," my shadow said. "No good waiting for Baldy to trot one out. He's only got one good story to tell and even then he comes out of it looking like a cry-baby. Did Baldy tell you that he set fire to a school?"

"Shut up," I said. "Shut the hell up about that."

"No Baldy," my shadow said, letting his hand rest on the butt of the pistol concealed beneath his shirt, "I don't think that I *will* shut up about that." He gave me a warning look.

Meanwhile, the remainder of Anushka's cider vanished down her throat in one draught and my erotic hopes for the evening vanished right along with it. She looked at the empty glass with glazed eyes and then seemed to belatedly catch the tail of a thought.

"But I think you say that it was Sidney who set fire to the school," she said.

"Is *that* what he said?" my shadow said, in mock outrage. "Well, that's just typical of Baldy …" His eyes closed and his head wagged for a few seconds and when he recovered he'd totally lost his thread.

Anushka, however, remained just about sufficiently compos mentis to seize the conversational initiative.

"I think it was to be *my* life story that we tell. No?"

"And show it is, my dear," my shadow slurred, "Show it is."

Anushka reached for the cider flagon with one hand and held the first finger of her other hand aloft. "I was born in Saratov!" she declared. Then, her face went slack and without any superfluous theatrics, her head thumped down hard on the table. I winced and prayed that there would be no bruise in the morning. A bruised forehead might be a thing she'd hold against me.

"Well, fuck me, Baldy, I thought … I thought …" my shadow said said, struggling visibly, " … I thought these Russians could drink." And with that and not before time, his head too thumped to a definite standstill. His hat flipped forward like the lid of a peddle-bin.

"And that's that," I said, in the fresh and mostly-welcome silence. "What a perfect end to a perfect day."

21

One thing was clear: I couldn't leave Anushka with her head resting on the table for the entire night. Over and above the fact that it would be uncomfortable for her (and thus un-gentlemanly to do so) there was simply no way I was going to leave her in the unsupervised company of my shadow while I took my own much-needed sleep. It was true that he'd imbibed enough of the horse tranquiliser to put most men into a coma for the entire night but he was *not* most men and I thought that his constitution was too robust and supernatural a thing to conform to anyone's idea of the average. God alone knew what awful molestations he might visit upon Anushka if he managed to shake himself free of the drug's influence. With that in mind, I lit a cigarette and watched over him for a while.

Thinking it was a good time to reclaim my hat I eased the brim from beneath my shadow's forehead. I twirled it on my finger a time or two but stopped short of putting it on. It felt a sullied thing and, deciding that I may as well let my shadow keep it, I returned it right-side-up to the table. It made me feel disproportionately sad to finally let go of that hat.

While Anushka snored softly I watched my shadow's head and shoulders twitch as if he were making one last doomed stand against sleep on some battlefield of his inner landscape.

Once he was finally still I stubbed out the cigarette and stole around the table. I got to my knees and probed delicately around the waistband of my shadow's jeans until I found the butt of the pistol. As I began to ease it out, he shifted his position slightly and released a loud snore. I froze but he didn't wake. After a second or two I pulled the pistol clear and got to my feet. I looked the pistol over until I found the release lever for the cylinder and then I swung out the cylinder and tapped at it and shook it until the bullets dropped into my waiting palm. They were of a bigger calibre than I'd expected and I realised that the pistol had only looked puny to my untrained eye because of its stubby barrel. I put the bullets in my trouser pocket and tucked the pistol into my own waistband.

Turning my attention to Anushka, I thought it best to try and get her upstairs so as to lay her on my bed where she could sleep off the horse tranquilizer in comfort. I would sleep on the couch, where I could keep an eye on my shadow. Of course, I would have to sleep too but I was certain that a selfish bastard like him would make more than enough noise on waking to wake me in turn.

So that's what I did. And how different was this version of taking Anushka to bed compared to how I'd previously envisioned it when she'd first allowed the possibility back at Billy's cottage. Like all unconscious people, she was very heavy. There was also the (literally) delicate matter of that off-the-shoulder dress. I had the feeling that the thing had only been held in place by some act of will-power on her part – which, of course, no longer applied. I was terrified that her breasts would somehow tumble free and that she would awaken at exactly that moment and so forever see me as a ravening, advantage-taking monster.

But for all that I managed to part carry, part drag her up the stairs and into my bedroom, where, with a sigh of relief, I lowered her onto my bed. I stretched and nursed my aching back. Then, feeling my way around to the other side of the bed, I tucked the pistol beneath the mattress, groped a sock from my sock drawer, dropped the bullets into the sock and then put the sock back in the drawer along with all my other paired and un-paired, matching and un-matched socks.

On impulse, I tiptoed back around the bed and sat beside Anushka. The moonlight at the edges of the curtains provided just enough light for me to make out her face. I gently brushed her hair away from her lips and then – because the moment demanded some gesture from me – I kissed my first and second fingers and touched them briefly to her forehead as if to soothe the knock it had taken. I wanted so badly to hold her that I daren't linger and so I made myself stand and tiptoe to the door.

It was then that I remembered Hendrix and, not wishing Anushka to go out that or any other way, I returned to the bed and shifted her dead-to-the-world body onto its side. All of which served little purpose because on my way back to the door I heard the bed springs creak as she – through some instinct of habit – re-adjusted her body back to the supine position. Then she began to snore – and not softly this time. It was more the kind of snore you'd expect to be unleashed by a drunken navvy (or, indeed, my reprobate shadow) rather than a Russian princess and so I, being a gentleman, hurried from the room and pretended to myself that I couldn't have and *hadn't* heard it.

Downstairs, I turned out all the lights except for the wall lamp that illuminated my shadow. It was important that I could see him clearly should he rouse himself. I took off my soiled jacket and hung it from the back of a chair and then I lay on the couch and covered myself with the blanket left there from the night before.

I closed my eyes. It had been a long and eventful couple of days and, of course, I'd slept very little. I *needed* sleep but at the same time I was reluctant to give in to it because of my obligation (and desire) to protect Anushka from my shadow, should he wake. After a while, however, these competing imperatives became academic because my shadow's snoring grew so loud that sleep became impossible. It was the kind of snore that had several parts to it and was graced by a hacking inhalation which I swear sucked the hem of the curtains six inches clear of the window sill.

I suffered in silence (or, at least, bad-tempered muttering) for half an hour or so and then gave up the idea of sleeping on the couch as a lost cause. I supposed that I could go and sleep on the couch in the living room but that would seriously compromise my efficacy as self-appointed guardian. No, I decided, there was only one viable alternative to this torturous situation and that was to return to my bed and sleep beside Anushka, fully-clothed and ever-so-chastely and somehow vigilant all at the same time. So that's what I did.

Anushka's snoring had either a) diminished in volume or b) now seemed as nothing compared to the cacophony emanating from my shadow. Either way, I deemed it tolerable and so, taking care not to let the bedsprings creak, I lay down beside her. I turned this way and that for a bit and than settled on my back with my arms folded across my chest – not so much for the sake of comfort (it wasn't comfortable, particularly) but more as a way of underscoring my pure intentions.

By and by, fatigue returned to mind and body and, as uncomfortable as I was, I soon dozed off.

I was awakened some time later by Anushka, who'd begun to moan and twitch in her sleep, as if in the grip of a potently unpleasant dream. (And how wrong I was about that.) Once I was fully awake, I turned onto my side so that I faced toward her and propped myself up with my elbow.

"Anushka …." I whispered. She let out a deep groan which startled me. "Anushka," I tried again. "Wake up," I said, shaking her shoulder gently, "you're having a bad dream." She groaned again and began to switch her head side to side on the pillow.

I thought of that old wives' tale about the dreamer dying if he or she was unable to wake before whatever frightful dream-fiend had snared them in the dream. I didn't believe there was any truth in that but, even so, being trapped inside a nightmare seemed like a terrible enough experience and, given the large draught of horse tranquilizer she's drunk, it wasn't likely that she'd be capable of waking herself.

"Anushka," I said, shaking her with more vigour this time.

She moaned again and I felt her legs begin to writhe. The more I shook her, the more animated she became and still I could not release her from the nightmare.

A little awkwardly, I reached behind me and managed to snap on the bedside lamp, hoping that might do the trick. It didn't. It did, however – once my eyes had adjusted – afford me a good look at her face. Which was not the face of a woman harassed by terror. No. Her breath had quickened and a twitching smile inhabited her lips. Her hands clenched and unclenched, gathering up handfuls of bed covers while her legs continued to writhe. She looked, in short, like a woman having a very good time. As she began to thrash her head side to side, her teeth chattering lightly, I was forced to contemplate the hitherto unmentioned aphrodisiac properties of the horse tranquilizer.

Then movement in my peripheral vision snagged my eye. I looked up. There they were, the two of them, naked, floating free of context and totally unrestrained, projected (if that's the word) on the span of wall between my wardrobe and my bookcase. I remembered my shadow's new trick – his shadow's hand lifting the shadow of the gin bottle free of its origin. It was now horribly clear that he could do much more than that.

My shadow's shadow's head was buried in Anushka's shadow crotch, doing things to her shadow pussy with his shadow tongue. Needless to say, Anushka's shadow body was a beautiful thing to behold. I watched in awful fascination as my shadow's shadow reached up to caress a shadow breast and tweak a shadow nipple.

Beside me, Anushka ululated a moan of pure and deep delight. I gave her a hard shake but my shadow's shadow had obviously hit a definite sweet spot. "Oooh," she whispered, in her off-kilter English, "is sooo good."

I couldn't take any more. "You dirty bastard!" I screamed. I threw a pillow at my defiled wall but the gesture was as ineffective as it was fuelled by fury and the shadows just kept up their shadow fore-play regardless.

I tried one more time to wake Anushka – this time pinching the skin of her arm and giving it a mean and vindictive twist – but to no avail. Alright, I thought, if I can't wake Anushka

I sprang from the bed and tore downstairs, where my shadow was still sleeping soundly.

"Wake up, you bastard," I yelled in his ear. "Wake up!"

He failed to comply.

A pool of drool had dribbled from the corner of his sleeping mouth and his tongue lapped at it obscenely. I was filled with revulsion and disgust and – as another cry of pleasure drifted down the stairwell – envy.

I shook my shadows shoulder and gave his ear a vicious twist. I bellowed and raged at him – all to no effect. He just remained slumped over the table, licking his own drool, lost in his dream-sex tryst with the sexy woman of my dreams. Christ, how I hated him.

"Right, you fucker," I said, "no more Mr Nice Guy."

I fetched half a pan full of cold water from the kitchen which I then poured – quite carefully and accurately considering the circumstances – over my shadow's head and the back of his neck. He didn't even flinch.

I raised the empty pan high enough for it to make a light *ding* against the ceiling. For a good few seconds I stood in this coup de grace attitude while I struggled against the urge to bash the bastard's brains in. For better or worse, I won the struggle and had to satisfy myself with a hard slam of the pan against the unyielding table. Which, of course, had no effect on my shadow whatsoever.

Then came the moment when all the world's mockery was distilled into a few seconds of interminable length and came rolling down the stairwell in the form of the loud and unmistakable groan of a woman within a few panting breaths of a profound orgasm. I was visited by an antithetical but equally potent desire not to let that happen. Selfish bastard that I am, he, she, *they*, were not going to have it all their own way.

Carrying the pan with me, I bolted back up the stairs. I filled the pan brim full in the bathroom so that a good part of it had slopped onto my socks by the time I was back in the bedroom.

My shadow's shadow had started to give it to Anushka good and hard now – in, out, in, out, in, out, it went (and he would have to be bigger than me, wouldn't he?) – while Anushka's lovely shadow back was arched all the better for him to jam it in up to the hilt. The bed was rattling in its frame as the dream played out its physical manifestation. Anushka's sumptuous mouth was wide and expectant and pre-ecstatic and her own back was arched and, as I watched in reluctant fascination, her ass began to pump against the mattress.

I positioned myself so that my back was to the shadows – casting no shadow of my own, of course – and then poured the water over Anushka's face. She spluttered against it briefly but the water did nothing to stifle the huge and lustful groan which rolled out of the very depths of her.

"Wake up …. *please* …." I said, somewhat pathetically.

But it was too late. The orgasm ripped through her and she began to scream in ecstasy, loudly and frantically enough to wake the roosting birds. I stepped back, somewhat awestricken and, not being able to help myself, turned just in time to see the denouement played out on the wall.

Exhausted and utterly defeated, I dropped wearily down onto the corner of the bed, where I was kicked by one of Anushka's toe-curled feet. I let the pan fall to the floor and buried my head in my hands. I was slightly ashamed – if not at all surprised – to find that I had grown a fine erection. I felt as if *I* were the one in violation of privacy and decency. When I finally looked up, the shadows were enjoying a post-coital cuddle.

I made it around to my side of the bed. I lay down with my sulking back toward Anushka and turned out the lamp. The pillow was wet but I didn't care.

Anushka's breathing finally slowed until she resumed a soft snoring. I tried not to hold the shadow-sex against her – it was not a thing of her making, after all. But I *was* angry with her and I would have to watch that. It was the kind of bitter anger – tinged with humiliation – which had once driven me to set fire to a school. (No, I reminded myself; not me, *him*. The same *him* who had just shadow-fucked my new girlfriend while I had done little more than kiss her.)

But, at some time in the night, Anushka threw an arm around me and hugged me to her (close enough that I could feel her wet hair) and told me that she loved me. And, even though I knew that she didn't mean me, but rather that darker portion of me slumbering away in his own drool, it was at least some kind of compensation to carry with me into sleep.

22

Two American Phantom jets screaming low over the moors. Another hot day in the making. Beside me, Anushka stirred.

"David?" she said, uncertainly.

"It's me," I said.

"My head hurt," she said. "And I am wet. What happen last night?"

"Nothing much," I said. "You drank too much, that's all." I'd already decided not to tell her that I'd drugged the cider. It was my only means of keeping my shadow out of mischief and out of my way and I was not about to compromise that by blabbing about it to Anushka, especially since she was on such good shadow terms with my shadow.

Anushka groaned. "I feel like head slammed in door," she said.

"Why don't you sleep a while longer," I said. "I'll go down and check on Sidney. With any luck he's died in his sleep."

"You should not be so rough on Sidney," she said, drowsily. "He is your brother. Besides, he has good points. No?"

"Well," I said, rising and trying to keep the rancour from my voice, "you *would* say that, wouldn't you?"

Downstairs, my shadow was still sleeping. He'd barely moved a muscle save that he'd turned his head at some point so that his right ear now rested where the pool of drool had been (and would be still if it hadn't been subsumed into the larger puddle I'd made when I'd poured the water over his head).

I drew back the curtains and looked for shadows. My shadow's shadow was sleeping beneath my shadow and acting impeccably like a normal shadow.

I fetched a couple of tea towels from the kitchen (putting on the kettle as I did so) and mopped up the water around my shadow's head as best as I could and then mopped up the water that had drained onto the floor. Unable to resist it, I snapped one of the wet towels into my shadow's face with a deft flick of the wrist. He cracked one bloodshot eye and groaned. Then, like a weary colossus, he raised his head slowly from the table.

Despite how bad he looked, he was cheerful enough. "Morning, Baldy," he said. "By fuck, that cider packs a punch."

"There's plenty left if you want some more," I said, indicating the flagon.

"Maybe later," he said. He rubbed at his incipient beard and felt the water there and then patted at his damp hair. "Any good reason why I'm wet, Baldy?" he said.

"I threw water over you," I said.

"What, was I on fire or something?"

"You were dreaming," I said. "Making all kinds of hideous noises. I tried to wake you but you'd drunk too much for that."

He thought about that until a slow smile dawned. "You're right, Baldy," he said. "I *was* dreaming. Why don't I tell you all about it and you can do some of that Freudian analysis bullshit. Give your brain some exercise. It started like this —"

"I don't want to hear about it," I said, cutting him off. "What's more, the next time you have a dream like *that* one, I'll fucking shoot you."

"That's a bold threat, Baldy," he said, "for a man without —"

This time, he didn't need me to cut him off. His cocky smile fled his face, routed by a sudden look of alarm which, I have to say, I enjoyed immensely. He clapped his hand to his waistband, where the pistol should have been.

"Never figured you for a thief, Baldy," he said.

"I didn't steal it," I said. "I confiscated it. For your own good."

"That's what I like about you, Baldy," he said, "all charity."

"I do my best," I said, relieved that he'd decided not to make an issue out of it. "I'm making coffee. Would you like some?"

"Coffee would be good, Baldy," he said, "Coffee would be just the ticket, in fact. I've got a lot planned for today. I'm running a bit behind what with one thing and another and it's time to stoke the engine and spin the wheels."

"You'll want it good and strong then," I said.

"The stronger the better, Baldy," he said, "and don't be shy with the sugar."

I made two mugs of instant coffee, holding off making one for Anushka - partly because I thought it best to let her sleep a little longer; partly because I had no idea how she took coffee. It was a remarkable thing to have a too-intimate knowledge of what she sounded like when in the throes of ecstasy while not knowing whether she took milk or sugar in her coffee.

As to my shadow's coffee, I had a very good idea of how *he* was going to take it. There was half a flagon of the drugged cider left and I had little doubt that he'd get around to drinking it eventually. But I feared that the sense of purpose he'd just revealed would give him enough impetus to commit some or other outrage before he decided to have a drink and I was taking no chances. I snuck out to the plastic pig and retrieved my haversack and the jar of horse tranquilizer and when I returned to the kitchen I spooned in a heavy dose of medicine along with some sugar.

I set the coffee on the table and sat opposite my shadow. His eyes were an especially evil shade of red and I could tell that his hangover was brutal but I didn't expect him to admit it. He picked up his coffee and sniffed at it. He pulled a face and set it down again. Then he lit a smoke and, to my relief, finally took a sip of coffee.

"Baldy," he said, grimacing, "you make lousy coffee. I'd better put that on my list." He slid one of his sheets of paper towards him and reached for his pen. He frowned at the wet patch in the corner of the paper and tutted to himself a couple of times and then – saying it aloud as he did so – he wrote "Remind Baldy to get a coffee machine."

"Remind Baldy where he'd get that kind of money," I said, dryly.

But my shadow had stopped listening. He was puffing on his cigarette and perusing his list of drunken ramblings. He underlined a couple of items but when I craned forward to see what they were he drew the sheet of paper closer and shielded it with his hand, like a schoolboy fending off an exam-room cheat.

"Why so coy all of a sudden?" I said.

"Because, Baldy," he said. "Just because." He scribbled something on the list and then tore off the damp patch, folded what was left, and then tucked it into his breast pocket before getting up to use the toilet, his shadow dutifully leading the way.

"Use the downstairs loo," I told him. "And if you piss on the seat, make sure you wipe it."

"It's *you* who sprinkles when he tinkles, Baldy," he said. "Me? I can piss like a fire hose."

Grateful to be left alone, even if only for a minute, I sipped my coffee. This brief respite, however, was almost immediately ruined by my ringing telephone. It was still early for my phone to be ringing and I felt a degree of trepidation as I went into the hallway to answer it.

"Hello David," my caller said, "Charles Mason here."

My heart sank. Mr Mason was about to tell me that the sun had blistered the gloss on his bargeboard and that the blisters had failed to shrink back and had in fact split so that the paint had already begun to peel and would I mind taking another look at it – all for no extra cost of course. What with the stolen grocery money, the busted bicycle and my wrecked van, I felt financial ruin circling my little camp.

As it was to turn out, however, Mr Mason's bargeboard was the furthest thing from his mind.

"Good morning, Mr Mason," I said. "Another nice day."

"I'm afraid I'm calling on a matter of some urgency," Mr Mason said, brushing aside my pleasantry. "I wonder," he went on, "that is, *we* wonder, Margaret and I, if you could find time to call in at the house today. Sooner rather than later might be best." Then, sensing my hesitation (I had a lot to do after all – even if I didn't yet know what the doing would look like), he added: "It really is rather important. I gather, from the little I know, that it could even be to your advantage." He lowered his voice. "It's about Aunt Alsey," he said.

"Oh," I said, "that *is* important."

"Margaret will be able to tell you more," Mr Mason said, "but I'm afraid she can't come to the telephone … or rather … well, you'll see why when you get here."

"I can be there in an hour or so," I said, without actually performing any kind of calculation.

"Splendid," Mr Mason said. "And thank you, David," he added, sounding very unlike himself. I hung up to the sound of the flushing cistern in the downstairs toilet.

I'd just set foot back in the dining room when the phone rang again. I turned back to answer it and met my shadow in the hallway. He was still buttoning his flies.

"Coffee's getting cold," I said. I waited until he'd entered the dining room so that I could close the door behind him and then I picked up the phone.

It was Silas Crabtree.

"Mornin', Professor," he said. "Didn't wake you I hope."

"No," I said, "it's alright; I've been up for a while."

"Up for a while, eh?" Silas said. "Don't suppose you tried any o' that sleeping draught then?"

"No ..." I said. Truth be told, I'd forgotten all about my fictional insomnia. "Didn't need any last night. Out like a light," I lied.

"That's good," Silas said. "It don't do a man no good not sleepin'."

"You're right about that," I said, acutely aware of my own fatigue. All this talk about sleep and sleeping draughts prompted a question. "How's Jed?" I said.

"Oh, Jed's right as rain," Silas said. "Fire brigade got 'im down an' he's sleeping off the dose in hospital. Said they'd never seen a man in such a deep coma that hadn't had a bridge fall on him or some such so they called out an ambulance. Seemed best all round to keep Jed under observation. 'Course, weren't easy getting the first ambulance out o' the pig waller but we did her in the end."

"How did the ambulance get stuck in the pig wallow?" I said, curiosity getting the better of me.

"Oh," Silas said, "Jed's leg started acting up. I told 'em to strap it down. I said, just 'cause *Jed's* asleep don't mean nothing. That leg don't need sleep, I said. Not even a cat-nap. Course, they knew best. Anyway, Professor, about your van ..."

"Yes," I said, "how's *that* going?"

"Well, Professor," Silas said, "I'm afraid it's a tad worse than when you fetched her in."

"Worse?" I said. "How can it be *worse?*"

It took Silas five minutes to tell me how it could be worse and when he was finished I had to concede that not only was it worse, but that it was worse than worse.

When I'd hung up I went to check on my shadow. He was just draining his coffee mug and I suddenly felt bad about drugging him. If what Silas had just told me was true – and I had no reason to doubt him – then my shadow was going to need his wits about him. But it was too late for regrets and certainly too late to do anything about it. In fact, he was already showing signs of being freshly drowsy. Even so, he had something on his mind.

"Bad news, Baldy?" he said.

"Just a customer," I said.

"Both times?" he said.

"Both times," I said. "Forgot to tell me something the first time."

"A customer?" he said. "Jeez, your customers are early birds, Baldy."

Which was his way of calling me a liar. Still, I persisted. It was likely that I'd been overheard but I could hardly admit the truth.

"He's a farmer," I said. "You know how they are. Wants me to creosote a fence."

"Does he now?" he said. He studied me with his sleepy eyes for a moment or two and then said: "I want that gun, Baldy."

"Why in God's name would I let *you* have a gun?" I said.

"So's I can protect myself, you fuckwit," he said. His eyes closed and he rocked forward but managed to start himself awake again.

"Protect *yourself?*" I said. "It'll be the rest of the damn county that'll need protecting if anyone was ever stupid enough to turn *you* loose with a gun."

"Something's coming," he said.

"What something?" I said, wondering how much he knew, or at least sensed, about Silas's unwelcome news.

"*You* know," he said. "Something's coming, Baldy. And it's coming for both of us. You know it too. It's why you want the gun … while …" his eyes closed again; opened again. "While I'll be … you *fucker*, Baldy. It'll rip me to fucking shreds." Then, just as last night, his head hit the table with a solid thump.

"Now what the hell am I going to do?" I asked the room.

Then I knew. It wasn't the answer to everything but there was a pressing urgency to it all the same. With my shadow now asleep it seemed prudent, in order to avoid a repeat of last night's display, to make sure that Anushka was awake.

She was indeed awake and sitting on the edge of the bed, smudging her eye make-up with balled fists. For all of her recent oneiric frolicking, her woman's body, she looked just like a little girl rubbing sleep from her eyes. She sensed my presence and lowered her hands.

"Are you alright?" I said.

"Yes," she said, with a forced smile. "I feel better after shower."

"I'm afraid I've only got a bath," I said. "I can make you some coffee though, if you'd like some."

"Is alright," she said. "You take me home. I have shower. Some breakfast. Then we go find this Aunt Alsey and return to her the lark mirror. You will get back your shadow and then we can be together."

"You make it sound so easy," I said.

"I make it sound possible, is all," she said, with a shrug.

"I hope you're right," I said. "There's just one thing. I need to be back here before dark. Whatever happens, I *have* to be back here before dark."

"Is plenty of time," she said.

I'd brought my haversack into the bedroom with me and she glanced at it. "You are ready now?"

"I just need to get changed," I said.

"So. I use the toilet and wait downstairs."

She was still slightly unsteady on her feet but she moved at a purposeful pace. I watched her go and then I retrieved the gun and bullets and stuffed them inside the haversack. While I was at it I took out the lark mirror and wrapped the towel around it more carefully so that the gun wouldn't damage it. Then I changed into jeans and a light cotton lumber shirt and then, hearing the downstairs toilet flush, hurriedly laced my Doc Martin boots.

"Your brother," Anushka said, when I stepped into the dining room, "you let him sleep like this all night?"

"It doesn't bother him," I said. "He woke for a bit and then went straight back to sleep. He's tough, my brother. He can sleep anywhere. Besides," I added, as if it meant something, "he wants to join a circus."

When I led the way to the door, Anushka lingered long enough to touch my shadow's hair fondly. Too damn fondly for my liking.

I, for my own part, kept an eye on my shadow's shadow, making sure that we weren't followed.

23

On the way to Billy Makepiece's I told Anushka about the phone call from Mr Mason and how it would save time if I went out there alone while she took her shower and ate her breakfast and did whatever else she had to do. Anushka agreed.

After that, we lapsed into a silence which was pregnant with unspoken questions. However, not wanting to get into a protracted conversation which could delay my visit to the Masons, I decided to leave the subject of last night alone for now.

For all of that it was a pleasant drive, punctuated with snatched glances at Anushka who, though a little dishevelled, looked as wonderful as ever. On top of that, the larks were rising, the buzzards wheeled, the sheep looked happy amongst the gorse and heather and the ponies which crossed the road seemed to be of good cheer. The only thing which marred the drive was the guilt I felt when we drove through the patch of country which still smouldered from the fire I'd set with my carelessly discarded cigarette. The fire had chased along the road for a full half a mile until its progress had been checked on reaching the parched bed of a brook.

I turned the plastic pig outside Billy's and then pulled to a halt to drop Anushka off. Without knowing I was going to do it, and throwing my earlier reluctance to the wind, I blurted "Anushka, about last night …"

"We speak later," she said. "You are right. Is not good *not* to speak of last night. But now is not the time."

She leaned towards me (which wasn't a lot of leaning within the close confines of the plastic pig) and almost devoured me with a long, lingering kiss. "We speak later," she reiterated. "Is my promise."

She pulled away and opened the door and it was then that I remembered the gun. I had no desire to carry it around with me, especially while driving the kind of vehicle that might pique the curiosity of a bored country constable. I could, of course, have disposed of it at any number of locations but the fact was that Silas's phone call had rendered the gun not entirely superfluous (my shadow's instincts were bang on the money on that score). And so it was that I made my faux pas with Anushka.

"Oh, wait," I said, reaching behind my seat for my haversack. "Can you keep this somewhere safe?" I delved into the haversack and took out the pistol and the bullet-filled sock.

Anushka's response was immediate and visceral. She all but leaped from the plastic pig, as if I'd offered her a live snake. She even held out her hands to fend off the pistol as she backed away. "No, no, no," she said. "I cannot touch gun. I *hate* guns."

"It's not loaded," I said, rather weakly.

"It make no difference. I cannot touch gun," she said. "How come you have gun?"

"It's *his*," I said, jerking a thumb roughly in the direction of home.

"Is Sidney's? Why for Sidney want gun?"

"He *doesn't* want it," I said. "Not any more. That's why I need a safe place for it."

She considered for a moment. "Alright," she said. "But I will not touch it. You will have to carry it in."

Which was hardly an onerous task.

"We put gun in Billy's safe," Anushka said, as she unlocked the cottage door. "Is only way it remain here."

"But we can't open the safe without Billy," I said, following her in.

"Is alright," Anushka said. "I have number."

"Really?" I said.

"Yes. I bring little cash with me and when Billy is called away and I say I will stay a little longer he tell me to borrow from the safe. Don't worry. Billy trust me."

"He'd have to," I said, with the now-familiar feeling that something didn't quite ring true.

The safe was in Billy's tiny cellar. Though I thought it more likely to be some kind of root cellar, Billy called it, somewhat romantically, his "priest hole" and had ambitions to turn it into a wine cellar (we both knew he'd never get around to it).

Anushka opened the door (which was beneath the stairs) and snapped on the light and then descended the steps. She clicked the dial on the safe door back and forth until the door opened and then she was obliged to climb out of the cellar to afford me the room to enter.

In the safe was a plastic banking envelope containing cash – hundreds, if not a couple of thousands of pounds; a considerable sum back then – along with a Manila envelope with the words, The Last Will and Testament of William James Makepiece written across it. The envelope was lying flat on the floor of the safe and I placed the gun and bullets on top of it. It was a dark and premonitory juxtaposition and it felt like a suicide waiting to happen.

"I am sorry," Anushka said, as she saw me out of the cottage. "I have deep aversion to guns. My father … when I was little girl … I find him dead … he shoot himself."

"I'm sorry," I said.

"Sorry in first regard – it make no difference. Is too late. Sorry in second regard – is no need. You were not to have known."

She kissed me again but it was a hollowed-out version of that earlier kiss, as if there was now something between us. Life, it seemed, was simply in the mood to dump as many complications on my head and pitfalls in my way as possible and there seemed to be little I could do about it.

As sleep-deprived and preoccupied as I was, I'd driven a few hundred yards before the coincidence of what just happened struck me. Billy Makepiece also had a deep aversion to firearms. I discovered this quite by accident and relatively early in our relationship. I'd had a rat problem in my garden and had been loaned a nine millimetre garden gun, with the option of buying it (which I never did). It was a small and un-intimidating weapon – slightly less dangerous than a decent air rifle, I'd been assured. I, of course, knew very little about guns so, before I'd even fired a shot, I'd taken it to Billy's to seek his opinion on it. With his penchant for fly fishing and his occasional lapses into playing the country gent, I'd felt certain that Billy would be au fait with pheasant drives and grouse shoots and all of the shotgun paraphernalia that went with them. I couldn't have been more wrong. I'd wrapped the gun in an old Hessian sack for want of a proper carrying case and when I pulled it clear of the sack – clumsy galoot that I was - Billy let out a cry and jumped backwards and, just as Anushka had done, he'd held out his hands to fend off the gun. It was perhaps the most embarrassing moment in our shared history. For one thing, there was the girly nature of Billy's little cry. Then there was the fact that Billy had been painting his garden gate at the time and his backward spring had upset a half can of paint which was not only wasted but made a mess of his garden path.

Billy had recovered well and made his usual offer of tea but he was a little off with me for the remainder of the visit. But he'd phoned the next day and invited me over. When I got there he said that he'd felt bad about the way he'd treated me. "It was the gun," he said. "I can't be near the damn things. The fact is," he went on, "my old man, father, paterfamilias ... Daddy ... well, the fact is, he shot himself. Have you any idea what a goose gun does to the humans cranium? No? Well I have. And it's an awful fucking mess, I can tell you."

As, no doubt, could Anushka.

24

As I drove on, my mind turned to other matters – most prominently, the content of Silas Crabtree's early morning phone call. Silas had told me that he was working late last night in order to get some jobs out of the way so that he could make a start on my van first thing in the morning. He was slapping a coat of under-seal on the belly of a Ford Zephyr which, he said, was a relatively quiet job for him, otherwise he might not have heard it.

"Heard what?" I said.

A snarlin', Silas said. No, more of a snufflin'. No. Let's say it was more a sort of a snufflin' snarl. At first, he didn't pay much attention to it, he said, because he often heard animal sounds out in the yard when he worked late. He was curious, he said, because whatever was out there didn't bark like a deer not sneeze like a hedgehog nor cough like a badger – but not so curious that he could be bothered to drag himself from beneath the Zephyr to go and have a look, especially as he was so close to finishing and in any case didn't want to pause and let the brush go hard.

But then, he said, a new thing. The creature began to snuffle along the gap at the bottom of the workshop doors (which he kept closed at night to keep out the moths). He said that from where he lay he could see that the creatures snufflin' and sniffin' was so powerful that it stirred up the dust there. But that wasn't all, Professor, he went on. It's snout or muzzle or whatever it was pushed at the doors so hard that they began to creak against the latch. Well, I know foxes can be cheeky devils, he said, but they aren't big enough nor strong enough to do that, so I knew it weren't no fox. But what bothered me most, Professor, is that it *knowed* I were there. Don't ask me how I know but I do. It *knowed* I were there and it didn't bother it one jot. A thing like that can make a chap nervous, he said. So – and keep this to yourself, mind – I got out from under the Zephyr and went and fetched my old dad's service pistol which I keeps in back o' the workshop. By the time I'd done that, though, the creature had moved away from the doors.

I crept over and looked through the glass. The moon was bright and it threw the shadders o' the trees and that's where it were – the creature – sniffing around in the moon-shadder. It was a damn queer thing to watch, the way it paced back an' forth, sniffin' all the while, as if it were trying to sort out a particular scent from all the others.

"What did it look like?" I said.

Job to say really, Silas said. It looked like a lot o' different things an' it looked different again every time it moved. It had a hump back, he said. Bit like a wild pig. Long back legs – something like a hare, only bigger o' course. Powerful chap in the shoulder, he looked. Long tail that kept swishing the ground an' curling around his hind quarters.

Anyhow, he went on, like I say, sniffin' an' snufflin' around out there he were. An' then, just like a switch had been thrown, he yawps back his head an' starts 'owlin. Fit to chill the blood it were, that 'owlin. Then, down goes his head again and he starts loping off towards your van – which was where you left it, far side o' the yard. He'd lope a bit, sniff a bit, lope some more. Then he sniffs all around your van. The van were in the moonlight so's I could see him well enough. Then ... well, he gets up on his hind legs, which didn't seem to suit him at all, an' tries to open the door. Clever 'ands, he's got. Not paws, but clever 'ands. So, when I say that he tried to open the door, Professor, I mean just that; that he pulled on the door handle. But o' course, it were locked. (I know you didn't lock it, Professor, but I did – not good policy to 'ave customer's cars stolen.)

Anyway, Silas went on, he gave up on that, an' he kind of raises up his arms or front legs or whatever you'd call 'em an' I see, plain as day in that moonlight , I see these big, evil-looking claws spring out o' the ends of his fingers. Marvel of engineering it were. Just sprung out of his fingers as big as knives. Then, he drops back on all fours an' lets out a wild screech and then goes at that van door like a fucking threshing machine.

Course, I weren't goin' to stand for that so I opens the door an' takes a shot. I'm sorry to say, Professor, that I missed the bugger and hit the front tyre instead. Anyway, it didn't bother him one bit an' that were that as far as that went 'cause I only 'ad the one bullet. So I pulls up the door and watches through the glass. Well, pretty soon your van door was just so much rusty tinsel an' the bugger was inside your van, sniffin' at the seats. Takin' the scent, see? Then he pulls hisself clear an' starts sniffin' around the ground again 'til he finds your trail, which leads him to where the pig were parked afore you borrered it. He has a good old sniff around the spot an' then he throws back his head an' gets off a good howl and then goes sniffin' off along the lane. I stepped into the yard to watch him go. He'd lope an' sniff just like before only he's picked up the pace a bit now 'til he's fair boundin' up the lane. Seems to me he were followin' the scent o' the plastic pig. Which is to say, Professor, your scent. Wouldn't think a creature'd be able to follow the scent of a vehicle like that but I'm dead certain that's what he were doing alright.

I'm no expert, Professor, Silas said, by way of peroration, but it seems to me that there are two possibilities here. Either you've got yerself a hell-hound on your trail or else yours truly got himself a good long look at the monkey-dog. Either way, he added, you've got something on your trail. An' I can tell you, Professor, it's a very *nasty* something. *Very* nasty indeed.

It was not the kind of news with which any sane person would wish to start their day and I was no exception. I'd had questions, of course, but I hadn't been able to voice them for fear of being overheard by my shadow. And, in any case, the most pertinent question was not one which Silas could answer. Who's trail was the monkey-dog on? Mine? My shadow's? Both?

The monkey-dog's movements (as related by Silas) suggested to me that he wasn't simply and blindly following a trail, but that he was making some kind of deductive reasoning. Otherwise, having followed the van's trail over several miles of road, from the late Major's house to Silas's workshop, why the need to tear his way into my van? My shadow would have left plenty of scent in the commission of his theft of the gin and the gun just as he would have left scent in my van. But he hadn't been with me when I'd gone to fetch the plastic pig and, of course, during my previous visit he'd been just a shadow. A semi-autonomous shadow, perhaps, but a scentless shadow for all that. So my shadow had left no scent at Silas's, while I had left plenty. In which case, if he were looking for me, all he'd need do was to simply follow my scent to the point where I'd climbed inside the plastic pig, and then follow the pig's trail thereafter.

And if he possessed enough intelligence to link man-scent to two separate vehicles then he would most likely have enough of that faculty to link two separate man-scents together. Both required the same kind of narrative reasoning, after all. All of which seemed to point to my shadow having been the one selected as a tasty chow-down, while I was just the means by which the meal had so far eluded him.

I thought back to what the Major had said about the monkey-dog – that, having selected a particular quarry, it would ignore all other opportunities in single-minded pursuit of that quarry. Which was bad news for my shadow and so bad news for me. I might be spared an awful death, but if the monkey-dog ever got hold of my shadow then I would be condemned to spend the rest of my life as a society-spurned freak.

Then another thought struck me. Before I'd dumped my van at Silas's yard, I'd dropped my shadow off at the cottage. Why hadn't the monkey-dog simply followed us there and then attacked at the cottage. Why had he followed the van back to Silas's yard? There were two possibilities as far as I could tell. Either – since I'd had to drive back along the same road to Silas's – the monkey-dog had picked up the fresher scent, which had turned him around and led him back to the workshop, *or*, it was me that had become the selected quarry after all. Which wasn't a comforting thought. What was of some comfort, in my straw-grasping frame of mind, was that, according to the Major, the monkey-dog was strictly nocturnal by inclination. (It was true that we'd seen it venture into the daylight, but only because, I reasoned, it had been angry enough to throw its natural proclivities aside.) We were, in that case, safe until dusk. By which time (call it desperate hope), bearing in mind my imminent visit to the Masons to receive information relating to Aunt Alsey, the situation may have been resolved. If, that is, it was my shadow that the monkey-dog sought. If it were *my* scent that he'd latched onto, then I would be pursued far beyond the termination of the curse.

By the time I'd worked through these various permutations, I was almost grateful that my shadow had stolen the gun. You did good, Sidney, I thought. You did good.

25

I had a choice of two routes which would deliver me to the Masons' house – the longer of which had the merit of taking me past my own cottage door. Tempting though it was to take advantage of this in order to check on my shadow, I was mindful of the press of time and so elected to save this dubious pleasure for the return journey.

Mr Mason wasn't casting a dry fly line down the length of his lawn when I drove between the stone lions and up the gravel drive. Instead he was standing on the terrace, rather lugubriously sucking gin through a too-generous helping of ice. He eyed the plastic pig with mild disapproval and then came down the steps to meet me. He took another suck at his gin while he stared in at me through the windscreen, vaguely quizzical that I'd yet to step out of the pig. The fact is, I was reluctant to do so until I'd had a chance to explain about my absent shadow.

I rolled down the window. "Morning, Mr Mason," I said, breezily enough. "There's something you need to know before I step out of this contraption-"

"If you're referring to your lack of shadow," Mr Mason said, "then there's no need to worry. We know all about that."

"You do?"

"Of course. You're locally famous for it. Why else do you think Margaret had me summon you here?"

The news was depressing but there was no point dwelling on it. I clambered out of the plastic pig and followed Mr Mason up the steps and through the French windows. I caught him snatching a quick glance at the place where my shadow should have been but he was discreet about it and had the good grace not to say a word more on the matter.

"Margaret is in the drawing room," Mr Mason said, upon pausing in the hallway.

"The green room?" I said. This was my shorthand to identify the rooms of the house. To me, the whole thing had been colour-coded with the various applications of paint which I'd slapped on during our lengthy and so far happy association.

"Yes," Mr Mason said, "the green room. David," he went on, lowering his voice, "try not to appear too shocked when you see her. She's in a bit of a way at the moment. To tell you the truth, I can barely bring myself to look at her. David, you will help us, won't you?"

"Of course," I said, not knowing exactly what it was I was agreeing to.

"Good," he said. "Perhaps we can get her through this after all. Now," he said, his spirits rallying, "can I get you some tea? No – you're a coffee man in the mornings, aren't you? Tea in the afternoon. Very civilised. Oh, and since it's you, feel free to smoke. Only don't smoke too close to Margaret will you; probably a little sensitive to it at her age."

"It's alright," I said, slightly puzzled by his reference to Mrs Mason's age, "I'm not smoking as much these days."

"Well, that's something," Mr Mason said. "Why don't you go and say hello while I make the coffee?"

He turned before he disappeared into the kitchen. "Oh," he said, "meant to say: splendid job on the bargeboard."

Mrs Mason wasn't in the green room when I entered. Or, at least, I thought she wasn't. But, wearing a dressing gown and sitting in a high-backed wicker chair by the window, where she could catch the sun, was an old woman – older even (in appearance at least) than Aunt Alsey.

"Oh, I'm sorry," I said. "I was looking for Mrs Mason."

"Look no further, David," she said in a thin, creaky voice.

"Mrs *Mason*?" I said, squinting.

"I'm afraid the years have not been kind since last we met," she said. Her shrunken, all but bald head wagged back and forth as she sawed out a chuckle. "Come closer," she said, "where I can see you. I'm afraid my eye-sight is starting to fail me. Please, David, sit down."

I sat down – *dropped* down – into a matching wicker chair so that there was just a small coffee table - which held some writing materials - between us.

The transformation that had been visited upon poor Mrs Mason was awful. Every trace of her former beauty had vanished. She was now just a frail sack of paper-yellow skin and bone, her luxuriant hair reduced to wisps, her veins blue and all too visible, her eyes like dead lights.

"What *happened* to you?" I said.

She managed to lean forward a little. "You know … the answer … to that," she said, with another wheezy chuckle.

"Aunt Alsey?" I said.

"Aunt Alsey," she said, with a nod.

"But when?" I said. "*How*? You of all people –"

"I'm afraid it was my fault," Mr Mason interjected from the doorway. He walked in carrying a tray with two mugs and his gin glass and set it on the table. His swift return from the kitchen was just more bad news; it meant that the coffee could only be instant.

"Coffee for you, David," he said, graciously turning the handle of the mug in my direction. "And here's your hot water, Dear," he said, placing the other mug on a coaster where it could be reached by Mrs Mason. "It's all she can drink now, poor old thing," he said to me, in a confidential tone.

The Lark Mirror

"Don't talk about her as if she wasn't here," Mrs Mason said and I was glad for her that she still had some spirit.

"Sorry, Dear," Mr Mason said, slightly chastened.

"Oh, don't look so glum, Charles," Mrs Mason said. "Why don't you tell David what happened?" she suggested. "I'm afraid I'm not up to delivering a long narrative."

While Mr Mason drew up a third chair and settled into it, Mrs Mason reached for her mug of hot water with a very shaky hand. The mug tipped unsteadily from side to side as she drew it towards her. Instinctively I leaned forward and was about to steady the mug for her when Mr Mason fired a warning glance in my direction which reminded me that Mrs Mason was a proud woman. I sat back and was relieved to see that Mrs Mason steadied the mug considerably once she'd managed to draw it closer to herself.

"It was Saturday night," Mr Mason said, with no preamble whatsoever save to suck some more gin through his ice, "which was, I believe, the night before your own … visitation?" He raised his eyebrows into question marks.

"That's right," I said. "It was on Sunday evening that Aunt Alsey stole the lark mirror –"

"Ha!" Mrs Mason said. "Is *that* what it was? I wondered about that. You didn't say. Wonderful things, lark mirrors. Why, do you know, when I was a girl –"

"Perhaps we can get to that later, Dear," Mr Mason said, kindly. With the mug settled in her lap, Mrs Mason had a free hand and Mr Mason took it in his and held it and stroked the back of it tenderly.

"Oh dear," Mrs Mason said, "was I being naughty again?"

"No, Dear," Mr Mason said. "It's just that I think it best if we stick to the point for now. Her mind wanders, I'm afraid," he said to me. (That Mrs Mason did not reprove him for lapsing back into the third person seemed testament to the fact.) "But don't worry, she'll snap out of it."

All the while, Mr Mason continued to stroke the back of her hand with an affection and gentleness that I would have thought beyond him. I can't begin to tell you how touched I was by that. I took a big gulp of coffee to wash down the lump in my throat. (Mr Mason had forgotten to sugar the coffee but I didn't bother to mention it.)

Before Mr Mason could resume his story, I felt the need to pick him up on an obvious point. "But if Aunt Alsey visited you on Saturday ..." I said.

"Then why wasn't Margaret in this sad condition when you were here on Monday... ?" Mr Mason said, anticipating my question.

"Not ... always .... Immediate ... effect," Mrs Mason said, rising from her brief fugue.

I thought of the delay between the Sunday evening that Aunt Alsey had cursed me and the Monday afternoon on which my shadow began his antics.

"It was *late* on Saturday night," Mr Mason said, picking up his narrative thread. "If it had been just an hour earlier then Margaret would have been still awake and downstairs with me. She might have been able to warn me and so nip this whole terrible business in the bud. But we'd had friends round for dinner and for one reason and another it hadn't gone terribly well – everything seemed off-kilter somehow; not quite right. Anyhow, it was not simply tire*some*, it was tir*ing* as well. So, instead of having a late drink with me in order to talk over the evening, as is our usual custom once our guests have left, Margaret retired earlier than usual. Well, needless to say, it was a warm evening so I took a brandy out to one of the benches on the terrace. And I hadn't been sitting there long when I saw someone crossing the lawn. The moon was close to full so I could see this figure quite clearly. It was stooped over with some kind of bundle on its back and some kind of hood or cowl covering its head. I must say I was more surprised and intrigued than alarmed and I perceived no threat. I couldn't be certain of this person's sex of course, but the loose clothing suggested a woman and the somewhat stooped physical attitude suggested that in that case it was an *old* woman – some old country woman, I thought, who'd perhaps lost her faculties and had wandered in from the road by mistake. But that thought dissolved when I realised that, far from being aimless, there was a definite sense of purpose about her. Are you okay dear?" he asked Mrs Mason.

"Yes, do go on, Charles," she said. "You're telling it beautifully."

"Thank you, Dear," he said. "Now, as you know," he went on, "this damned weather has not been kind to the rivers and so I've been reduced to casting on the lawn, just to keep in practise. As was the case on Saturday. In fact, I'd been happily casting away when our guests arrived. I wish now that I hadn't been. Or, at least, that I'd bothered to pack my fly rod away." He glanced at Mrs Mason.

"Not your fault," she said.

He smiled ruefully. "Very kind of you to say so, Dear," he said. "But we both know that it *was* my fault. Me and my blustering and bad temper."

"The story, Charles," Mrs Mason said. "Stick to the story." She looked at me and said, "His mind wanders you know." And damned if she didn't tip me a conspiratorial wink.

Mr Mason acknowledged the joke with a good-natured grunt and then continued with his story. "Anyway, I *had* been casting and I *hadn't* packed the rod away. I'd been so eager to greet our guests that I'd simply leant the rod against the apple tree, with the intention of seeing to it later. The real agony of it is that twice during the evening I'd remembered the rod and had made my excuses to go and deal with it and on both occasions I'd allowed myself to be sidetracked with another drink; another conversational tangent."

"He really is so terribly hard on himself," Mrs Mason confided to me.

"Anyhow," Mr Mason continued, "as I stepped down from the terrace it dawned on me that the figure was making a bee-line for the apple tree. Even then, I thought that this old woman (I was satisfied about that by now) was simply looking for apples and that her age-addled brain had failed to remind her that it wasn't yet the season. I was disabused of this notion soon enough, however, when I saw her very deliberately pick up the fly rod. I'd been drinking, of course, and, as I say, I perceived no threat and so I'd been watching up until then as much in the spirit of curiosity as anything else. It was only when I saw the risk to my fly rod that I finally pricked myself into action.

"'I say,' I said, 'would you mind putting that back? It's really rather delicate.' A beautiful thing," he said, almost dreamily and almost to himself. "Hardy," he said. "Built cane. Wonderful craftsmanship. Better than any amount of fibreglass rubbish."

"Don't worry, Dear," Mrs Mason said. "We'll get you another if it comes to it."

"Oh, blast the rod!" Mr Mason exclaimed. "I'd shed a million bloody Hardy fly rods to restore your beauty."

"Am I so very ugly, Charles?" Mrs Mason said.

"Oh damn," he said, "I didn't mean ..." He broke off, noticing her chuckle.

"Oh Charles," she said, "you've always been so easy to tease. Please, go on. And let's have no more foolishness about blame."

"Alright," he said, "but I know who did this to you, even if you're too sweet and kind to admit it." He took a deep breath and went on. "So, as I say, I called for whoever it was to put down my fly rod. Politely, I felt. But the old woman took no notice. She just brought the rod up

The Lark Mirror

to her face and – don't ask me how; you've seen her – bit through the line. Then she cranked the reel to wind the line down through the eyes. She wanted to break down the rod, you see, to make it fit into her bundle.

"The cheek of it! I thought. By now I was striding across the lawn. 'I really must insist that you put that down,' I said, a little more sternly. Again, she ignored me. By the time I'd reached her she'd separated the tip of the rod from the rest of it. Very expertly too, I might add.

"I tried again. 'Please,' I said, 'Just put down the rod and we'll say no more about the matter.' But, to my total dismay, she simply broke down the next section of the rod. Which was when my temper also broke. 'Really,' I said, 'this is too much.' I grabbed her by the shoulder – firmly, I'll admit, but without violence. Which was when she finally turned around. The moonlight caught her face and I'm sure I must have gasped audibly. I felt a chill run up my spine and, I don't know how you felt when you saw her, David, but all of those old childhood names came back to me. Hag. Witch. Crone. Hob."

"Yes," I said, "me too."

Mr Mason nodded. I felt very close to him then, like some old war veteran finding another from the same campaign. He surprised me a lot that day, did Mr Mason. He'd displayed kindness and humility to touching effect and now his eloquence was another unexpected trait which shored up his credit as a human being greatly in my eyes and I already knew that, if nothing else, I would leave the Masons' house with a much-improved opinion of Charles Mason.

"She said," he went on "'What do ye want, ye piss-pot?' I ignored the insult and, as calmly as I could, I said, 'Now look, that's my fishing rod. I'd appreciate it if you'd hand it over to me.'

"'Eren't yourn,' she said.

"'I'm afraid that it very much *is* mine,' I said. 'And what's more, you're trespassing.'

179

"She spat on the ground. '*That* to yer peck o' dirt,' she said. 'Aunt Alsey don't need no permission to go where she goes. An' this be *my* fishing rod, for I to catch nice tasty trouts with.'

"Of course," Mr Mason went on, "I'd heard the name. Aunt Alsey is part of our local folklore, as you know. And I've heard Margaret mention her both in conversation and in lectures – I listen to Margaret more than she thinks." He smiled at his wife. "Anyhow," he went on, "I don't know if it was the amount I'd drunk or the sheer effrontery of her insistence that the fishing rod was hers, or the audacity of her appropriating (as I then thought) this name out of folklore in order to scare me off … whatever it was, I'd not only reached the end of my tether; I'd broken it in two.

"'So,' I said, 'you're the famous Aunt Alsey, terror of the moors. Why don't you conjure up your own bloody fishing rod? Better yet, a ready-cooked trout. With peas and new potatoes. *Aunt Alsey*,' I scoffed. 'Why, you're just some crack-brained gypsy-turned-thief.' I snatched the rod from her – I had to tussle for the tip section. 'I ought to use this to whip you with,' I said, once I had the rod in my possession. 'Get the hell off my property,' I said, 'before I do just that.'

"She began to shuffle off, leaving me breathing hard and already ashamed of myself. Then she turned back toward me. 'Ye take from me,' she said. 'I'll show ye what it be to watch beauty decay. And tonight ye'll couple fer the last time.'"

He paused and picked up his drink and sucked gin through the ice again. He looked terrible. "Damned ice," he muttered. Then, he said: "Interesting word, 'decay'. I'm not much of a scholar but I looked it up this morning. It comes from old French, and its root is 'to fall'. And look at us. Look how we've fallen." He took his wife's hand again. "You must understand, David," he said, "that I didn't believe in Aunt Alsey. I thought she was just some conflation of old wives' tales cobbled together to scare the children. If only I'd *believed*."

Mrs Mason was smiling kindly. "Charles," she said, "I thought we weren't going to apportion blame any more. Please go on with the story. We're wasting time."

"Yes" he said, "yes, of course. Well, I didn't tell Margaret about the incident –"

"Though we did ... *couple* ... on Saturday night," Mrs Mason said, mischievously.

"Yes," Mr Mason said, as close to blushing as I'd ever seen him. "And that *was* the last time –"

"Until we get out of this frightful mess," Mrs Mason assured him. "Which we will."

"I certainly hope so," Mr Mason said. Then he went on. "As I say, I didn't tell Margaret about the incident. Partly because I was ashamed of myself for threatening an old woman in that way, thief or not. Partly because, since I'd recovered my fishing rod, there was no harm done. And partly, I suppose, because Margaret did believe in Aunt Alsey on some level and I didn't want to worry her needlessly." He sucked at his drink again but his glass now held only ice.

"Why don't you get yourself another drink, Charles?" Mrs Mason said. "I've rested enough to be able to tell it from here. Besides, it's more my story from now on, don't you think?"

"Yes," Mr Mason said, standing. "Yes, I suppose it is. In that case you won't mind if I take a saunter in the garden for five minutes. I'm feeling a little edgy."

"We don't mind at all, do we, David?"

"No," I said. "And thank you."

"I'm hoping," Mr Mason said, "that *we'll* be thanking *you*." And with that, he left the room.

"Poor Charles," Mrs Mason said, in his wake. Considering that her husband's impetuosity had been at least partly responsible for her miserable condition, Mrs Mason's generosity of spirit was awe-inspiring. If *her* shadow had gained its independence and then metamorphosed into a creature of flesh and blood it would be a beautiful thing, numinous and angelic. Neither she nor Mr Mason would have to go hunting it out of the dens of Corny Cross. No, they would be rightly proud of this wonderful addition to their lives. The comparison inherent in this speculation shamed me.

Luckily, Mrs Mason began her story before my thoughts could travel very far along that road.

"I suppose I first noticed on Monday evening – Sunday passed as it usually does after a dinner party; with me feeling under par from the wine and Charles blustering and groaning in his bear-with-a-sore head manner. So, there was nothing unusual about Sunday. But on Monday evening, after my bath, I was combing my hair and I noticed how grey it was. Not just the odd grey hair, but streaks of grey. Which I knew had not been there before, not even that afternoon. Then, on Tuesday morning, I felt dreadful ... tell me, David, was that yesterday?"

"Yes," I said, "yesterday was Tuesday."

"I get confused sometimes," she said.

"It's alright," I said. "Take your time."

"But it isn't alright, is it?" she said. "I need to remember. I need to remember everything ..... now, where was I?"

"Tuesday morning," I said. "You felt dreadful."

"Yes, that's right. So I did," she said. "And I felt dreadful because someone tried to steal Charles's best fishing rod. Did he tell you about that?"

It was an alarming question and it was hard not to let my discomfiture show.

"Yes," I said. "He told me."

Mrs Mason looked confused for a moment and then she laughed and leaned forward to place her mug on the table. This time, I took it from her and set it down.

"Thank you, dear," she said. "You must think me very foolish. I *know* that Charles told you about his fishing rod and about Aunt Alsey and about how she cursed us. He sat right there and told you all about it and now he's gone for a drink in the garden to steady his nerves. I *know* that. It's just that it keeps ... well ... slipping from my grasp, so to speak. The fact is, David, I've aged even in the time that you've been sitting there and I'm terribly afraid that soon I won't even know my own name. Never mind," she said, rallying. "Now ... Tuesday morning, *yesterday*," she said, triumphantly, "I felt dreadful. By the time I went to bed I looked seventy years old.

"Charles wanted to call the doctor of course but I'd already suspected that this was not simply some terrible ailment; that it had all the hallmarks of a curse. I asked Charles if anything out of the ordinary had happened in the last few days. Which was when he told me what happened on Saturday night. And then ... well, as you can see ..."

"Yes," I said, "I'm sorry. It must be awful for you."

Mrs Mason chuckled again. "I've had better days," she said. "But let's not get all maudlin about it. What we have to do is find Aunt Alsey and give her back the fishing rod and the ... oh dear, what was it again?"

"The lark mirror," I said.

"*That's* right," she said. "Wonderful things, lark mirrors."

I felt suddenly crestfallen. I'd been hoping that in coming here I'd be handed some informational key with which to spring the lock of my curse but Mrs Mason's contribution amounted to little more than my own plan read back to me with a fishing rod thrown in. The only information I'd gleaned so far which had any practical value was the fact that Mr Mason had encountered Aunt Alsey on Saturday evening, which allowed for a reasonably accurate estimate of her rate of travel – about twelve miles per day.

"You will help us, David, won't you?" Mrs Mason said, pulling me out of my reverie.

"Of course," I said.

"That's good," Mrs Mason said, "because I trust you to see the job through. There's something special about you, David. Something you hide under a bushel. You're more than you appear to be. Do you think I haven't noticed the way you browse our book shelves? Appreciate our paintings? Use words which *aren't* the ones that spring to mind. Well, if you want to hide your own intelligence then that's entirely your business. But it hasn't gone without notice. Charles thinks very highly of you."

Which came as news to me. "Well," I said, "I'll do my best. I'll do my best for both of us. But where do we start? I know that Aunt Alsey was heading west the last I saw of her but that's *all* I know. I haven't got the first clue what to do or where to look for her. Meanwhile," I griped on, "my shadow has turned into a man of flesh and blood and it's a full-time job keeping him out of mischief." I stopped, realising I'd just told Mrs Mason more than she already knew. "Charles – sorry, *Mr Mason* – says that it's all over the moors how I lost my shadow. Has anyone mentioned that he's now a man?"

"No," Mrs Mason said, "this is the first I heard of it."

Or perhaps you've just forgotten I speculated, a little meanly but realistically.

"Does he look like you, your shadow?" Mrs Mason said.

"A little bit," I said. "He's better looking than me and stronger and more robust but he's got an ugly mouth on him. I've been passing him off as my brother but I can't get away with that forever. He's got his own shadow now and he can make it do tricks. If I don't find Aunt Alsey and give her the lark mirror he's going to tear my life apart."

"Would you say that he's all bad? The worse part of you?"

"Oh, he's the worst part of me alright."

"And is he what you've been trying to hide all this time?"

"In a way," I said. "He's the reason I don't drink anymore and the reason I came to live here." My gaze fell. "I set fire to a school," I told my boots. "I used to work there. It was over a woman. She used to work there too. She broke my heart. I was drinking too much. Drugs too, I'm afraid. I was very confused and I ended up setting fire to the geography room, which was where she worked. There wasn't much damage and the school pretended that the fire was started by accident. They didn't want the scandal. Which was what kept the police out of it. Which is why I wasn't jailed for arson like I should have been. The school settled for a resignation with no references. But everybody knew what really happened. After that, I came to live here. To start again."

"But it was your shadow that set fire to the school, wasn't it?" Mrs Mason said. "And you thought you'd left him behind."

"Yes," I said, "but now he's back. And, according to him, he's back for good."

"But not if you can find Aunt Alsey," Mrs Mason said, brightly. She'd been enjoying a well-timed moment of lucidity and seemed determined to make the most of it. "To the point then," she said. "There's one thing I haven't told you yet. Very late last night, a man came to see me. A farmer. Erskine Cotteral. Do you know him? No? Well, he said he had to talk to me. He was in some kind of trouble, he told Charles, and, as far as he was concerned, I was the only person who could help him. Of course, Charles wasn't about to let Mr Cotteral see me in my condition – as I say, I looked about seventy years old. But Mr Cotteral was very insistent. He said he'd been to one of my lectures – Rural Folklore in Peasant Art – and it was right apparent, he said, that I knew more about Aunt Alsey and her curses than anyone else alive and so I ought to be able to help him in some way. The poor man was desperate. Of course, at mention of our tormentor Charles knew that whatever pertained to poor Mr Cotteral also pertained to us. So, he jotted down some particulars and told Mr Cotteral that we would be in touch the next day. Today."

"And Aunt Alsey had cursed him?" I said.

"Oh yes," Mrs Mason said, emphatically. "She visited him on Monday evening. His curse – whatever it is – took effect almost immediately. The poor man was in a terrible state, according to Charles. He kept talking about things that would shame him somehow. But don't you see? We now know where Aunt Alsey was on Monday evening. Which puts us within a few miles – perhaps a dozen or so - of Aunt Alsey's whereabouts. *If*, she carried on walking in the time since. Mr Cotteral will also be able to say in which direction she was travelling once he'd ejected her from his farm."

"That *is* good news," I said.

"Isn't it," Mrs Mason said, brightly. "So, will you go and see him?"

"I'll get over there as soon as I can," I said, already rising.

"Here," she said, clawing through the writing materials on the table. "You'll ... now where did I put that? ... oh yes, here it is." She handed me a sheet of Basildon Bond writing paper. "Here's where he lives."

I glanced at the paper, which was enough to tell me that I had a reasonable idea of where Erskine Cotteral's farm was, and then folded the paper and stuffed it in my shirt pocket.

"Is it true that Aunt Alsey is centuries old?" I said.

"Yes," Mrs Mason said, "I think it is. She's certainly been in the literature for at least three hundred and fifty years. The rational consensus is that there have been several Aunt Alsey's, stretching through the centuries, with a new Aunt Alsey to pick up the mantle when the incumbent passes on."

"A bit like the Pope?" I said.

"Yes," Mrs Mason said, "very much like the pope. But I'm not convinced by the theory. It's plausible and logical and rational but … well, as we both know, those things are pretty meaningless when it comes to Aunt Alsey."

Which I agreed with wholeheartedly.

"And what about sleeping in ponds and turning herself into smoke?"

"Perhaps you should ask her," Mrs Mason said, "when you find her."

I appreciated her confidence in me but I had a terrible feeling that it was misplaced. Seeing Mrs Mason in that sad condition only confirmed how powerful Aunt Alsey was – if killing the Major hadn't been sufficient evidence. And on top of that, I felt that, if *I* didn't find a way to fuck things up, then my shadow surely would. Then, of course, there was the monkey-dog to worry about.

I was about to ask Mrs Mason if she knew anything about the monkey-dog and then changed my mind. "Maybe I will," I said.

But then, just like that, I lost her. She gave me a queer look and in, a high, pleading voice said, "Oh, Ralph, stop telling tales. You know Mummy doesn't like it. She'll be cross with us and I *hate* Mummy when she's cross."

I didn't quite know what to do about this sudden shift in her mental state but luckily Mr Mason came back into the green room.

"It's alright, Margaret," he said. "Ralph's just leaving. He won't get you into trouble again. Don't worry, It's alright."

I met him halfway across the room and he whispered for me to wait in the garden.

"Daddy," Mrs Mason wailed, "make Ralph go *away*."

"It's alright, darling," I heard Mr Mason say, as I closed the door. "Daddy's here. It's alright."

When I stepped outside, the lump in my throat was so big it felt like I'd swallowed a chair.

I was a good way into a cigarette when Mr Mason came outside. He carried the fly rod tied in a cotton rod bag.

"All clear on what to do?" he said, sounding a little more like his old self (which I didn't hold against him one bit). "Here," he said, handing me the rod, "take the damn thing. With any luck, I'll never have to look at it again."

"You know, don't you," he said, "that if I didn't have to be here for Margaret then I'd be coming with you?"

"Yes," I said, "I know."

He stared out across the lawn for a few moments and then said: "It's just as well I'm not. If I were to ever lay hands on that old woman after what she's inflicted on Margaret I'd skin her alive. And this time, there wouldn't be any damn guilt about it either. Goodbye, David. And good luck. Whatever happens, I won't forget this."

26

On my way back to Billy Makepiece's I swung by the cottage, as planned. My shadow was still sleeping – I could hear him snoring as soon as I opened the cottage door. I gave him a nudge just to make sure he was sufficiently comatose to sleep through the remainder of the day. The nudge didn't even break the stride of his snore, neither did it rouse his shadow, which was also sleeping.

The drugged cider was still on the table and it was not beyond the realm of the possible that my shadow's first act upon waking would be to down some more of the stuff, which would of course knock him out afresh. As much as I would have liked to, it didn't seem wise to let that happen. If the monkey-dog were to come for us that night, we would both need our wits about us. With that in mind - and with some misgiving – I took the cider with me when I left.

When Anushka let me into Billy's cottage she was wearing the blue, paint-spattered boiler suit which Billy sometimes wore when he painted. Her fingers were smeared with paint of various colours and there was a streak of black paint down her cheek.

"I feel urge to paint," she explained. "Billy has new fast-drying acrylic paint I wish to try."

I remembered that Anushka had mentioned that she too painted as a hobby and I'm sure it was all very interesting but I couldn't help thinking there were more pressing concerns than her desire to experiment with a new medium. She seemed to sense this.

"Is all right," she said. "I clean up, change clothes. Be ready in jiffy. You have eaten?"

"No," I said. "I haven't really had time."

"But you *must* eat," she insisted. "We have long search for Aunt Alsey ahead of us. You must keep strong. No? So. Go to kitchen, make sandwich."

"Alright," I said, as my stomach began to grumble, "I've just got to fetch something from the plastic pig first."

I'd remembered the cider. I didn't want to leave it in the pig because it would be rendered tepid and unpalatable and though I suspected that my shadow would have few such qualms when it came to quaffing alcohol I didn't want to take any chances, just in case I needed to dose him up again.

So, as Anushka climbed the stairs, I let myself out of the cottage and fetched the cider. When I took it into the kitchen what I saw there stopped me dead in my tracks. Anushka had been painting in the light of the kitchen window, as Billy sometimes did, with the easel close to the sink. Brushes, trays and pots of water, a palette and several tubes of acrylic paint were scattered over the draining board while, resting on the easel, was a medium-size and hastily-executed painting. The painting featured two shadows, projected high on a wall. The shadows were making love in the missionary position. The composition would have had a very two-dimensional feel to it if not for the inclusion of a chest of drawers in the bottom right corner of the canvas. On the chest of drawers was a small mirror – a shaving mirror in fact – which held the reflection of a face. It was rendered with just a few deft strokes and was more hint than definite statement. Even so, it was a face I recognized as my own. The eyes were fixed in a position which made it plain that "I" was standing in the room, impotently watching the two shadows making love. I thought that, all in all, it was a cruel use of my image.

I stood and stared at the painting for some time, trying to decide what it meant, if, indeed, it meant anything at all. My appetite had pretty much bit the dust and so I just put the cider in Billy's fridge, lit a cigarette and then went into the living room to wait for Anushka. She took longer than she'd implied and, still smarting as I was from seeing that painting, my growing impatience did little for my mood.

When she finally entered the living room, Anushka was wearing some kind of cream-coloured blouse - which looked to be made of silk - and a pair of fawn-coloured trousers tucked into the tops of her long, lace-up boots. She looked like a figure in a Russian folk painting. Or would have, if she hadn't bothered to apply fresh make-up.

"You have eaten?" she said.

"Yes," I lied, "I had a cheese sandwich."

"Is good. Then we are ready to go. You have new plan now, yes?"

"Yes," I said, "we have a new plan now." But I wasn't ready to go. "Anushka," I said, "why did you paint that awful picture?"

She shrugged. "I tell you; I have urge to paint."

"But why *that*?"

"Is what I wish to paint. Is how I wake up feeling. No, I wake up feeling like head slammed in door. But after ... is how I feel."

I stubbed out my cigarette. "What do you remember about last night?" I said.

She shrugged. "Everything? Sidney offer gin. You fetch water. Sidney make joke about scars. We drink the gin. Then we drink cider. Cider hit me like ton of brick. Then, I think, we make love. But when I wake, I still have clothes on. But also, Sidney is there. I do not make love to Sidney." She shrugged again. "Or, perhaps I do. Maybe you know more than me."

"And maybe you know more than you're telling," I said, peevishly.

"You think Sidney has turned my head?"

It was my turn to shrug.

"No," she said, "Sidney has not turned my head. But I no longer believe that Sidney is your brother."

"Really?" I said. "Then who is he?"

"You will tell me when you trust me enough. You know what Sidney say about scars? For every scar on his face, he say you have one on your soul."

That stung enough to make me pause for a moment, not sure whether to press on or to give it up. In the end, my mouth just started moving. "Anushka," I said, "doesn't it bother you that you may have made love with me – or even with Sidney – and you don't remember it?"

"No. Why should it? If we make love then is what I would have wanted. Why would I complain?"

"Well," I said, standing, "just so you know, we *didn't* make love."

"Then that is thing we rectify later. Yes?"

It wasn't easy in the face of that promise but I succeeded in mustering an air of practicality. "We've got a lot to do first," I said.

"So. We leave now. Yes?" she said. "Wait one moment. I fetch things from kitchen."

When she returned she had a small, greaseproof packet (which would turn out to be duck sandwiches) and the US Army canteen which Billy had wheedled out of one of the servicemen from the base at the close of an afternoon's drinking.

"By the way," I said, "have you heard from Billy?"

"No," Anushka said. "Please not to worry about Billy. Billy is fine."

As we made our way to the door, Billy's phone rang. To my surprise, Anushka totally ignored it.

"Aren't you going to get that?" I said.

"No. Is not important."

"But it might be Billy," I said.

"Is not Billy," she said, with unassailable finality.

27

Erskine Cotteral's farm was in a remote spot in sight of Blowing Stone Tor and less than a mile shy of Witchfall Woods, a great, dense swath of woodland which held the moor's western edge like a cupped hand. I only knew about the farm because I'd once worked on a forester's cottage within the woods and so had spent half a winter driving past it on my way to work and back.

As I drove, I adumbrated to Anushka how things stood. I explained where we were going and why, and I told her about the curse inflicted on Mrs Mason and what I had been charged to do about it.

"Poor Mrs Mason," Anushka said. "Such a nice lady."

Which, needless to say, were words that surprised me. "You know her?" I said.

"No," Anushka said. "How could I know her? No. I do not know her. But Billy has told all about her."

"Billy tells you everything about everything, doesn't he? It's starting to seem as if all you and Billy can ever find the time to do is talk. I mean," I went on, aware that I may be pushing too hard but unable to still my tongue, "seriously, how do you find the time? How the hell does Mrs Mason's name just happen to crop up in conversation?"

"Billy has wide range of interests," she said. "You are cross with me."

"No," I said, crossly. "It's just that … well, sometimes it seems as if there's so much overlap between you and Billy that you could almost be the same damn person."

"You are jealous of Billy," Anushka said. It was a statement, rather than a question.

"No," I said, "that isn't what I mean."

"First Sidney," Anushka said, ignoring my denial and letting a petulant tone creep into her voice, "and now Billy. Everything I tell you about way I feel about you – you dismiss this as lie?"

"*No*," I said. "It's just that … well, how *can* you feel that way about me? We've only just met, for Christ's sake."

"But you are interesting and attractive man. Why you no believe a woman wish to be with you?"

"I've had lots of woman who wished to be with me," I said, "but none of them looked like you. None of them acted like you. You could have any man you want. Any man at all. Why would you want me?"

"Do you think so little of yourself? I have just told you why. If you choose not to believe then there is nothing more I can say."

But I didn't believe and I said as much. "Sidney," I added. "Now, *Sidney* is an attractive man…"

"Here we go with fucking Sidney again," Anushka said. "Please to stop the fucking car."

I was shocked by the language but even more so by her vehemence. I pulled into a passing place on the narrow road. Anushka prised my left hand from the wheel and took it in hers so that I was forced to face her.

"I tell you in beginning," she said, melting my heart with her beautiful soulful eyes, "that we can know without knowing; that we have waited, one for the other, for a very long time. I ask you before. So. I ask again: is this not a thing which pleases you, David?"

"I'm puzzled by it," I said.

"Is no need," she said. "*Here* is what matters." She kissed me, giving me the all of herself. She put her hand on my crotch and squeezed, gently and expertly – and, I have to admit, there was more for her to squeeze than there had been a few moments ago.

When she finally pulled away I was breathing hard and trembling with sexual excitement. All of my troubled and puzzled thoughts were driven from my head and I wanted nothing more right then – not even the restoration of my shadow to its rightful place and status – than to lay with her in blissful embrace.

"This afternoon," Anushka said, "we make love. No more delay. Then you will see what you mean to me." She gave the back of my hand a tap which felt like a full stop and said, "First, we proceed with mission. Is better if you have shadow. No?"

"I could probably manage without him for a bit longer if I had to," I said.

"Perhaps," she said, with a smile. "But is our job to find Aunt Alsey. Only," she said, growing serious again, "when we find her, I do not wish to meet. She is dangerous. Besides, she is your affair."

All of which seemed reasonable enough to me.

I had a failure of memory which caused me to take two wrong turns but once in sight of Blowing Stone Tor I found it easier to get my bearings and, just before midday, we got our first glimpse of the farm, nestled in a shallow valley to the north-west of the tor. Beyond it lay the arboreal world of Witchfall Woods, so dense and rich in foliage that it seemed to swallow the daylight. As steeped in legend as it was in shadow, you could hear as many dark and cautionary folk tales about Witchfall Woods as you'd hear about any place on the moors. Looking at the woods now, I hoped against hope that Aunt Alsey had gone north or south or even doubled back east, the way she had come. If she had gone west, into the woods, and, for whatever reason, chosen to linger there, then she could well prove impossible to find. On top of that, I remembered how I'd once got lost in those woods and it was not an experience I relished repeating.

It had been my third or fourth day working at the forester's cottage and, curiosity getting the better of me, I'd decided that that lunchtime, rather than sitting in my van and munching my way through a small packed lunch followed by Thermos tea and a cigarette (which was my usual custom when working on an empty property) I'd go for a walk in the woods. I'd followed a path which led from the back garden of the cottage and pretty soon I ran out of path. I'd persevered however, and, because it was winter and so the nettles and most of the ground cover had died back, I found that I could progress by following deer trails. Which was all very well until I decided that it was time to head back to the cottage. It soon became apparent that I was hopelessly lost. Worse – queer, flitting shapes began to trouble my peripheral vision. I would jerk my head this way and that but I tried in vain to get a good glimpse of them. Now and again I thought I could hear a mocking laughter. Other times, I felt as if I were being stalked. I'd spin around to confront my pursuer only to find nothing there. Nothing visible, at any rate.

By the time I'd managed to locate the cottage I'd lost three hours and dark was settling in. I'd built up such a head of panic that I'd arrived back at the cottage with badly scratched hands and face and wild, half-mad nonsense jerking from my mouth. My only consolation was that the cottage had been between tenants and so there had been no witnesses to add to my shame.

All of this came back to me as we drove slowly toward the farm, surveying the landscape below.

Meanwhile, Anushka had decided she was thirsty so she unscrewed the cap on Billy's canteen. She took a good pull on it (Christ, I thought, she even slurps *water* like Billy) and then handed it to me. As I was taking my own gulp, she suddenly exclaimed: "David, look at the smoke!"

I lowered the canteen from my field of vision, glanced at the road to make sure I was still steering true and then glanced to where Anushka was pointing, which was toward the Cotteral farm. The place had the same abandoned and derelict look about it that I remembered from before – it's only pleasing feature being quite a large pond about fifty paces from the farmhouse – and, if not for the smoke rising from the chimney you would think its former inhabitants had long since fled to comparative civilization.

"They still haven't got electricity out here," I said, missing Anushka's meaning entirely. "They have to keep the stove lit no matter how hot it gets. It's the only way to cook and heat water."

"No," Anushka said, "I tell you *look* at the smoke."

I slowed the van to a crawl in order to study the smoke without driving off the road. Then, when I saw what Anushka meant, I braked the plastic pig to a halt. The smoke *wasn't* rising from the chimney at all. It wasn't doing *anything*. It's true that there was no breeze so you'd expect the smoke to be a little tardy about its movement. But the smoke had no movement whatsoever. It just leaned from the chimney, static and immutable, in roughly the shape of a cartoon speech bubble.

I didn't drive into the farmyard, the entrance of which was to the right of the farmhouse, because the ground looked too deeply-rutted for the poor plastic pig to deal with. So, instead, I parked in a small lay-by beside some milk churns on a wooden staging at the front of the house. It was eerily quiet. No sheep baahd, no cattle lowed, no chickens clucked, no geese honked and not a duck muttered.

When we closed the doors of the plastic pig – quietly and almost reverentially – they sounded to me in that silence like the first stirrings of bones in a crypt.

"I no have good feeling about this place," Anushka said.

"Me neither," I said.

On that side of the house was the garden with the pond. We entered quietly through the garden gate and just as quietly closed it behind us. We'd walked a little way up the garden path when Anushka stage-whispered: "David, look at pond."

We both stood gaping at it for several long seconds. As told, the day was still and yet there were enough small waves disturbing the surface of the pond to suggest a moderate breeze. But if you looked at the pond carefully you could see that, despite the waves, there was no actual movement to the water. More strikingly, a duck and drake pairing of mallards were suspended in flight a few feet above the pond's surface where they had burst from the cover of some bull rushes. Water dripped from their feet yet neither the ducks nor the water moved.

"The bird table," Anushka said. "Look- is same."

The bird table was on the far side of the pond. A small throng of jackdaws had been arrested there, mid wing-beat, in a bad tempered squabble over a few chunks of bread.

"Perhaps we go now," Anushka said, uneasily. "Is dangerous here. Maybe we end up frozen like the birds."

"No," I said.

"Please, David- is bad place."

"You go back if you want to," I said. "But I have to know."

But she didn't go back and we walked stealthily on toward the farmhouse. After a few more paces I happened to look down and spot a vole, frozen mid-scurry in the act of crossing the path. I stooped down and picked it up. It was stiff and it had no heartbeat that I could feel and its breathing was utterly still and you'd have thought it dead the way it just lay stiffly in my palm. Save for the brightness in its eye. Save for the fact that it was warm.

"Feel it," I said. "I don't think it's dead."

Anushka took a step back. "If we go to house we go to house. We not stop to play with mice."

"Actually," I said, gently placing the creature just off the side of the path where it wouldn't be trodden on, "it's a vole."

"Mouse. Vole. What difference?" Anushka said.

And, despite everything, I thought what a very Billy Makepiece kind of thing that was to say.

***

Even on such a bright day there was an air of oppressive gloom about the house. The curtains were drawn over every visible window and it now seemed not so much as if had been abandoned but more as if its occupants were sick and dying or perhaps already dead. I gestured for Anushka to wait a few paces behind me and then I walked tentatively up to the door. I took a deep breath and knocked. There was no answer and, after a brief wait, I knocked again. Still no answer. There were six small panes of frosted glass in the door and I peered through one of them, cupping my hands around my forehead to shield off the sunlight. I could make out a long hallway receding into near-darkness and then, dimly, something stirred from the shadows. I leaned down to the letterbox, pushed it open with two fingers and then spoke through it.

"Mr Cotteral?" I said.

"Go away," a voice called back. "Leave me alone."

"Mr Cotteral," I said, "Mrs Mason sent me."

My words were greeted with silence but it was the kind of silence people make decisions in. A full half minute later I heard Mr Cotteral approach the door.

"Who are you?" he called.

I straightened up and spoke directly through the glass. "My name's David Chambers," I told him. "I'm a friend of Mrs Mason. I'm here to help."

"Don't need yer help," he said.

"Oh, but Mrs Mason says you do," I said. "She says that you went to speak to her about Aunt Alsey."

"Oh, she did, did she? Been spreadin' it all over has she? Well, why don't miss high an' fuckin' mighty come herself then, eh? Not good enough for her, that it? That husband of hers ran me off like a fucking beggar. So, you go back an' you tell them stuck-up cunts that I don't need no blessed fucking help from them, thank you very much."

It hurt me to hear him talk about Mr and Mrs Mason like that but I could see it from his perspective. He was not to know what had befallen Mrs Mason. All he knew was that when he went to her for help he *had* been turned away. And while I doubted he'd been run off like a beggar, Mr Mason could be brusque and I could see why he'd feel the way he did about it.

"Mrs Mason's ill," I said. "It's why she couldn't see you and it's why she sent me instead. I've seen the ducks and I've seen the bird table. I know about Aunt Alsey's curses and how they work. Please, open the door. I can't help you unless you do."

Again, a ruminative silence. Then the door opened to the length of its security chain and Mr Cotteral peered through the gap. He looked dreadful. His eyes were red with big purple bags hanging beneath them. He'd obviously been cultivating a Bobby Charlton comb-over to cover his bald pate but it hadn't been combed over that day and it puffed out of the right side of his head like candy-floss. On top of that, he looked like he'd been drinking fairly steadily.

"Can I come in?" I said. "It'll be easier to talk if you let me in."

He stared at me for a few moments, his breath seething in and out so that I caught the full blast of alcohol it carried. Then something poked out of the gap between door and door frame. It was the twin barrels of a shotgun, held at waist height. "I'll let you in," he growled, "but don't you give me no trouble. You hear?" He emphasised the point with an upward jerk of the barrels. I doubted if Anushka heard him, or had even seen the shotgun - since I obstructed her view - and I had no time to warn her because just then Mr Cotteral fumbled the chain from its keep and swung the door open. Which was when he saw Anushka for the first time.

I blame myself for what happened next. It hadn't even occurred to me that I should have warned him that I wasn't alone.

"Oh, and who's this?" he demanded. "Why's she dressed like that? Who *are* you people?" A lifetime's familiarity with shotguns brought the butt to his shoulder so quickly I barely saw the gun move. At the same time, drunk as he was, he'd sprung back a couple of feet to give himself room to swing the barrels. First he swung them in my direction, then he swung them in Anushka's. I turned just in time to see her blench.

"No," she said, "please to point away."

"Don't move," I told her.

"Why's she speaking that way?" Mr Cotteral asked me, favouring me with the barrels again.

"I am from Russia," Anushka said.

Which wasn't helpful. As I've said, you didn't find many Russians on the moors in nineteen seventy six.

"Why are *you* here?" he asked her. "Why are the fucking *Russians* here?" he demanded of me.

"It's just one," I said, feebly.

"You're spies is what *you* are. I go to see Mrs Mason for help, and she sends out Russian *agents*?" he went on, in an outraged tone. "What are they," he said, meaning the Masons, "some kind of fucking sleepers?"

I couldn't really blame him for any of this. Quite apart from the fact that he was drunk; quite apart from the fact that his predicament had driven him crazy, it was a period in time when the papers were full of lurid tales of cold war espionage, from Mata Hari agents to poison-tipped umbrellas. Well, we were short of an umbrella but I could see how Mr Cotteral might think we were halfway there.

"I *knowed* there was something about that stuck-up bitch," Mr Cotteral ranted on. "You want to find out what happened here and use it as a weapon, don't you?" It was at that point that he got around to cocking one of the hammers on the shotgun.

What happened next astounded even me, given my natural pusillanimity. I took a quick step forward, knocked the gun barrels upward with my left hand and drove my right fist into Mr Cotteral's throat. The shotgun went off and blew a hole in the ceiling and the combination of its unexpected kick and my punch sent Mr Cotteral staggering backwards with a strangled little squawk. He tripped on the curled edge of a rug and smashed the back of his head hard against the newel post at the foot of the stairs. He left a smear of blood on the gloss-painted wood as he slid down it, as insensate as a stone. Somehow, without my consciously doing so, I'd grabbed the gun barrels just as Mr Cotteral had relinquished his hold of the stock so that the shotgun was now swinging from my left hand by its barrels.

"Are you alright?" I asked Anushka, who had just stepped up to join me.

"I am not the one in need of help," she said.

I looked at poor Mr Cotteral and had to agree with Anushka's assessment. "Jesus," I said, "I hope I haven't killed him." Then, recovering my wits, I shouted a general enquiry into the house. "Is anyone home?" I said. "We're not here to harm you," I added. As I listened for a response, I realised that anyone stumbling into that scene now would have good cause to question the veracity of that statement. Not that it mattered, since no-one answered my call and all I heard was the gun blast still ringing in my own ears.

"Please to put down gun and stand aside," Anushka said. I did as I was told, leaning the gun in the corner behind the door while Anushka knelt beside Mr Cotteral, who had come to rest more or less in a sitting position with one hand on a stair tread and the other in his lap. Anushka lifted that hand and felt for a pulse. She listened to his breathing and then she forced up an eyelid with her thumb to reveal the white (and red) of his eye. Then she gently tilted his head forward and examined the wound in the back of his skull. Her hand came away bloody.

"Is not hard enough to crack skull," she said, "but is bleeding badly. Please not to stand there like useless article. We need first to make him comfortable."

I opened two of the doors off the hallway and settled on a parlour with a large, old but comfortable looking couch in it. It was only when I turned away to say something to Anushka that I noticed the dog. He lay curled in front of the dead fireplace with his jaw resting on his hind quarters. At first I thought he was asleep but then I saw that his eyes were open. Just like the vole's, they held life. Yet they didn't move. And when I tried to prompt a reaction with a whistle and a 'good boy' and all the usual noises you make with dogs, neither did he.

It was seeing the dog that prompted the realisation that just because my earlier shouted enquiry went un-answered it didn't necessarily mean that the three of us were the only ones in the house, nor that the remainder of the Cotteral clan (whatever it was comprised of) were hiding. As soon as we'd made our unintended victim comfortable, I was going to have to make a search of the house.

By the time I'd stepped back into the hallway, Anushka had already fetched a towel from the kitchen – which was at the end of the hallway – and was tying it against Mr Cotteral's wound with the bailing twine he'd been using as a belt.

"You find place for him?" she said. "Good. Please to take heavy end of him."

Feisty he may have been but he was a small man for all that and we succeeded in getting him on to the couch without too much difficulty.

"Please to put him on his side," Anushka said. "I will need to stitch the wound. Fetch me please needle and thread."

I searched the downstairs house, finding nothing more out of the ordinary, until I came across a sewing machine in a room at the back of the house. On one of the room's many shelves was a sewing basket. I checked inside for needle and thread and there were plenty of both.

"Are you sure you know what you're doing?" I asked Anushka, when I returned to the parlour.

"Is simple job," she said, snatching the basket from me and searching inside for a needle of appropriate size. I watched her thread the needle, her hands sure and steady.

"Where did you learn to stitch a wound?" I said, feeling a little awed.

"You think now is good time for questions?" she said, stripping the bloody towel from Mr Cotteral's head.

It was a fair point. "I'm going to take a look around upstairs," I said, glad of the excuse to exit. I didn't consider my self squeamish, but I *did* have a thing about needles, even if it wasn't my flesh they were being driven into.

"Is good idea," Anushka said, the needle now poised at the ready. "But you come quick if I call. The pain, it may wake him."

"Don't worry," I said, "I will."

I considered taking the shotgun upstairs with me, having learned to expect the unexpected. Yet, I could sense no immediate malevolence waiting to spring, unless we were to be turned into living statues, in which case I didn't see what use a shotgun would be. Even so, I ascended the stairs carefully and quietly, alert for any sight or sound of movement.

I worked my way along the landing, opening doors and calling softly into various rooms. I saw no-one as I progressed from the back of the house to the front. Saw no-one and heard nothing. No birds skittered in the attic, no mice scurried beneath floorboards and no rats scratched behind walls. I saw nothing and nobody until I opened the door of the final room and discovered two people making love. Silent, stock-still love. They must have been going at it for some time when the curse struck because the quilt had slipped off to reveal their full, naked glory. They were both young - both still in their teens in fact — but they were far from a handsome couple. The lad (who was on top) was as hairy as an ape, with a fine pelt all the way up his back, while the girl was as pink and fat as a sunburned pig. But, for all that, they had jolly enough expressions on their faces. The girl was smiling and biting her lip at the same time, while the lad grinned broadly with his eyes open.

I stepped closer and (I couldn't help it) passed my hand back and forth in front of the lad's gaze a few times. There was no reaction whatsoever. I stooped down to pick up the quilt to restore their modesty and as I did so feathers spilled out of it. In the floor where the quilt had been was a hole, its edges splintered and ragged. Which was the destruction wrought by that recent and errant blast from Mr Cotteral's shotgun.

As I tucked the quilt around them, I noticed that a string of saliva dribbled from the boy's chin. It was frozen an inch shy of the girl's cleavage. But that wasn't all I noticed. I noticed now the familial resemblance between them. A resemblance they shared with Mr Cotteral. No wonder he was half crazy. It was bad enough having your world made inanimate around you without discovering your own offspring locked in a perpetual act of incestuous sex. 'Shame' was the word he'd used (according to Mrs Mason) and shame, as much as the curse itself, had driven him to despair.

I was just leaving the room when I heard a loud groan from Mr Cotteral, followed by a cry for assistance from Anushka and so I hurried downstairs to do what I could. Which wasn't a lot.

Mr Cotteral was rocking back and forth and holding his head, groaning all the while.

"Please to keep still," Anushka pleaded, "I need to cut cotton."

But Mr Cotteral had no intention of keeping still. He sensed my presence and looked up.

"You," he said accusingly. "*You* hit me."

"Well," I said, "you *were* about to shoot us."

"Look!" he said, ignoring my response and holding up a bloodied hand. "Look what you did –" He stopped abruptly. "You've been upstairs," he said, "haven't you? Is that why that bitch sent you – to find out about *that?*"

"Mrs Mason doesn't know about that," I said. "And neither does anyone else. Not even Anushka here. Just you and me. And I'm not going to tell if you don't. Not even to Anushka." I gave her a meaningful look.

"I will not ask," she said.

That seemed to placate Mr Cotteral a bit. "Do you promise?" he said, a tear rolling down his cheek.

"We already have," I said. "I told you why I'm here. Believe it or not, I *am* here to help you. And I was also hoping that you'd be able help me."

"What's wrong with *you* that you need my help?"

"Let me draw back the curtain and I'll show you," I said. "Though I'm surprised you haven't heard by now – everybody else seems to know."

"Don't see no-one much out 'ere," he said, somewhat defensively.

There were two windows to the room and I chose the one which would let in the most direct sunlight. I drew back the curtain and the light flooded in. Mr Cotteral winced – you could *feel* his headache coming off him. The dog didn't blink.

When he'd recovered a little I asked Mr Cotteral what he noticed about me. "No," I said, "don't look at me. Look at the floor around me."

Which he did. It took a moment for the penny to drop. "You eren't got no shadder!" he said.

"No," I said, "and that's because I had a visit from Aunt Alsey."

With Mr Cotteral more or less mollified, Anushka was able to do various things with her fingers in front of his eyes to check for concussion. Meanwhile, I interrogated him, sweetening him with constant reminders of my intent to help him while exaggerating my own knowledge and sagacity and expectations of success. His condition meant that he was short on detail – which suited me, since I was short of time.

With his stitches stitched and his head properly bandaged; with a diagnosis of mild concussion and advice to take aspirin and plenty of rest, we left Mr Cotteral with a little more hope in his heart than he'd had when we'd arrived. Whether that was a fair exchange for a king-size headache would depend entirely on whether that hope came to fruition and since (my worst fear realised) he told me that Aunt Alsey had entered Witchfall Woods I had some doubt that it would.

And the object Aunt Alsey had coveted?

It was, much to Anushka's displeasure, the very same shotgun that Mr Cotteral had threatened us with. "For I to shoot nice, tasty rabbits with," Aunt Alsey had told him, before he'd so disastrously snatched his gun back.

"You should perhaps start career as arms dealer," Anushka said, acidly, as I placed the reloaded shotgun beside Mr Mason's fly rod in the back of the plastic pig and then covered both items with an old blanket that Silas had left in there.

28

"You find rest of family?" Anushka said, after I'd started the engine.

"Yes," I said.

"They are alive?"

"For now," I said. All of the Cotteral clan were accounted for. While Anushka had washed the blood from her hands and changed into a tight-fitting shirt that Mr Cotteral had given her, the farmer had informed me that his wife was in the wood-shed, where she'd been fetching logs for the stove when the curse struck.

"I ask no more," Anushka said.

"Thank you," I said.

As I drove towards Witchfall Woods we maintained a thoughtful silence. Then, as if catching the drift of my disappointed musings, Anushka said: "You did not gain as much as you'd hoped."

"I don't know *what* I'd hoped for," I said. "But I do know that Aunt Alsey went into the woods."

"Is big wood?"

"It's about six miles across," I said. "There's a road which runs straight through the middle. If she took that and just kept going she'll be well out the other side by now."

"And you think is what she did?"

"No. There are people who live in here. Foresters. Game keepers. Recluses. They're scattered, but I'm pretty sure there's a circular road inside the wood which links them all together. Plus logging tracks, footpaths and deer trails. I think Aunt Alsey would make the most of it."

"You mean she would make visit?"

"It's what she does," I said, with a shrug.

The Lark Mirror

"Then we will knock on doors," Anushka said.

"Correction," I said, "*you* will knock on doors. Only, if anyone asks, this time, tell them you're from Norway. Or Denmark. Or any damn place save Russia. Okay?"

We entered the woods, the air heavy with shade and pollen. It was cooler in there – which was something of a relief – but in some of the sunken bottoms in the road the air seemed depleted of ozone and it was hard to breath.

In places the canopy was so dense that a dusky light prevailed; in others it was less so and the road was sun-dappled and jays flitted tree to tree and magpies flew in shallow swoops ahead of us. The road surface was patchy, metalled in some stretches, bare and rutted in others so that the front wheel of the pig had to ride between the ruts, forcing up the front end like the prow of a boat.

Occasionally, the banks would sheer away from the road precipitously and you could look down and see the treetops which covered the hidden valleys and gullies below. In most places, however, the woods were so thick, the brambles so choking, the fern so dense, that the eye did well to penetrate more than fifty paces. What if Aunt Alsey had gone to ground in here? I thought, gloomily. What if her peregrinations were over and she had simply come here for seven years of rest? How would I ever find her if that were so? The answer was, of course, that I wouldn't. Seven years of freakery suddenly loomed larger than ever in my future. Mrs Mason would surely die and Mr Cotteral, in his despair, would burn down his house after locking himself inside. And none of this even factored in the monkey-dog, which, if it shredded my shadow like it had shredded that leg of lamb, would make my condition permanent.

"You have bad thought?" Anushka said, sensing my mood.

"I'm worried that I'll never find her," I said. "Not in here. *Look* at it."

"Is no time to quit," Anushka said. "Is time only to try harder. No?"

The first house we visited – since it was the first house we came to – was the forester's cottage which I'd painted. Anushka went to the cottage while I remained in the plastic pig and had a half-hearted smoke. In truth, my shadow's absence may well have gone unnoticed in such a sun-deprived spot but the people who lived in these woods would keep dogs and I was taking no chances with that kind of dog.

I lost sight of Anushka when she went around the side of the cottage and to help while away the time I took the lark mirror from my haversack and held it up in front of my face, very much like Hamlet with Yorick's skull. "You've caused me a lot of trouble," I told the lark mirror. The lark mirror said nothing back. It just stared at me with its myriad eyes. I ground out my cigarette in one of them. Then I had another drink from Anushka's canteen. I wondered idly how Aunt Alsey was going to carry a shotgun, a fishing rod, a lark mirror, plus whatever else she'd appropriated in the course of her wanderings. But when you're dealing with a four-hundred year-old sorceress reputed to sleep in ponds a consideration like that seemed almost absurdly pedantic. Besides, her luggage was her own affair.

"Forester not home," Anushka said, on her return. "But wife is home. She never hear of Aunt Alsey. They come here from different place, I think. She tell me, however, that washing was stolen from line."

When we struck the circular road I turned left so that we would travel around the wood in a clockwise direction. I'd been on the moors long enough to know that to travel widdershins around something – *anything* – was to invite bad luck, and I certainly didn't need any more of that.

As we circumnavigated the wood's interior, Anushka continued to knock on the doors of the few cottages we happened upon. The response was mixed. Some of the cottages were empty, their occupants busy with their outdoor lives (we would hear the occasional bite of an axe, the far-off growl of a tractor, a barking dog). Of those cottages where someone was at home, most had heard of Aunt Alsey but had never seen her, while some said that yes, they had had small items of little worth stolen only yesterday. As the reports of these thefts mounted, I began to feel a renewed surge of hope. We were close, closer than I'd been since I'd begun my reluctantly embarked-upon quest. Yes, she would be hard to find, but she was, I sensed, still here. And her recent activity suggested that she hadn't gone to ground as I'd feared. Not yet, anyway.

I was about to tell all of this to Anushka when she suddenly cried out: "You smell that? Stop the car!"

I slowed the plastic pig and sniffed at the open window.

Wood smoke.

***

Having ascertained the direction from which the smoke was emanating, we abandoned the plastic pig and made our way along a narrow but fairly well-trodden path. I carried the haversack on my shoulder but I thought it impractical to carry the shotgun and the fly rod. I don't know what either of us were expecting to find at the terminus of that smoky trail, perhaps Aunt Alsey herself – in which case, Anushka would have to return to the pig for the other items while I parlayed with the old woman as best I could. It's more likely though, that we expected to find exactly what we *did* find, which was a woodsman about his work. If you could call what he was doing at that precise moment 'work'.

The trail brought us into a partial but still-shady clearing (so I was not too concerned about my lack of shadow). Sitting on a tree stump beside a large kiln was an old charcoal burner. He had a jug of cider planted between his boots and a pipe clamped in his mouth. His face was as black and soot-pocked as that of a powder monkey's in the heat of battle.

"Aft'noon," he said, mildly.

"Afternoon," I said.

"Don't usually get many visitors," he said. "Come to think of it, don't get any."

It was only when I noticed the ramshackle lean-to built around the trunk of a tree on the far side of the clearing that I realised this old axe-waddler lived out here.

The old man spat through his beard and wiped his mouth on the back of his hand. "Well," he said, "I knows ye eren't lost, otherwise ye'd be cryin' an' carryin' on by now. So, I reckon ye must be lookin' for summat."

"Have you heard of an old woman by the name of Aunt Alsey?" I said.

The old man sucked on his pipe and nodded. "I've heard of her, alright," he said. "Seen her too."

"You *have*?" I said, eagerly. "Where?"

"'Ere an' there," he said, gesturing vaguely with his pipe. "In the woods."

"Yes," I said, "but *where* in the woods?"

"Just told ye," he said, "'ere an' there. Likes it 'ere see. Nice an' cool after all that trampin' around on dusty roads."

"Look," I said, tiring of his rustic ramblings, "I hate to push the point but it's very important that I find her."

"Is it now?" the old man said.

"Yes," I said. "Lives depend on it. So, I wonder if you could be more specific."

"Specific?" he said. "That's a long word."

"It means-"

"I knows what it means," he said. "It means ye wants me to be more particular."

"Look," I said, growing irritable, "can you tell me where to find her or not? Do you happen to know, by any chance, where she is right now? Or can you at least tell me where you saw her last."

"I *could*," he said. "Wouldn't do ye much good though."

"Why not?"

"'Cause she won't be there *now*, will she? But I can do better'n that anyway; I can show ye where she sleeps."

"And where's that?" I said.

"No use tellin' ye. I'd 'ave to show ye. Ye'll ne'er find it, see. Not without me showin' ye. Seems to me though, that if lives depend on it, then it ought to be worth something fer my trouble."

"Yes, yes," I said, eager to dispense with this trifle, "of course. I've got money. How much do you want?"

The old axe-waddler reached down for his cider jug, uncorked it and had a good pull while he ratiocinated his way towards a price he could get away with. When he was done, he slapped home the cork and wiped his mouth.

"Twenty-five guineas," he said.

"Twenty-five *guineas*?" I repeated.

"I likes the old way o' business," he said. "What do ye think my dear?" he asked Anushka. "Think that's a fair price?"

"Is what it is," Anushka said, with a shrug.

"It's a lot of money is what it is," I said.

"It's a long walk," the old man said.

"In that case," I said, "we'd better get started."

"Can't," the old man said.

"What do you mean, you can't?" I said, exasperated with the crack-brained old fool. "You just said you could."

"An' so I can," he said. "but not today. Ye'd best come back tomorra."

"But you're not doing anything," I protested. "You're just sitting on a stump, drinking cider."

"That's 'cause I eren't workin' at the moment. The *kiln's* workin'; I eren't. But when the kiln's finished *its* work, then it'll be time fer me to do mine." He chewed on his pipe. "Don't know much, do ye?" he said.

"I'll double the money," I said, ignoring his barbed rhetoric.

The old man spat. "Won't make nary a difference," he said. "I needs to keep an eye on things, make sure she don't flare up. I eren't lettin' two day's cuttin' go to waste. Besides, I got some laths to make. No, best all round if ye was to come back tomorra, like I said. Don't you worry, young-un; she'll still be here."

Back in the plastic pig, Anushka rested a hand on my arm. "Calm, David," she said. "Please to be calm."

"*Calm?*" I said. "I've got a good mind to take that shotgun in there and shoot that recalcitrant, intransigent, mercenary-minded bastard. Oh, and burn the fucker's shack down while I'm at it."

"Is typical of man with gun," Anushka said. "You and these bloody guns," she went on, smacking her forehead in frustration. "Is because you no think straight. We are in better place than we have been so far. No? Is true or false?"

"He could be lying," I said.

"No. He was telling truth. That she is still here. So. Tomorrow we find out where to find her, you give her lark mirror. You get shadow back and we are together with no more troubles." She took a deep breath. "You see this as hiccup? I see this as blessing in disguise. How much sleep you have in past few days? How much food you eat? So, we go and recuperate. Tomorrow you fire on all sparks and you no mess things up."

"What about Mrs Mason?" I said. "What about Mr Cotteral? Do they have that kind of time?"

"You cannot do what you cannot do," Anushka said, pragmatic as ever.

I sighed. "Maybe you're right," I said. Anushka was not to know of my other complications. "I've got to be home before dark anyway," I reminded both of us.

"So," Anushka said, "we rest now. We spend remainder of afternoon together. Yes? Then you go see Sidney. Tomorrow night, you will be rid of curse."

***

On the way back to Billy's - wouldn't you know it? – the plastic pig began to falter. At first, a jerky quality – almost imperceptible – crept into the higher rev range. I wasn't unduly alarmed. The pig's engine was not large and it was a hot day and I'd had to work the engine pretty hard in low gear while I'd been driving through the woods. The engine had a right to be tired. But pretty soon the pig started to go into spasms, running smoothly one moment, almost kangarooing to a stop the next.

I tapped at the fuel gauge like a concerned aviator and the needle held steady at half a tank. I had no reason not to trust it. Silas had told me the fuel tank was full when I'd taken possession of the pig and I had no reason to distrust Silas either. Besides, these weren't the symptoms of an empty fuel tank.

"Is dirt in fuel line?" Anushka said, as we came to a puttering, stuttering halt on an uphill section of road.

"It could be," I said.

"You can fix?" she said, anxiously. "We must not waste whole afternoon."

"Don't worry," I said, worrying, "these things often sort themselves out." I cranked the engine. It coughed. Fired. Died.

"Is this your plan?" Anushka said. "To let it sort itself out?"

"I just don't want to –" I started. But just then the engine caught. It misfired once and almost died but picked up healthily. I took a run at the hill. The pig accepted the challenge – rose to it beautifully in fact – and we reached the top of the hill with little more than a mild judder which faded entirely once we started down the other side.

"It was just tired," I said.

"Is as I say," Anushka said. "Is what happens when you fail to take rest."

29

We made it back to Billy's cottage without further trouble with the plastic pig. The first thing I did when we got there was to phone Mr Mason to report my progress. He was calm at first but when I explained about our frustrating delay he advocated thrashing the old axe-waddler with a birch limb. When I asked after Mrs Mason his tone turned grave. "She doesn't even know who I am anymore," he said. "Please don't fail me, David," he pleaded. I assured him that I wouldn't and, for the first time, didn't feel like a liar in saying it.

I hung up the phone and found Anushka in the kitchen. She was staring at her painting.

"You are right," she said. "Is awful painting." Without another word she took a carving knife from a drawer and slashed the canvas to ribbons. "Now it can no longer hurt us."

"What made you think it could?" I said.

She put the knife back in the drawer.

"Paintings have power," she said. "Sometimes they even change lives. Why to paint them otherwise?"

"Why indeed?" I said. Then, as casually as I could, I said: "Oh, before I forget, I'm going to need that pistol. Can you open the safe?"

I was expecting to have to come up with some kind of explanation (in which case I would just say that I intended to throw the pistol into a bog) but Anushka just shrugged.

"Is your gun," she said.

"It's for the best," I said. "Billy hates guns too. If he came home now and found it in his safe he'd be very upset."

"Then you put gun in plastic pig and we say no more about it."

Which is what I did.

As I was making my way back up the garden path I heard Billy's phone ringing. Four rings and then it stopped. This time, Anushka had answered it. Closing the door quietly behind me, I heard her say: "I tell you last time – is not well." A pause. "No. He will call you when he is well again. Please to call no more." She slammed down the phone with the force of ill temper.

"Who was that?" I said.

Anushka started and turned and a slight blush flushed through her cheeks. "You make me jump," she said.

"Sorry," I said.

"Is wrong number," she said, gesturing at the phone.

"They *are* a nuisance, aren't they?" I said.

"I leave phone off hook," Anushka said, "so we are disturbed no more."

But the phone call had bothered me. "Anushka," I said, "there are some things that I've been meaning to ask you –"

Anushka had moved closer now and, employing her usual method, she stopped my next words from spilling from my lips.

We kissed and sought each other with our hands.

For minutes we kissed. Minutes during which all my concerns and problems and vague suspicions were driven from my mind.

"Now is not time for talking," Anushka said at last, breathing warmly into my ear. "Now is time for *not* talking."

In Billy's bed I loved her. In Billy's bed I took her. In Billy's bed I did all the things that my shadow's shadow had done to her shadow and she responded in like spirit. Gently at first, a slow breeze of pleasure building toward a scirocco of bliss – a whirlwind tumble of sucking, biting, scratching animal pleasure that rendered us into little more than shaved apes groaning our hunger for one another.

When it was over we were left panting and stunned. We *would* be together forever, just as we had waited, one for the other, for a very long time. Anushka was right about that and I had been a fool to think otherwise, a fool to harbour my petty suspicions.

Once we had finally disentangled ourselves Anushka lay on her side so that I could stroke the fabulous musculature of her back, kiss her beautiful, cream-white shoulder, tease her lustrous hair back from her perfect ear into which I poured words of love.

A delicious fatigue washed over us and we dozed like that for a while, my hand resting on her thigh and her warm ass pressed against my crotch.

"Was good for you?" Anushka murmured, drowsily.

"Was very good for me," I murmured back and on we dozed.

At some point the heat of the day, the heat of love, must have forced us apart because when I next woke Anushka was laying on her back, staring at the ceiling, an odd, disbelieving smile on her face. I stroked her stomach and then moved my hand lower and she squirmed against it and groaned out a subsidiary orgasm.

We were still again for a while and then, in that way that I'd forgotten about (it had been so long) my thoughts rose unbidden to my lips and didn't stop there.

"Did Billy ever tell you that he was in the army?" I said. "Very briefly," I qualified, "but he was in just the same."

Anushka said nothing but I felt her tense up.

"He comes from an old military family, does Billy," I went on, "and so he felt obliged to do his stint. But his heart wasn't in it. He knew that he wasn't soldier material. He didn't particularly like guns, for one thing – even before his father shot himself. After which, he became positively phobic about them. Just like you. And, on top of that, he didn't particularly like discipline either. Not *that* kind of discipline anyway."

"Why for you tell me this?" Anushka said.

"Because I feel like talking," I said. "And so anyway," I went on, "Billy hit upon a compromise. How to please his father while staying true to his own nature. Billy couldn't kill anyone, could he? So, what he did, was he joined the medical corps. Even then, it was still a huge mistake. So, much to his father's disgust, Billy pulled out before his probational period (or whatever you call it) was up. Before he had to sign on the dotted line, so to speak. He was only actually in the army for a few weeks. But it was long enough for him to do some basic medical training. He told me that that was the only good thing to come out of the experience – that he'd learned, for instance, to stitch and dress a wound, check for concussion … that kind of thing."

"Is all very interesting," Anushka said, peevishly, "but I ask again: why for you tell me this?"

"Oh," I said, "it's just seeing you do those things to poor old Erskine Cotteral made me think of it. That's all. Is that something else Billy told you about? How to deal with a head wound?"

"Yes," Anushka said, sarcastically, "first time I meet Billy he say: 'Come see my paintings. But first, I show you how to dress head wound.' You lay and think of Billy if you want," she said, throwing back the covers, "I go down for glass of water."

I felt her absence keenly and immediately and so I began to back-peddle. "Hey," I said, "I was just teasing."

"I am Anushka Pavlova from Saratov," Anushka said, apropos of nothing. "In Saratov there are twelve fountains in the square and the clock on the Institute of Culture is always five minute too fast. In winter, dogs and old men die from cold. You buy roast nuts and vodka in the street. My father used to take me to the museum. The museum was dull but it was good to be with my father on those days. Now, you would like something to eat? To drink?"

She'd succeeded in making me feel foolish. "A glass of milk would be nice," I said, humbly.

I closed my eyes again and quickly slipped into another doze and the next thing I knew was that Anushka was prodding me awake with a cold glass of milk. I took it drowsily and sat up to drink it. Anushka climbed into bed and closed her eyes. I noticed that she hadn't brought up a drink for herself and so offered her some milk.

"Is alright," she said, already slipping into sleep, "I drink downstairs."

I finished the milk and set the glass on the floor and settled down for another doze. Half an hour, I thought. Just half an hour and then I'd better get ready to go and check on that bastard Sidney. Maybe, I thought, I'd find just enough time for more love first.

But when I awoke to the sound of Anushka's heavy snoring the sun had moved on and the light was draining from the day.

"Jesus Christ!" I said.

I tried to shake Anushka awake but she wouldn't be woken. She lay on her back with her face turned toward me. Her mouth was wide open and her snoring breath hacked out of her.

"Come on," I said. "Anushka, wake up. I have to go."

For answer I received only her next snore. Then, the last words she'd spoken drifted into my mind. *Is alright; I drink downstairs.*

"Oh fuck," I said.

I leapt out of bed and pulled on my underwear and jeans. "Oh fuck," I said again. I took the stairs several treads at a time and hurried into the kitchen. The flagon of cider was in the fridge where I had left it but the handle – and I noticed this kind of thing – was now turned towards the right of the fridge, whereas I'd placed it turned towards the left.

"Oh fuck," I said again and then scanned the kitchen for further evidence. Which I found in the form of a glass on the draining board. The glass hadn't been rinsed and still held a film of amber liquid in the bottom. I picked it up and sniffed at it. It was cider. Anushka would have spotted it in the fridge when she went there for my milk. And why not have a nice cool glass of cider after making hot love? But how much had she drunk? I hadn't smelled it on her breath and when I went back to the fridge to check it didn't seem to me that the contents of the jug had been greatly diminished. I relaxed a little. Anushka had survived last night's dose with little ill effect. I didn't think there had been any great harm done and besides, the rest would probably do her good.

When I looked out of the kitchen window I saw that the shadows were long and the light had taken on a rosy hue. I would have to get moving. I would finish dressing, I would write Anushka a note to the effect that I would be back for her in the morning and then I would leave. But then my eye found and lingered upon Anushka's destroyed painting and I remembered what she'd said – that curious statement about paintings having the power to change lives. Which, in turn, made my thoughts tend towards the unseen masterpiece in Billy's studio. Yes, time was pressing. But this was too good an opportunity to pass up. Besides, how long could it take?

Telling myself that Billy would *want* me to see his painting, that Anushka had been over-protective in refusing to allow me to view it when I'd asked, I nevertheless felt like a thief when I stole back upstairs with unnecessary stealth. Pausing only for a furtive look into Billy's room to check on Anushka (which was also unnecessary since I could hear her snoring before I'd even reached the head of the stairs) I turned left on the landing and padded towards Billy's studio door on my bare feet. I turned the door handle and pushed. The door was locked. There was a small table on the landing – kitty-corner from the studio door – which held a vase of artificial flowers. Billy had let the flowers go dusty and dull. But I wasn't interested in the flowers. A small drawer was built into the table and I opened it and rummaged beneath various layers of detritus until I found the key which I knew to be there. It was a very Billy-like thing to do, leaving the key to a locked room in such an obvious place. I inserted the key into the lock and turned it. The tumblers tumbled and slid obligingly. I paused and listened. Anushka's snoring continued without interruption. I took a deep breath and swung the door open.

And there was Billy. He was more or less life-size and he stared out of the painting with a look of surprise or perhaps puzzlement on his face. He wore a three piece suit and his right hand was extended towards the viewer, as if reaching out to touch something or someone beyond the world of the canvas.

I walked past the painting, which was supported on an over-sized easel, and searched for the picture of Anushka. I lifted sheets from various other canvases until I was satisfied that no picture of Anushka was to be found in the room.

I returned to Billy's self portrait. His context in the painting was very much like that of Anushka's portrait when I had seen it in embryonic form, when it had been little more than charcoal lines and blocks of ground colour. Which is to say that he was in a bedroom, possibly a hotel bedroom, rendered in tones that managed to be warm and lugubrious at the same time. On the bed behind him was an open suitcase but no clothes spilled out of it. In the right hand side of the painting was a window, slanted by perspective. The window framed a view of a minaret – the usual kind, guaranteed to bring Moscow or any other Russian city to the mind of the un-travelled westerner.

"Billy," I said, overwhelmed by the implications of what I was looking at. "Oh my god, Billy."

There was a hard-backed chair just inside the door. Billy had told me that the distance between the chair and the easel was what he considered to be the optimum distance for viewing a painting and that he would sit there to appraise his own work while composing or when considering final touches. And sometimes, he'd added, I just sit and stare. I dropped into that chair as if winded and I too just sat and stared.

When I'd recovered I left the studio and locked the door and tossed the key back inside the drawer.

Back in Billy's bedroom I kicked the mattress beneath Anushka with the sole of my foot. "Wake up!" I said. I didn't really expect her to and I wasn't disappointed. Her body rocked with the kick but her snoring went on unabated.

I stood over her for a while, my whole body trembling.

"Who are you?" I said. "Who are you *really*, Anushka Pavlova from Saratov?"

I tried to leave her an anodyne note, matter of fact in its contents. That I would pick her up in the morning but if I was able to return to her later that night then I would. But it wouldn't do, so I tore up the note and started again. I could still feel the lingering glow of our love-making in every cell of my body. Could feel love in my heart – a sick, troubled and confused love, but love for all that – and I said as much in my note. But we have to talk, I ended it. There are things I have to know.

And then I left, taking the cider with me.

30

I drove back through the gloaming, the moon rising out of the moors as broad as a dinner plate. For the first half a mile or so the plastic pig coughed and jerked but the problem soon resolved itself and I began to suspect that Anushka had been right about there being dirt in the fuel line and so managed to convince myself that the dirt had now been flushed out of the system.

It was a beautiful evening and my gaze was naturally drawn from the road to the surrounding moors. Which was how I came to notice the sheep, a huge flock of them which must have been comprised of smaller flocks gathered here from other parts of the moors. They'd amassed at a break in a stone wall, as if herded there by an invisible sheepdog. They squeezed bleating through the gap in ones and twos before trotting on towards the south west. It was a curious thing to see but even then I might not have thought any more on the matter if, a mile further on and not far short of home, I hadn't been met by three deer springing down the road towards me. They behaved like creatures fleeing a forest fire, coming at me in such a blind panic that I had to swerve hard against the verge to let them pass safely. I watched their white-flashing hind quarters bobbing westward in my rear-view mirror and then, with a now-familiar sense of trepidation in my heart, I drove on towards home.

When I pulled up outside the cottage I saw that the dining room light was on and that the curtains had been drawn against the coming night. I distinctly remember having drawn back the curtains that morning which meant that my shadow had roused himself from his slumber, which, in turn, could mean anything at all – a thought which not only further stirred the trepidation in my heart, but had it doing forward rolls and back-flips.

I killed the engine and had just swung open the door of the plastic pig when I heard it - an otherworldly howl that could only have come from the monkey-dog himself.

"Oh Christ," I said. Instinct made me reach into my haversack for the pistol. I had to delve in deep for the sock-full of bullets and my hand came up greasy from a leak in the packed lunch which Anushka had made and which we'd failed to get around to eating.

But if instinct made me reach for the pistol, common sense made me reluctant to take it inside. My shadow really wanted that pistol and if he was still at large in the cottage, god only knew what kind of ambush he'd have had time to construct in order to take it from me.

I thought the matter over for a second or two and then shoved the pistol and bullets behind the seat. Then I got out of the pig, slammed the door and rushed up my garden path. As I did so, another howl from the monkey-dog made me duck and flinch like a Tommy under shell fire.

I'd been expecting all kinds of things from my shadow but what he served up so confounded my expectations that it may as well been a dish from a distant and alien culture.

"Baldy?" he called from the dining room. "Is that you?"

"Yes, Sidney," I said, "it's me."

He came to the dining room doorway with the air of a man who'd been relentlessly pacing back and forth in an agony of waiting. He was hatless and his hair stuck up in unruly tufts. The horse tranquilizer had worn off and he was as edgy as hell.

"Where the fuck have you been?" he said.

"Out," I said. "I had things to do."

"You are one selfish bastard, Baldy. You leave me asleep all fucking day and when I wake up you're not here, my *gun's* not here and … there's that *thing* outside."

I noticed that though his shadow was in its proper place and was slanted at its proper angle, it was doing a nervous, on-the-spot jig, like a man who badly needed the toilet.

"Which is why we've got to go," I said, ignoring his complaints. "Come on, we haven't got much time."

"I'm not going out *there*," he said.

"We can't stay here," I said. "We'll have no chance." I thought about Silas's description of how easily the monkey-dog had made a ruin of my van. I didn't think the cottage door would slow him down for even a minute. "If we stay here," I said, "one of us is going to die."

"Why not both?" he asked, suspiciously.

"He only wants one of us," I said. "The Major told me all about him. It's how he works."

"Well, which one?" he said.

"I hate to say it," I said, not hating it at all, "but I think it might be you."

"*Me?*" he said. "Well what the fuck have *I* done?"

"I don't know," I shrugged. "Maybe he just hates a gin thief."

His shadow had become more agitated now and he looked at it with shame and contempt. "Look at this fucking coward," he said. "He's been like that since I woke up."

"Can't you control it?" I said.

"What do you think, Baldy? You think I *want* him to show me up like this?"

"He needs a drink," I said. "*You* need a drink. There's a full jug of cider in the fridge –"

"No there's not," he said. "I already found it."

"Then you'd better fetch it," I said. "Come on, let's go."

The monkey-dog howled again and my shadow flinched. "I told you, Baldy," he said, "I'm not going out there. That fucking thing could be anywhere. You go if you want. Just give me back my gun and I'll fort up here. If it turns up then I'll just shoot the fucker." Which was all just empty bravado.

"I've seen one desperate stand end badly this week," I reminded him. "I really don't need another."

"Alright," he said, "I'll come if you give me back my gun."

"No," I said. "You come, and *if* it comes to you needing it, then *maybe* I'll let you have it."

The monkey-dog howled again.

"Listen to that thing," my shadow said. "I'd like to know, Baldy, since you're so fucking smart, in what way could we possibly *not* need a gun in a situation like this?"

But I was done arguing with him. "You'd best fetch your cider," I said, with finality, "it's time to go. Oh," I added, "and keep your shadow under control. He's getting on my nerves."

That hit home. "Alright, Baldy," he said, "but you'd better have a fucking good plan."

"Plan?" I said. "There's no plan. There's just you and me and the monkey-dog and probably a long night ahead. But there's no plan. I'll wait outside. Pull the door up behind you. Oh, and turn the lights out; you've wasted enough of my money."

I started the plastic pig, noticing what I'd missed before – that not a single rabbit bobbed its tail along the bank. The monkey-dog seemed to have thrown a scare into the whole of the surrounding moorland.

I turned the van around. Since the monkey-dog's howl was in the east, in so far as I *did* have a plan it was simply to travel west and maintain the distance between us. But as I executed a three-point-turn, the plan evolved a little in my mind. If I could lead the monkey-dog all the way to the coast by as diverse a route as possible so as to arrive there at dawn, then it would be stranded out there all the next day by its aversion to daylight, forced to hole-up in whatever refuge it could find. The plan would require nerve and good judgement and may even involve letting the monkey-dog get too close for comfort in order to be sure that it was following but if I could pull it off then I would have placed considerable time and distance between the monkey-dog and my business with Aunt Alsey.

When my shadow finally emerged from the cottage he had his moon-shadow in tow. They must have had words because his shadow was behaving more or less like a regular shadow.

My shadow jumped into the pig and slammed the door. He clamped the cider flagon between his ankles, tugged his hat firmly onto his head and then pulled one of my carving knives from his belt and tossed it down beside the jug.

"What's the knife for?" I said but he just gave me a look which told me not to ask such damn fool questions.

At that moment the monkey-dog issued another blood-curdling howl, one which told me that it was perceptibly closer.

My shadow seemed to think so too. "For fuck's sake, Baldy," he said, "don't let's sit here all fucking night."

I put the pig into gear and pulled away. My shadow was so relieved to be moving that he lit a smoke, unstopped the cider and tipped a fair amount of it down his gullet.

"Listen, Baldy," he said, punctuating his utterance with a belch, "I may have been a bit hard on you. Truth is, I thought you'd run out on me. That was hard to take, since I thought we were pals and all. But you came back, didn't you? You did good, Baldy. You did good."

"Is that an apology?" I said, dryly. "From you?"

"I'm just glad you came back is all I'm saying. We're in this together, Baldy. And it's a comfort to me that you've got my best interests at heart and that you're not just concerned with saving your own skin."

Despite his being an obnoxious shit and a major inconvenience to boot, I felt a stirring of guilt when he said that, given that all of my recent travails and the travails to come were dedicated to his destruction.

"Well," I said, lamely, "God hates a coward."

"And so do I, Baldy," he said. "So do I," before helping himself to more cider.

I drove on until I was on the burned section of road and then slowed to a stop. From there I could see for the best part of a mile behind. The moon had climbed higher and was bright enough to read by. Well, I didn't feel much like reading but I *did* want to make sure that the monkey-dog was unerringly on our trail.

"What the hell's wrong now?" my shadow said. "Drive the fucking thing, can't you?" He turned to look out of the rear window.

"Don't worry," I said, "I know what I'm doing. There's a bigger picture here." It was the same picture as before with a few more lines and squiggles drawn in. I would lead the monkey-dog out almost to Blowing Stone Tor and then criss-cross south to the coast from there. Once the bastard had skulked off with the dawn, I'd drive a big loop back via Corny Cross, thus locking the monkey-dog into a journey which would eat up most - if not all - of the following night. None of which was information I was prepared to share with my shadow.

"So you *have* got a plan," my shadow said. "Well, Baldy, I hope it involves more than just sitting here until we get eaten alive."

"Shut up," I said, "I'm trying to concentrate. If you're a good boy, I might even let you play with the gun." I had no intention of doing this, despite what I'd said earlier.

"Fat fucking chance," my shadow said, sensing as much.

We sat there for perhaps twenty minutes, both of us smoking. The more my shadow drank, the more mean and mischievous he became.

"Where's the Russian, Baldy?" he said.

"Never mind the Russian," I said. "The Russian's my business."

"You're right, Baldy," he said. "I'll stay out of it."

"Good," I said.

Then he began to sing. "*Anushka, Anushka,*" he crooned, "*she ain't no old babushka. Young and sweet, and what a treat, when on the wall I took her.*" He got off a good chuckle at that.

"Shut your filthy mouth," I said.

"Why don't you make me, Baldy. Let's see how *that* goes."

"You're like a kid," I said, bitterly. "Like a fucking kid."

"*Anushka, Anushka,*" he crooned again, "*now Baldy's gone and bushed her.* Get it, Baldy?" he said. "*Bushed* her."

I tried to ignore him and was just deliberating how I could get him to switch to the drug-laced cider without arousing his suspicions when I saw it. The Monkey-dog.

"Hate to ruin your fun," I said, "but we've got company."

My shadow turned in his seat and we both watched it approach. At first it was little more than an erratically-moving dot at the road's far end but it ate up the distance with terrifying speed and soon we could see it more clearly. It had a sort of lolloping gait and its body seemed to articulate in the middle in some queer way so that its back end would swing out and almost overtake its front end. All the while its head was lowered and even at that distance and in that light you could see its tale lashing the air. When it had drawn within a few hundred yards it lifted its face from the road and seemed to see us for the first time. It let go a terrible yawp and then shifted gear and bounded towards us.

"Fuck's sake, Baldy," my shadow wanted to know, "what the fuck are we waiting for?"

I pulled slowly away, my eye fixed on the monkey-dog in my rear-view mirror.

A couple of miles further on I stopped and waited and then pulled away again once the monkey-dog was in sight. I drove slowly past Billy Makepiece's cottage, noticing as I did so that all the lights were out which meant that Anushka was probably still sleeping, in blissful ignorance of our plight. I stopped again, at a place just on the edge of the hamlet from where I could still see Billy's cottage. When the monkey-dog lurched around the bend, I watched it and saw that it totally ignored the scent of my earlier comings and going in and out of the cottage and was intent only on catching up with the plastic pig. I smiled wordlessly. Its ignoring my raw scent like that must surely mean that it was my shadow and not *me* that the monkey-dog hunted. Which meant that if I could keep my shadow safe until I found Aunt Alsey then the monkey-dog, like all my other problems, would just go away.

I'd taken a big risk letting the monkey-dog get that close and I compensated for it by gunning away from Billy's hamlet at top speed. Then, the immediate danger having passed, I slowed again to let our pursuer catch up.

On we went in that fashion for mile after mile, the monkey-dog almost always in sight. My shadow no longer seemed to mind. He'd made impressive progress with Silas's notoriously strong scrumpy and he now seemed to be having a fine time, serving up renditions of various blues songs. "*Sucked and weaned on chicken bile*," he sang. I have to admit he didn't have a bad voice so I let him get on with it. His singing was less irritating than his talking (so long as he didn't start singing *that* song again) and besides, weak with hunger and exhaustion as I was, having that chimerical hell-hound on our trail as we did, I was, nevertheless, in good spirits. My plan was working and working well.

And it was working well right up until the moment that the engine began to jerk and splutter. Even my shadow noticed.

"What's wrong with this heap of shit?" he said.

The Lark Mirror

"It's nothing," I said. "Dirt in the fuel line. It'll clear in a minute."

But it didn't clear. Neither did it die altogether. We limped on, almost reduced to walking pace at times, the monkey-dog closing the distance between us with every cough and splutter from the engine. We were far to the west by now, not far short of Blowing Stone Tor and close to the turning which would lead us zig-zag to the coast. But the coast now seemed very far away.

And then, on a long, uphill stretch of road, the engine quit altogether and we came to a standstill. I yanked on the hand break and cranked the engine desperately but it wouldn't catch.

From a quarter of a mile behind, the monkey-dog unleashed one of its long howls. I thought I heard triumph in that howl.

As drunk as he now was, it took a moment or two for the seriousness of the situation to dawn on my shadow. "Well, Baldy," he said. "Now what?"

"Don't worry," I said, still cranking the engine, "it'll start." But I was wrong.

I glanced in the rear-view mirror and saw the monkey-dog appear on the rise of the hill behind us. It saw us and howled again and then ran headlong into the dip between us as fast and avid as we'd yet seen it. It hit the bottom of the dip and bounded up the hill towards us, the gradient slowing it not one jot.

"Well, Baldy," my shadow said, "look's like the time's come." He held out his hand, affecting "gimme" gestures with his fingers.

I looked at him steadily for a few moments. "Alright," I said, "I'll trust you. But don't you fuck this up."

"You worry too much, Baldy," he said, as I reached for the pistol and bullets. "What's to fuck up?" He took the pistol and flipped open the cylinder. "This thing's got six shots. I ought to get the fucker with one of them."

It was encouraging watching him load that pistol. His hands were steady and he seemed to know what he was doing and I could only marvel at what half a gallon of Silas's scrumpy could do for a man's courage.

31

"Don't look so glum, Baldy," my shadow said, snapping the pistol closed. "There's nothing to it. I'll go down there and kill it, then we'll hit the spots. What do you say?"

"Sounds good," I said, indulging him.

"That's the spirit," he said, clambering out of the pig.

"Good luck, Sidney," I said, and meant it.

I never thought I'd ever feel admiration for that pernicious bastard but at that moment I was full of the stuff.

"Oh, and Baldy," my shadow said, popping his head back in, "if it doesn't work out, my advice to you is to cut your throat." It was typical of him to spoil the mood.

After cranking the engine one more time without success I gave up and climbed out of the pig to watch the spectacle. I have to confess that my shadow was a picture of ragged magnificence as he walked down that slope, his cider flagon swinging from his left hand, the pistol pointed skywards in his right.

The monkey-dog had seen him by now and had slowed to a sneaky-looking trot as it evaluated the situation.

"Nice doggy," my shadow taunted. He'd gone about a hundred yards down the hill when he reached the place at which he'd make his stand. He stooped to set the cider flagon in the road, like a knight planting his standard, and then he stretched and jabbed out his elbows and flapped them like a bird by way of limbering up before gripping the pistol in both hands and readying his aim.

The monkey-dog, obviously game for the challenge, lashed its tail and threw back its head and cried a terrible battle screech. And then it charged. My shadow didn't seem the least bit fazed, and neither did *his* shadow, which stood its ground right beside him. He let the monkey-dog come on until it was in range and then he fired.

Ker-*chew*!

An impressive flame leapt from the pistol and the shot echoed for miles around. The bullet kicked up dust to the left of and far behind the monkey-dog.

It's alright, I thought, he's just getting his aim in and he's got five shots left.

Ker-*chew*! Went the pistol.

Ker-*chew*!

And still the monkey-dog came on and still my shadow held his nerve.

Ker-*chew*!

Ker-*chew*!

Ker-*chew*!

And that was that. The inept fool had missed with every shot. He threw down the pistol and snatched up his cider and began to run back up the hill, his hand clapped to his hat to keep it in place, snatching glances over his shoulder as he ran.

The monkey-dog was a few short bounds behind him, growling and snarling in anticipation of the night's first taste of meat.

"Help me, Baldy!" my shadow cried. In the moonlight his face was a white mask of terror. His shadow had slipped loose of his control again and was running ahead, making urgent gestures for him to catch up.

So this is how it ends, I thought. What the monkey-dog had done to that leg of lamb back at the Major's he was about to do to Sidney and I doubted it would be pretty. Moreover, my not-so-golden future as a shadow-less freak now seemed secure.

Except that it didn't end that way at all. With my shadow screaming in terror – *really* screaming now – the monkey-dog closed the last few feet between them, then it closed the inches and then ... it kept right on going. It bounded past my shadow without even a sideways glance. Its head was up again now, its eyes fixed on me.

"Oh Christ," I said, "it's *me* he wants!"

Squawking out my own expression of terror, I swung myself inside the plastic pig and slammed the door. Not that I expected that fragile, fibre-glass shell to protect me – no, I was just operating on pure blind instinct. I cranked the engine uselessly. I thought of Mr Cotteral's shotgun but the butt end of it was at the back door and the barrels were too long for me to be able turn it around in such a tight space, trapped in the driving seat as I was. No, going for the shotgun would mean opening the back door and there was no way I was going to get out of the pig again. And besides, there wasn't time. Then, not because I was clever, and certainly not because I was calm, but simply because it was the only thing I *could* do, I let off the handbrake.

A muted groan creaked out of the wheel hubs and then the plastic pig began to roll backwards down the hill. I turned in the seat and looked over my shoulder so that I could steer.

The monkey-dog was just thirty yards behind me and getting closer - much closer – by the second, since I was now rolling towards it. There was little weight to the plastic pig and I doubted I'd built up enough speed to do much harm but the pig was now the only viable weapon I had and so, using the centre of the back window as a sight for that weapon, I aimed straight for the monkey-dog.

Meanwhile, having perceived that the shape of the game had altered, the monkey-dog had slowed and then stopped. It seemed mesmerized by the approaching vehicle and, though I lacked experience at reading the expressive range of the monkey-dog, I'd have to say that the look on its face was one of surprise. Either way, it was a boost to my morale and I allowed myself a smile as I anticipated the impact.

But the impact didn't come.

At the very last second, the monkey-dog executed a neat little sidestep and snatched itself from my view. There was a thump on the side of the pig, close to the back door on the passenger side, and then a set of claws – claws which were very much like knife-blades - punched their way through the side panel and into the pig's interior. There was a horrible cracking sound and, with the pig still moving, the claws cut their way toward the front of the vehicle. All of this happened very fast. Even so, I distinctly remember that when the claws reached the passenger door and the door was ripped off, the monkey-dog was quick enough to shove its face inside the pig and snap its teeth at me. Then the side of its head hit the glove box and it was spun back out of the pig to land sprawling in the road.

I was still rolling backwards but I risked a glance through the windscreen and watched as the monkey-dog picked itself up and shook itself down. Then it howled and started to chase the pig back down the hill.

I looked over my shoulder again so that I could steer. My shadow was in the road, stooped over with his hands on his knees, trying to catch his breath. He straightened as I drew close and stuck out his thumb like a hitch-hiker by way of a joke and readied himself to jump into the pig but I rolled right on past him, gathering speed. He jumped clear when he realised I wasn't going to stop and, with the engine dead and a gaping hole where the passenger door should be, I distinctly heard him shout, "Baldy, you *cunt!*"

I didn't hold it against him. He wasn't to know that this particular cunt had a last-ditch plan up his sleeve. I glanced forward again. The monkey-dog was lolloping along as avid as ever now and my shadow was running along in front in a vain effort to catch up with me. Then, judging that I was going as fast as I could go in free-wheel mode, whilst also wanting to save some hill for a second attempt, I slammed the van into reverse gear and popped the clutch.

The engine almost sheered free of its moorings but it coughed and choked and then, almost miraculously, burst into vigorous and healthy life. I put the clutch back in and gunned the engine to make sure that it wasn't going to quit and then I braked, put it in first and drove back up the hill towards my shadow and towards the monkey-dog.

I stopped to let my shadow aboard.

"Get in," I said, but he really didn't need telling. He swung himself inside and put his cider on the floor.

"What the fuck did you do to my gun, Baldy?" he said. "You bent the fucking sight."

"I didn't do anything, you idiot," I said, working my way into third gear. "You were just too fucking drunk to hit anything."

"Don't be a cunt, Baldy," he said. "A good drink steadies your aim."

Having more pressing concerns, I decided to abandon the debate.

The monkey-dog was running straight at us and I was driving straight at it. At the last moment, I switched on the lights to dazzle the bastard and then swerved so that its claws swiped the empty air just inches from my side window. We shot past it and on up the hill. When I looked in the mirror the monkey-dog was striking the road with the heels of its paws. It looked to be in a terrible temper.

It recovered his composure quickly, however, and before we'd breasted the hill it was once more in pursuit. My shadow was trying to light a cigarette but the wind tearing past the open doorway kept snuffing out his matches. Eventually he got it lit and, evidently perceiving that the immediate crisis had passed, rewarded himself with a good guzzle of cider.

"So, Baldy," he said, smugly, "it was *you* he had in his sights all along. Guess that means I just saved your skin."

"How the fuck do you work *that* out?" I said. "You missed with every fucking shot."

"I told you," he said, "you bent the sight. Now, don't try and tell me otherwise, Baldy, because I know my way around a gun. When I worked on the Carney-"

"You never worked on the Carney," I said.

"Oh yes I did, Baldy. Worked on the Carney for years. Now, as I was saying-"

"Oh shit," I said, cutting off the rest of his lies.

"Jesus, Baldy," my shadow said, "just why *are* you driving this pile of shit anyway?"

The pile of shit had begun to falter again. We were on another downward stretch with a hill coming up. If the engine were to die in the dip between then there would be no coasting out of trouble. Not this time.

First it faltered and then it shuddered and juddered. I put in the clutch to take advantage of our downhill run, all the while pumping the accelerator to try and clear the fuel system. In the mirror, I saw the monkey-dog come over the hill behind us.

By the time we hit the dip the engine was revving freely again and so I let out the clutch and we powered up the next hill at an encouraging pace. But as we hit the crest of the hill, the engine was once more afflicted.

For another mile it went on like this – with the engine losing power and then recovering just in time to prolong my un-eviscerated existence for another minute. It became horribly clear that the monkey-dog was gaining on us, just as it became clear that the engine was taking longer and longer to recover each time. It was not a good ratio.

I'd long since given up on my plan to give the monkey-dog its night-long run-around. Now it was just a matter of short-term survival. Which was why, when we reached the junction where I'd intended to take the road for the coast I just kept going, barely conscious of what I was doing. I drove straight past Blowing Stone Tor and on towards Witchfall Woods.

On a level section of road before it began to drop into the valley, the van puttered down almost to walking pace with the monkey-dog a mere four hundred yards behind. If I could make the slope before the engine died altogether then I could pick up enough speed to outrun that unbound abomination for a few more minutes. But then what? The situation looked hopeless.

"It's going to be hard breaking it to the Russian, Baldy," my shadow said, less than helpfully. I sighed with the knowledge that I was going to have to trust him again.

"Get in the back," I told him.

"Don't be a cunt all your life, Baldy," he said. "This is no time to take a nap."

"Just do it, you idiot," I said. "There's another nice toy back there for you to play with. It's under the blanket. There's a fishing rod in there too – for fuck's sake don't break it."

He made sure that he kicked me in the ear as he did so but he managed to climb over his seat and into the back of the pig without too much fuss. Then, kneeling in the low space he threw back the blanket.

"Well, Baldy," he said, "why didn't you tell me about this in the first place? I'm much better with one of these. It's what I used to use when I was a trick-shooter for the Carney."

"Never mind the fucking Carney, you lying bastard," I said. "Do you think you can hit it this time?"

"No problem," he said, breaking the barrels to make it easier to turn the shotgun in such a close confine.

"Good," I said, "because remember: if I die, *you* die."

"Maybe, maybe not," he said, snapping closed the breech.

We'd slowed to a hopeless crawl, the monkey-dog gaining with its every misarticulated lope and bound.

"You'd better open the door and get ready," I said.

My shadow fiddled about with the door for several seconds and then said: "Baldy, you daft cunt, there's no catch on the inside."

Which was a serious flaw in my plan.

There was no time for him to crawl back in the front and there was no time for me to stop and open the back door. I was forced to simply watch as the monkey-dog grew in size in my wing mirror and then disappear from view when it was too close to even fall into the mirror's ken.

"Shoot through the door!" I yelled in desperation.

My shadow fired from the hip and there was a flash and a bang and there was smoke and most of the door fell away behind leaving the remainder swinging on its hinges.

I stared at this mess like a pilot who'd just had the tail shot off his plane. The one thing I couldn't see which I was expecting to see was the monkey-dog and for a second I thought that my shadow must have nailed the bastard.

But then there was a huge and heavy thump on the roof of the pig and four claws pierced the roof close to my head. I flinched away and screamed in terror and just then the engine hit one of its good patches and perked up considerably. I stuck my foot down and veered side to side in an effort to dislodge the monkey-dog from the roof. Its claws cut rents into the fibreglass and the rear wheels lifted clear of the road on every swerve so that I thought we were going to roll over.

Suddenly the monkey-dog's awful, upside-down face appeared in the windscreen. It grinned in at me and then its other paw came into view. It was a paw very much like a hand and indeed, the monkey-dog wiggled its fingers as if to wave at me. Then knife-blade claws sprang from the ends of those fingers and the monkey-dog drew back its fore-limb with the claws pointing directly at my face, poised to strike through the glass.

And then there was another blast from the shotgun. The monkey-dog's eyes widened in pain and surprise and then it was gone, taking a chunk of the roof with it.

In the wing mirror I saw the creature roll and then get up and then half its guts spilled out into the road. Its legs buckled under it and it went down, all but finished.

The Lark Mirror

"Good shot!" I told my shadow.

"Didn't I tell you, Baldy?" he said. "When you've got me, you've got the best."

I stopped the plastic pig and got out. The monkey-dog was crawling toward the ditch, trailing its guts behind it. It was mewling in agony but I couldn't find it in myself to feel the least bit sorry for it.

My shadow popped his head up through the hole he'd shot in the roof. Between the two of them, my shadow and the monkey-dog had left Silas with very little cover on his courtesy car.

"Hey, Baldy," my shadow said. "I can see the pole star from here."

I reached back into the pig and fetched the cider from the floor. I handed it to my shadow across the roof. His shoulders were through the hole now, his arms resting on the roof – what was left of it. "Here," I said, "have a drink. You deserve it."

"Why, thank you, Baldy," he said.

The monkey-dog was still mewling pitifully. It had made it over the bank and only its hind quarters were visible above the ditch.

"Listen to him," I said. "Bet he never thought it would turn out like that."

"You want me to go and finish the fucker?" my shadow said. "I'd be happy to oblige."

"No more cartridges," I shrugged.

"Well then I'll stove his head in," he said.

I thought about that for a moment. "Nah," I said. "Fuck him. He's as good as dead anyway."

32

We smoked and took in the night air and listened to the sounds of the monkey-dog's dying. When it grew quiet I checked that Mr Mason's fishing rod hadn't been lost in the chaos and then stowed the shotgun beside it and covered both items with the blanket.

I'd left the engine ticking over and when we'd both taken our seats I drove on to the start of the long slope into the valley, telling myself it was the best place to turn around.

The engine ran smoothly enough at that point (though I didn't expect it to last) but the pig's bodywork, having lost its structural integrity along with a good part of itself, creaked and flapped in the low wind of our passage.

I braked to a halt at the top of the slope. Witchfall Woods lay below us, vast and dark and as moon-silvered as an inland sea. Not a light could be seen in the woods and the only light at all in all that panorama was a single lit window at the Cotteral house. I thought of Mr Cotteral in there, his sanity being steadily eroded by shame. I thought of Mrs Mason and how that lovely woman no longer even knew her own name. I thought of the Major and his valiant but doomed last stand and I thought of Anushka who only wanted me to be a whole man again. And then I thought about how the agent of all this misery was perhaps less than two miles from where we sat. And I just wanted it all to end. And so I drove down into the valley.

"Where are we going now, Baldy?" my shadow said.

"We're going to see a friend of mine," I said. "But don't worry, I'll get you home. One way or the other, you're going home."

The engine foundered again close to the Cotteral farm and we passed in a spasm of flapping fibreglass. I thought – but couldn't swear to it – that I saw Mr Cotteral's anxious face pressed against the glass of the lit window.

As we entered the woods and lost the moonlight my shadow grew uneasy. Of course, he tried to hide it with bluster.

"Why are we fucking around in these woods at this time of night, Baldy?" he wanted to know. "Why don't we just go home?"

"I told you," I said, "we're going to see a friend of mine. You'll like him – he's got cider."

"I'm tired of cider," he said, and to emphasise the point he tossed the third-full cider flagon out of the doorway.

"Well, not to worry," I said, "I expect he's got whisky too."

"If you say so, Baldy," my shadow said, with a troubling lack of enthusiasm.

Given that I was now better-acquainted with Witchfall Woods and given that it was a freshly renewed acquaintance, I'd expected to find the charcoal-burner's camp without too much difficulty. But the woods began to play their old disorienting tricks – as if they had effected some geographical swaps and shifts once darkness had descended. Moreover, my search was somewhat hampered by the fact that the pig's rear wheels followed the wheel ruts, while the front wheel rode the ridge between, which meant that the headlamps shone into the tree canopy, rather than on the road ahead. On top of that, all that flapping fibreglass was a big distraction.

"What are you sniffing for, Baldy?" my shadow said. "You got a cold or something?"

"Wood smoke," I said. "This friend of mine; he's a charcoal burner."

"What's his name, this friend of yours?" my shadow said, catching me completely off-guard.

"I ... I'm not sure," I said, being just quick-witted enough to know that he'd sense the lie in the second or two it took me to conjure up a fictitious name for a charcoal burner.

"He's a friend of yours and you don't know his name?" my shadow said.

I didn't much care for his inquisitorial tone – in fact, it made me distinctly nervous and I started to feel as uncomfortable in his company as I'd ever felt. I decided to stick as close to the truth as possible.

"Well, the things is," I said, "I only met him today."

"Where?"

"Here."

"You've been in these woods *already* today?" he said. "Why, Baldy," he went on, "not only are you a sly old dog but you're a pretty dark fucking horse as well, aren't you? So tell me, Baldy, what brought you to the woods today?"

"A picnic," I said, suddenly inspired.

"A *picnic?*" he said, scornfully. "Why, don't *you* live the genteel life."

"Yes," I said, "I *like* doing things like that. Things that are pleasant and harmless and don't make me feel bad about myself." I knew he didn't believe me but by the time I'd served that up I at least felt as if I *had* been on a picnic.

"Who with?" he said.

"Who with what?" I said, playing for time.

"Come on, Baldy," he said, "even a dappy cunt like you wouldn't go on a picnic on his own."

"You know who," I said, knowing it was pointless trying to fend off the inevitable.

"Ah," he said, "the lovely Anushka." Then he began to sing his vile song. "*Anushka, Anushka, she ain't no old babushka. Young and sweet and what a treat, when on the wall I took her.*" He began to laugh.

"Shut up," I told him.

But he wouldn't shut up. "Let me tell you something as a pal, Baldy," he said. "She's not what she seems, the Russian."

"That's none of your damn business," I said.

"If you say so, Baldy," he said. "But I'll tell you one thing: she wasn't born in Saratov."

It was then that the engine threw another sulk.

"I don't know why we don't just burn this piece of shit," my shadow said. "Don't know about you, Baldy, but I miss a good fire."

We'd jerked to a standstill in a hollow in the road.

"If you can't say anything useful," I said, "why don't you just keep your mouth shut?"

I turned off the lights to save the battery and then cranked the engine. This time though, the malady seemed terminal.

"Now what?" my shadow said.

"I'm going for a piss," I said, "that's what."

I *did* need to relieve myself, but more than that I needed to extract myself from my shadow's company so that I could think clearly. It was for this reason, as much as for the sake of privacy, that I walked off a good way before unbuttoning my flies. I stepped off the road and pissed into a nettle patch.

The air was woefully free of wood smoke and I began to feel foolish and impetuous for entering the woods that night. Tomorrow, I could have come here sans shadow. I could have drugged him again and kept my rendezvous with the old axe-waddler unhindered. But it was too late for that now. As I re-buttoned my flies, I stood on tiptoe and craned over the bushes directly in front of me. I could see now that there was moonlight down there; that we had come to a halt above one of the hidden valleys. Far below, the moonlight lay a bluish hue over the canopy. If I were forced to guess then I would have said that it would be in one such valley – perhaps this very one – that Aunt Alsey would make her bed. But there were dozens of such places in Witchfall Woods and it would be a full night's work just to search this particular valley, never mind the rest of them. The task was impossible and though my impetuosity had left my original plan intact, I was now stuck a long way from home with no transport and a companion – if we can call him that – who was becoming more sly, unpleasant and quite simply un-nerving with every dark minute that passed.

And so it was with low spirits that I returned to the plastic pig and when I dropped into the driving seat my spirits sank even lower. It wasn't that my shadow was munching his way through one of the duck sandwiches that Anushka had made and which had remained, unloved and uneaten, within the sweaty confines of my haversack - for he was welcome to the duck sandwich. No. It was the fact that he now had the lark mirror balanced in his lap.

"What are you doing with that?" I said.

He looked at the sandwich. "I was hungry, Baldy. What do you think? Trouble is, I fucking hate cranberry sauce," and with that he tossed the rest of the sandwich into the road.

"Give it to me," I said, ignoring his deflection and reaching for the lark mirror. He pulled it from my reach and held it almost at arms length out of the doorway. "Don't snatch," he said. "It's rude to snatch. Thing is, Baldy," he went on, "I'm curious about this thing. Why do you carry it with you all the time?"

"It's valuable," I said.

"No it's not," he said. "It's just an old music box with a broken mirror mashed onto the top of it."

"It's valuable to *me*," I said.

"It's coming between us, Baldy, this thing. I can feel it. No, I can feel *more* than that."

"Can I have it please?" I said, with as much authority as I could muster.

"No, Baldy," he said, "you can't have it. And if you interrupt me again I'll make you sorry."

Oh yes, my shadow was revealing his true nature now.

"Know what I think, Baldy?" he said. "I think that this thing is the reason we're here. Part of it anyway. Why *are* we here, Baldy? And if you mention that friend of yours again I'm going to smash this thing into a million fucking pieces."

"We're looking for something," I said.

"Some *thing*? Or some *one*?

"Look," I sighed, "this has got to stop. It's all wrong."

"No it isn't," he said. "Its *good* to be alive again. It's good to drink and to fuck whores and to shoot guns. That's all the good stuff. It's all there *is*. And this thing – I don't know how, but It's going to stop all of that. *If* I let it. But you know what, Baldy? I don't think I *will* let it."

He made to step out of the pig and I grabbed his shoulder but he was ready for that. He smashed his elbow into my cheek and I fell back, stunned. Before I could recover he snatched the carving knife from the foot-well and pressed the blade against my throat.

I'd forgotten all about the knife.

"Try that again, Baldy," he said. "See what happens." His scars seemed suddenly more raised and livid, his teeth longer, his eyes black and liquid. If I'd ever come close to forgetting that he was a supernatural being then that glimpse of his face disabused me of such a notion.

"Alright," I said, "alright."

"You make me sick," my shadow said. "Carrying on about the little things when here you are, bringing me out here to do me in – just like a filthy common murderer. Christ, I even saved your fucking skin tonight."

"You did," I said. "Thank you."

"I'm not going back to being your slave, Baldy, you can count on that. I told you before, I'm back for good. Now," he said, "I'm going to get shot of this thing and then I'll be right back. You want rid of me after that then you'll have to do it the hard way. If you've got the guts." He eased out of the pig, holding the lark mirror by its base in his left hand, warning me off with the knife in his right. "Oh, and just to make it interesting," he said, "we'll fight for the Russian."

So I sat there, helpless and hopeless, as he strolled away from the plastic pig. There was a single patch of moonlight on the road and whether by accident or by theatrical design that's where he chose to execute his coup de grace. He cocked back his arm - his shadow dancing with glee – and then hurled the lark mirror into the valley below. As it pin-wheeled along the course of its arc it caught the moonlight and when the moonlight winked out of it and it went crashing through the canopy below it seemed a fitting enough metaphor for my spirits.

Or, at least, it would have been if not for the fact that I heard a distant splash as the lark mirror found water. It was (to keep the tropes marching along) like a splash of hope.

My shadow and his shadow both seemed satisfied with his work. As he stepped out of the moonlight his shadow dissolved in the moon-shade but I could see *my* shadow clearly enough. He was tossing the carving knife palm to palm like a knife fighter in a western.

"Alright, Baldy," he said, "your move. Are you going to fight? Or are you going to shit your pants and run away?"

I climbed out of the plastic pig as if to join battle. "No," I said, "I think it's time I finished you off for good." And with that I let out a wild yell – which threw him somewhat – and ran blindly into the brush. Low-lying brambles tried to shackle my legs but I just tore my way through them, unmindful of the thorns.

"Baldy," my shadow yelled after me. "Come back here you cowardly cunt!"

"Fuck off," I yelled back triumphantly and then I was falling through the air. My fall was broken by a mercifully soft and mossy ledge but I bounced straight off it and was once again falling. I landed again and the wind *whoofed* out of me and then I was rolling and tumbling through ferns and over tree roots until I slammed and splashed to a halt with one leg splayed out in water.

I lay there for a second or two. I'd bitten my tongue and I could taste blood. There was some pain in my left shoulder. Otherwise though, I thought I was more or less unhurt. I sat up slowly and began to take stock of my surroundings. There was no direct moonlight beneath the talus but enough ambient light filtered through for me to see that I was in a small clearing and that the water I was half in and half out of was not so much a pond as a hollow filled with rain water. I was in a place so steeped in shade that even the heat of that notorious summer had failed to burn off the water and this small fact made me feel very far away from the rest of the world.

As if to offer me some kind of perverse reassurance on that count my shadow called down from high above. "Baldy," he called. "Hey, Baldy, you cunt. I'm going to gut you like a fish. Then I'm going to fuck the Russian till she walks bandy-legged."

"Oh fuck off," I muttered.

Then, with my eyes now better adjusted to the gloom, I saw something protruding from the water on the furthest edge of the hollow. It was shaped like a globe. It was the lark mirror.

"I'm coming down there, Baldy," my shadow ranted on. "And when I do, you won't like it one little bit."

I ignored him. It sounded like an empty threat to me. It was one thing to launch yourself blindly off the top of a steep slope and find the bottom with little injury through pure blind luck; it was quite another to pick your way down the same slope in the dark, mindful of self preservation and with two thirds of jug of scrumpy in your belly. Besides, I was too overjoyed at being reunited with my lark mirror to let that bastard spoil the mood again.

I got to my feet and slopped and sucked my way through the mud and leaf mulch around the water's edge, tripping once on a tree root in my haste to recover my prize. I pulled it free of the water and let the water drain out of it. Then I shook it. It didn't sound to me as if it were damaged. I used the front of my shirt to wipe the mud from the box and then I opened the little door at the back of the box and turned the key twice. Sure enough, the globe began to revolve. I watched as the spring wound down. True, it was looking pretty grubby but as far as I could tell the lark mirror was fully intact. It hadn't even lost any of its glass.

It was then that I smelled wood smoke. I smiled, sensing a change of luck. I sniffed and sniffed again and then left the soggy clearing and began to make my way deeper into the valley. I threaded my way through a maze of trees, sniffing my way along the smoke trail as I went. The further in I went, the stronger the smell became and I was becoming increasingly convinced that I would find the charcoal burner's camp once I'd climbed out of the far side of the valley.

I'd progressed maybe five hundred yards when, from behind, I heard a cry of surprise, followed by the crash of a breaking branch, followed by a shriek of pain topped off by a howl of rage, all of which was perorated by my shadow, with his usual eloquence. "Baldy, you *cunt*," he screamed. "You're going to pay for that."

I listened for a moment or two more and then continued my slow and groping passage toward the heart of the valley where the canopy was thinner and where moonlight filtered through and where I could now see well enough to pick up the pace, greatly encouraged by the fact that the smell of smoke from the charcoal kiln was now stronger than ever.

But it wasn't the charcoal kiln I could smell at all. As I came to the far side of the moonlit ground I discerned a small fire winking amongst the trees. I made my way toward it cautiously, until I found myself in another clearing, staring out over another dank pool. On the far

The Lark Mirror

side of it was a small camp fire, the wood crackling in an oddly cheery way. And on the far side of *that*, sat Aunt Alsey.

Her head was covered by her cowl but I could see enough of her crone's face, eye-patch and chin whiskers and all, to know beyond doubt that it was her. She was roasting something on a green-wood spit and she licked her lips as she watched it cook.

"Aunt Alsey?" I called, softly.

She raised her head and peered over the flames, fixing me with her one good eye. "What ye want with Aunt Alsey?" she said.

"Look," I said, "I've brought you something."

She squinted over the flames. "Can't see that far, youngen," she said, "ye'd best fetch it yere."

I picked my way around the sump until I stood as close to her as I dared. "It's the lark mirror," I said, proffering it with outstretched hands like an inverted mendicant. "Here, you can have it. Its yours. I took it from you and I shouldn't have. I'm sorry. Won't you take it? Please? I just want my shadow back."

"Don't want no lark mirror," Aunt Alsey said.

"You *do*," I insisted. "You want it to catch nice tasty larks with."

"What'd I want with *larks*? Nice tasty squirrels is what I likes to eat," she said, shaking the thing on the stick. "*Larks*," she snorted, derisively, "nasty, bony things." She spat her disgust into the fire.

The conversation had the ring of familiarity about it and in my desperation I took perhaps the biggest gamble of my life.

"Fine," I said, drawing the lark mirror into a protective embrace, "I'll give it to Mother Priest. *She* likes larks."

"Ye?" she said, scornfully. "Ye wouldn't know where to find Mother Priest."

"Oh, but I would," I said. "And I've seen her and spoken with her. She keeps snakes in her skirt." Aunt Alsey's ears pricked at that. "Oh, and she asked me to tell you that she hopes the devil takes your liver."

Which galvanized her somewhat. "Give I that thing 'ere," she said, letting the squirrel fall into the fire and holding out both hands to take the lark mirror.

But just as I was about to place the lark mirror into her claws, my shadow called out from somewhere close by.

"Baldy," he said, "come on out and fight, you fucking coward."

Aunt Alsey's fingertips were two inches shy of taking the lark mirror.

"Please take it," I begged.

"Who be that?" Aunt Alsey wanted to know.

"It's my shadow," I said. "He's trying to kill me."

"And ye're runnin' away?"

"Yes," I said, "he's too strong for me and I don't want to die."

"Afeard of 'im are ye?" she said.

"Yes," I said, "He scares me."

"Told ye he would, ye young ronyon," she said. "I told ye ye'd be afeard o' yer own shadder." And then she took the lark mirror.

As she did so, my shadow began to issue another of his threats. "Baldy, you cunt," he said, "I'm going to-" And then he stopped.

And never said another word.

Ever.

"Thank you, Aunt Alsey," I said. "Thank you." I was looking at my shadow thrown against a tree trunk by the firelight. I scratched my head and my shadow scratched *its* head. I did a celebratory jig and my shadow did likewise.

"This thing'd best work, youngen," Aunt Alsey warned me, "else I'll turn yer 'ead on backwards."

"Oh, it works alright," I assured her. "Listen, I've got some other things for you," I went on, pressing home the advantage.

"Oh? An' what be they?" she said.

"Well, I've got a fishing rod for you to catch nice tasty trout with …"

"Oh, I *likes* nice tasty trouts," she said.

"And I've got a shotgun for you to shoot nice tasty rabbits with. *Or* squirrels," I added, hastily.

"Oh, I *likes* rabbits too," she said, smacking her lips.

"Shall I fetch them then?" I said. "Will you still be here?"

"Eren't got nowhere's else to go," she said.

I turned to walk away.

"There be more thing I wants, ronyon," she said.

I turned back to her. Here's the catch, I thought. "And what's that?" I said.

"I wants a swallee o' water," she said. "Can't drink this nasty bog water."

I remembered that Anushka's (actually, Billy's) canteen was in the plastic pig. I was so elated that I even managed to laugh.

"I can do that," I said. "I can fetch you a swallow of water."

***

On my way back to the road I found the jeans, shirt, socks, underwear and boots that my shadow had "borrowed". They were in a loose pile on the forest floor beside my carving knife. I took the boots and the knife with me and left everything else where it had fallen. I never did find my hat.

It was hard climbing out of that valley and, once I'd retrieved the other items from the remains of the plastic pig, it was hard climbing back into it -which meant that the best part of an hour had elapsed by the time I'd rejoined Aunt Alsey at the fire. She'd eaten her supper by then and the squirrel's discarded ribcage and other small bones were now popping and searing in the flames.

"Here," I said, handing over Mr Mason's fly rod. "Here," I said again, handing over Mr Cotteral's shotgun. "I'm afraid I haven't got any cartridges for it," I apologised.

"Don't matter," Aunt Alsey said, "they eren't hard to come by."

"Oh, I almost forgot … " I said, slipping the canteen from my shoulder. "Last but not least, a swallow of water." I unscrewed the cap and handed her the canteen.

She took it and drank deeply. "Ah .." she gasped, "I *likes* a nice swallee o' water."

"Keep it," I said, meaning the canteen, "you might find it useful."

"Thankee," she said. She stoppered the canteen and lay it by her side and then yawned. "Be-gone then, ronyon," she said. "Aunt Alsey's tired now."

"Of course," I said. I turned to go but turned back again. "Aunt Alsey," I said, "is it true that you're four hundred years old?"

"Oh," she said, "I be much older'n that. I'm older'n the rivers an' trees. Only the rocks is older'n Aunt Alsey."

"And is it true that you sleep in ponds?" I said, gesturing to the sump. "Ponds like this one."

To my surprise she threw back her head and began to cackle. "Sleep in ponds?" she said. "Why-ever would I? Nice comfy leaves an' straw is what I likes. Sleep in *ponds*? Whatever next? What *do* ye think I am, ronyon – a blessed frog?"

Needless to say, I felt very foolish.

33

Though I was enfeebled by hunger (I wouldn't touch the duck sandwiches since my shadow had had his filthy mitts on them) and worn down by fatigue I was also flushed with success and feeling pretty high and so I managed the long trudge home virtually without a rest, my moon-shadow pacing faithfully along beside me. I paused by Mr Cotteral's milk churns and listened for a few moments to the furious row that had broken out in the farmhouse. I smiled to myself and went on my way. As I walked my head was filled with many things but it was mostly the thought of being with Anushka again - being with her as the whole, shadow-endowed man that I now was – which sustained me throughout that long trek.

By the time I reached Billy's cottage there was light in the eastern sky and somewhere a nightingale sang an aria as if in mourning for Old Father Night.

The door was unlocked, which is how I'd left it, so I imagined that Anushka had slept through the night and was still sleeping now. I let myself in and flopped into my usual chair in Billy's living room. I smoked a cigarette and just sat there, listening to the first stirrings of the dawn chorus. Then, from upstairs, I heard someone weeping. Anushka, I thought.

As I mounted the stairs I heard the sob again. It sounded terribly hoarse, as if Anushka had been crying all night – and perhaps she had.

"Anushka?" I said, as I entered Billy's bedroom. "Anushka? What's wrong?"

There was enough dawn light in the room for me to see the huddled form beneath the bed covers.

I crept to the bed. "Anushka?" Still there was no answer.

I began to suspect that the situation was serious. Perhaps the horse tranquilizer had made her ill. And so I snapped on the bedside lamp with one hand and lay a comforting hand on her shoulder with the other. The covers were pulled all the way over her head. I shook her gently. "Anushka?" I said.

"Oh, go away and leave me alone," said the voice of Billy Makepiece.

I sprang away from the bed.

"Billy?" I said. "When did you get back?"

"I've been here all along, you fool!" he said, with a bitter anger I'd always considered beyond him.

"No," I said, "Anushka told me –"

"Anushka?" he said. "Do you want to talk about Anushka, David? Go and look at the painting. And don't worry about the key. You won't need it."

During that whole exchange, he'd not revealed himself once.

Billy was right about the key. The door had been smashed to pieces from the inside and the pieces were still scattered on the landing. I stepped over them, entered the studio and snapped on the light. And instead of finding Billy's puzzling self-portrait, I was confronted by Anushka. She was trapped within the same painting that Billy had been in. The same bedroom; the same scene of a minaret through the window. She was naked and she looked utterly beautiful – more ravishing even than she'd been in the flesh, if that were possible. Billy had made an excellent job of her; she truly was his masterpiece.

It was all too much for me and I landed heavily in Billy's viewing chair. I buried my head in my hands, just as I had done the previous day.

Eventually I looked up again. "Oh, Anushka," I groaned. I noticed, for the first time, that in the world of the painting the suitcase on the bed was no longer empty. Some clothes were now half spilling out of it. *There* was her black dress. *There* the fur stole. *There* the trousers and blouse. And there too, in that painting, was the mouth I'd kissed, the breasts I'd caressed.

In my own breast an unstoppable force was building. I resisted it for as long as I could but in the end I failed to stifle the long and anguished howl that rose out of me. When I'd quit howling, I put my head in my hands and sobbed.

I sat like that for a long time until I heard the pad of Billy's feet on the landing and felt Billy's comforting hand on my shoulder. He'd stopped crying and I could tell by his touch that he was no longer angry.

"Aunt Alsey," he said. "But then, you knew that."

"No, I didn't," I said, without looking at him. "I thought I did. Then I didn't. Then I didn't care. I just wanted to be … to be with *her*," I said, gesturing vaguely in the direction of the painting.

"She came here the same night that she stole your lark mirror," Billy said. "I was working on Anush- … I was working on my painting. I heard someone downstairs and when I went to investigate I discovered Aunt Alsey in the kitchen. Of course, I didn't *know* it was her. I just knew that there was a stranger in my kitchen and that I wanted her out so that I could finish my painting. And, of course, she cursed me. 'Ye'll get the thing ye most want,' she said, 'an' it'll break yer heart.' And I *did* get that, David," he said. "At first I was just in love with the woman I was painting – an artistic game, I told myself. But then I wanted to *be* her, to feel the worlds as she would feel it. And I did. And it felt wonderful. But no more. Now, here I am, just like she said, with a broken heart."

I looked at him for the first time. He was wearing the suit he'd been wearing in the painting but there was make-up or paint (to this day I'm not sure) smeared and tear-streaked down his face so that he looked like a balding drag queen who'd survived some fracas and had a good cry about it afterwards. Which is to say that he was a shocking sight.

"But I still don't understand," I said.

"She wanted a 'swallee' of water, David," Billy said.

I groaned and hid my face in my hands.

"And, since you've got your shadow back, I'm guessing that you found her and that you ... did you?" Billy said.

I nodded. "The canteen," I said. "She tricked me. The old bitch tricked me. She asked *me* for a 'swallee' of water ... she knew all along about the canteen and that it contained water from this house."

Billy patted my shoulder again.

"Come on," he said. "Let's have some breakfast. Then, perhaps, we ought to go and see how Mrs Mason is."

"Just leave me for a minute, Billy, will you?"

He left me alone and I rose wearily from the chair and stepped towards the painting. I touched it lightly with my knuckles, to check that it was dry. And then I kissed it. Kissed Anushka for the final time. Then I turned away from her and never saw her again.

END

Printed in Great Britain
by Amazon.co.uk, Ltd.,
Marston Gate.